The
Dream Stalker

‹ The ›
Dream Stalker

Margaret Coel

BERKLEY PRIME CRIME, NEW YORK

THE DREAM STALKER

A Berkley Prime Crime Book
Published by The Berkley Publishing Group
200 Madison Avenue, New York, NY 10016, a member of Penguin
Putnam Inc.

The Putnam Berkley World Wide Web site address is
http://www.berkley.com

First Edition: October 1997

Library of Congress Cataloging-in-Publication Data

Coel, Margaret, 1937–
    The dream stalker / Margaret Coel.
        p.   cm.
      ISBN 0-425-15967-1
      I. Title
    PS3553.0347D74   1997
    813'.54—dc21   96-54797
                                                                  CIP

Printed in the United States of America

10   9   8   7   6   5   4   3   2   1

For George, Kristie, Lisa and Tom

ACKNOWLEDGMENTS

My thanks to Ron Ross and Jo Clark of the Western Governors Association for pointing the way through the intricacies of interim nuclear waste storage facilities;

to Dr. Virginia Sutter of the Arapaho tribe for sharing with me much invaluable insight into her culture;

to the Rev. Anthony Short, S.J., for continuing to offer such good advice and encouragement;

to Carl Schneider, Maura Schneider, Michelle Sirini, and John Dix, baseball aficionados, for looking over my shoulder in the baseball scenes;

to Deborah Haws for teaching me much about horses and their ways;

to Karen Gilleland, Ann Ripley, Sybil Downing, and Dr. Carol Irwin, for reading parts or all of this manuscript and suggesting the ways to improve it;

to Jane Jordan Browne of Multimedia Product Development for believing in me;

and to Judith Palais of Berkley Publishing for guiding me with such a deft hand.

◄ The ►
Dream Stalker

◀ 1 ▶

Rain pattered against the window and broke through the quiet in the study. Father John Aloysius O'Malley closed the thick, red-bound report and glanced at the clock on his desk. A little after midnight. The evening had gotten away from him. He switched off the lamp and, out in the front hall, scooped the phone from the small table before starting up the dark stairs of the priests' residence. The long cord trailed behind. He always carried the telephone to the second-floor landing when he went to bed, in case someone needed a priest in the middle of the night.

The phone began to screech, sending a kind of electric shock through his hand. He felt his stomach muscles tighten as he sank onto a stair and picked up the receiver. "St. Francis Mission." He heard the edge in his voice.

A hollow sound came over the line, then a whooshing noise, like a gust of wind. Father John could sense the human presence. "Hello?" he said. The tone was meant to be encouraging.

"This the priest?" A man's voice, raspy.

"Father O'Malley. Do you need help?" He never got used to the late-night calls, although he'd been at St. Francis Mission on the Wind River Reservation now for seven years, the last three as the Jesuit pastor. He didn't want to climb back into the old Toyota pickup tonight.

He'd spent the day driving through the rain across the southern half of the reservation where the Arapahos lived. The Shoshones lived up north, outside of his parish. He'd visited a few of his elderly parishioners—the lovely old people, as he thought of them. And he'd stopped at Esther Willow's place to talk about the plans for her daughter's wedding next month at St. Francis. Then he'd driven to Ethete and had lunch with Bobby Red Feather. Bobby was having a tough time since Mary left.

Two hundred miles or more he'd probably put on the pickup. He didn't know the mileage for certain; the odometer had conked out a few months ago. But he didn't need an odometer to tell him that every ranch, meeting hall, gas station, convenience store, every cluster of houses on the reservation stood miles apart from everything else. Wherever the caller was, it was bound to be a long drive in the rain.

"Do you need help?" Father John asked again.

The man coughed, a muffled, distant sound, as if he'd laid a hand over the mouthpiece. "You could say I might be needin' some help," he said before the coughing came again. After a moment he continued: "I keep seein' it in my dreams. It keeps comin' back on me. I seen the old man get hit in the head with the shovel. Today's the day. Can't keep it inside no more."

"Who is this?" Father John was on his feet now, staring down the shadowy stairway, past the rain-blurred window next to the front door, trying to imagine the face of the man on the other end of the line. He was either drunk or sick—Father John wasn't sure which—but the caller was Indian. He could tell by the familiar flatness in the voice, as if the man were speaking into the wind.

"My ride's drove up. You come to Johnstown Road. A mile past the big curve, you'll see the old cabin I'm stayin' at."

"Wait. Can't you come to the mission?"

The hacking started again, strained and helpless. After a moment he said, "You come to the cabin. I'm dyin'."

The click gave way to the monotonous electronic buzz, the voice of a machine. Father John left the phone on the stair and hurried down to the front hall. In the gloomy darkness, he pulled on his khaki jacket and set his cowboy hat on his head. He stepped into the study and grabbed the small leather bag in the top drawer of the desk. He might need his sacred oils tonight, he thought, slipping the bag past his jacket into his shirt pocket, next to his heart.

As he came back into the hall, he heard the muffled scrape of footsteps. A dark figure towered in the shadows at the top of the stairs—his new assistant, Father Geoff Schneider. "What's going on?" The other priest's voice was sleep-filled.

"I have to go out."

"Hospital emergency?"

"Just somebody needing a priest." Father John had a sense he should hurry; there wasn't time for explanations.

His assistant started down the stairs, a dark robe cinched at his waist, pajama legs flapping at his ankles. His feet were bare. "At this hour? Who is it?"

"He didn't say." Father John yanked open the front door; the metal knob felt cool in his hand. The smell of moist earth floated into the entry. Rain drummed on the concrete stoop, a steady rhythm like that of horses racing across the hard ground.

"Wait a minute. Where are you going?"

"Johnstown Road." Father John pulled the brim of his hat low on his forehead as he ducked outside. He was aware of his assistant in the doorway behind him.

"Are you nuts? Going all the way out to Johnstown Road at midnight to meet some anonymous caller?"

"He said he's dying." Father John started down the sidewalk. He felt as if the caller himself were pulling him forward. Specks of moonlight danced in the rain, like sand blowing in the wind.

"He should've called 911!" the other priest hollered.

"He called a priest."

"Wait, I'll go with you."

"There isn't time!" Father John shouted into the rain as he slid inside the Toyota pickup parked where the gravel of Circle Drive butted against the soggy grass. He stabbed the key into the ignition. The engine groaned and fluttered into silence.

"Come on," he muttered, stomping on the gas pedal. The sense of urgency was like a physical presence beside him.

Finally the engine flared into life. Rain plunked on the roof, washed down the windshield. The wipers began carving out blurred half circles. He threw the gear into drive and wheeled past the buildings of St. Francis Mission: the old stone schoolhouse; the yellow administration building; Eagle Hall and the guest house; the new school; the baseball field, glistening like a black lake; the white church, its bell tower silver-blurred in the rain. It was the first Monday in May, the Moon When the Ponies Shed Their Shaggy Hair.

He turned left onto Seventeen-Mile Road, keeping the gas pedal to the floor as he passed two cars, the sense of urgency like a cold wind at his back. There was more traffic than he'd expected at this time of night. He slowed behind a 4x4 and waited for a line of oncoming vehicles before swinging again into the left lane. The Toyota vibrated around him. Past the 4x4, he pressed harder on the accelerator—a useless gesture. The Toyota was already wide open.

Keeping his eyes on the road, he pulled one of his opera tapes out of the glove compartment and slipped it into the cassette player wedged on the seat beside him.

The Toyota had never been equipped with a tape player, and the radio had conked out five years ago. He didn't care. He preferred the company of opera. The opening notes of the overture to *Faust* filled the cab. Music was what he wanted, to sort his thoughts by, to assuage the uneasiness inside him.

The call could be some kind of ruse. He'd heard enough confessions, counseled enough people—he knew what people were capable of doing. Maybe he'd been set up for robbery. The idea struck him as so ridiculous he had to stifle a laugh. He had a few dollars and some coins in the pocket of his blue jeans. Nobody would rob a priest from an Indian mission. Nobody who thinks straight. But drunks didn't think straight, he knew. When he was drinking, that was when he'd thought he made the most sense.

He turned north onto Highway 132, weaving past the traffic, pulling back into his own lane seconds ahead of oncoming vehicles. Another mile, and he let up on the gas and made a hard right turn, sending the pickup into a skid onto Johnstown Road. He'd left the traffic. Ahead was only the narrow gravel road caught in the headlights and the rainy darkness beyond. He passed an occasional clump of cottonwoods, an occasional oil pump—black shadows looming alongside the road.

Suddenly headlights flashed out of the darkness ahead and bore down on him. He jerked the steering wheel to the right, squinting to keep in view the edge of the barrow pit that ran like a ditch alongside the road. A dark truck passed, pelting the Toyota with wet gravel.

As he rounded a curve, he slowed down, scanning the darkness for a sign of the cabin. *A mile past the big curve*—he could still hear the caller's raspy voice. He guessed he'd gone farther than a mile and was about to turn around when he saw the black hulk standing twenty feet back from the road ahead. He hit the brakes and stopped at an angle to the ditch. The headlights washed over a log cabin huddled close to the ground, its tin roof shiny in the rain. It looked deserted; there were no vehicles in sight. He found it hard to believe this was the cabin, but it was the only structure he'd seen on Johnstown Road.

He grabbed the flashlight from under the seat and swung out into the rain, leaving the engine running, headlights bursting over the cabin. *"Avant de quitter ces lieux"* floated into the moist night air. His boots squished in the mud as he started toward the cabin. He could make out the squiggly patterns of tire tracks and boot prints. Somebody had been here a short time before. It crossed his mind the caller could have been in the truck he'd just passed. Maybe his ride had taken him to the hospital. Or maybe he had simply gotten tired of waiting and had decided the priest wasn't coming.

He waved the flashlight over the cabin: missing chinks; rotting logs; broken window pane; plank door hanging on its hinges, half opened. There was a faint odor of wet horses, a sense of life having passed by. Rain pinged on the tin roof.

He pushed the door open. It squealed into the night, protesting the effort. "Anybody here?" His voice reverberated around him.

The flashlight splayed across a room no more than twelve feet square, and he took it in all at once, like the jumbled flash of a dream: the plank table and wood chair toppled sideways, legs stiff in space; the cardboard carton stacked with a couple of cans of food and an orange box with white letters—Wheaties; the poster tacked to the wall, edges curled inward—an old pinup of a naked woman, the curving sweep of thighs and breasts; the red-black wetness next to the poster, like paint hurled against the log wall; and slumped beneath the poster, a man. A man in blue jeans and dark shirt, with half of his face blown off.

◀ 2 ▶

Father John heard the sound of his own heart pounding, of his own breathing—in and out, in and out—as he stepped into the cabin. He lowered the flashlight over the shattered face to the shirt soaked in blood, the blue jeans frayed and ripped, the brown cowboy boots, soles gaping at the toes. The man might have been pressing himself into the logs—cowering there—before he sank into death.

Then Father John saw the blood pooling next to the body, sending grisly fingers across the floor. He went down on one knee, careful to avoid the blood, and lifted the man's wrist, gently probing for a pulse. The skin felt warm and loose, like a branch dried in the sun, the bones close to the surface. It was the wrist of an old man. There was no pulse. Father John slipped one hand inside his jacket toward the container of the sacred oils—an automatic response. Slowly he drew his hand away. Sacraments were for the living.

He made the sign of the cross over the body and prayed out loud. "Dear Lord Jesus, have mercy on his soul. Raise him up and forgive him his sins, whatever they may be, and gather him into Your everlasting love." His voice mingled with the sound of the rain plinking on the roof, the music of an aria coming from far away.

He got to his feet, backed through the doorway, and, head down, ran to the Toyota, slipping in the mud, catching himself from falling. *Faust* rose over the drone of the engine, the shush of the rain. He threw himself inside the cab and rammed the gear into reverse, then drive. The pickup shot down the middle of Johnstown Road, mud splattering the hood and windshield. The nearest phone was at Ethete. It would take a good twenty minutes to get there.

He was filled with sadness and anger. Filled with regret. If only he'd arrived at the cabin a few minutes sooner. He'd known he must hurry; the sense of urgency had been like a physical presence beside him as he'd driven across the reservation. But he'd arrived too late. By some wordless logic, he knew it was the dead man who had called an hour ago. The thought left an acrid taste in his mouth, like smoke from a dying campfire.

He could never get used to the sudden deaths. The sound of the telephone breaking through the night quiet always made his stomach lurch, and left him with a feeling of dread. It was always a marker in someone's life: before, everything normal; then something terrible; then life never the same again. Tonight's call had marked the end of a man's life, a man he knew nothing about.

That wasn't true, Father John realized. From a two-minute phone call, he knew a lot. The man was an Indian, maybe an Arapaho. He'd seen something terrible: an old man being hit with a shovel. *Today's the day.* It must have happened today. And it bothered him so much he'd wanted to talk to a priest. And someone had come to pick him up, which meant he wasn't alone.

And? And? Father John thought of how Father Logan, one of his professors at Boston College, had prodded the students, urged them to examine their own thoughts, to reach further and understand more. It was in Father Logan's American history classes that he'd begun to dream about teaching American history at a Jesuit university himself someday.

And . . . the caller hadn't given his name, which meant he wasn't from around here. He'd have thought his name wouldn't matter. Nor did he ask for a specific priest. More proof he wasn't from here—he didn't know the names of the priests at St. Francis. One priest was the same as another. And the coughing and rasping, as if he were trying to catch his breath, hold onto life. He was dying. No priest could refuse to go to someone who was dying.

In the darkness ahead, he spotted the sprinkle of lights at Ethete. Another mile, and he wheeled onto the concrete pad in front of the gas station and coffee shop. An overhead light illuminated the island with three gas pumps and the front of a cement-block building with a wide plate-glass window. White letters marched across the glass: BETTY'S PLACE. Beyond the glass was a well of darkness. The shop was closed. He skidded around the island, stopped next to the telephone mounted at the far corner of the building, and jumped out.

Rain dripped from the brim of his cowboy hat as he slipped a quarter from the small pocket of his blue jeans, fed it into the phone, and punched in 911. The receiver felt slippery and wet against his ear. After a moment, the ringing stopped. "Wind River Law Enforcement," a woman droned. The same greeting every call, a thousand calls.

Father John identified himself and said there was a man shot to death in the old log cabin on Johnstown Road. He started to explain. Somehow an explanation seemed necessary—but the operator interrupted. Two police cars were on Highway 132. They'd be at the cabin in a few minutes. The police would want to talk to him. He said he would meet them there.

He heard the sirens wailing as he turned onto Johnstown Road. Just past the curve, he saw the blue and red lights pulsing in the darkness ahead. He drove toward the lights.

Drawn up at the edge of the road in front of the cabin were two white police cars with the gold insignia of the Bureau of Indian Affairs on the front doors. He pulled in next to the cars, shut off the engine, and hit the stop button on the cassette player. "Il était temp" shut off, leaving a blank quiet as Father John got out of the cab. The blue and red lights waved around him. Static and chatter erupted from the police radios. Three officers were moving along the front of the cabin, flashlights skimming the white-chinked log walls, the muddy ground. Another officer dodged past the police cars and came toward the Toyota.

"How come you found the body, Father?" Rain pattered on the gray slicker the policeman wore over the navy blue uniform of the Bureau of Indian Affairs police. Watery threads ran off his cap and down the sides of his face—the round, flat face of the Cheyenne, or the *Shyela*, as the Arapaho called the people who had ridden with them across the plains in the Old Time. The BIA police force was made up of Indians from various tribes, not just from the Arapahos and Shoshones at Wind River Reservation. Father John read the real question in the man's dark eyes: How come he was out here in the middle of the night?

He said, "A man called the mission about midnight. He asked me to meet him here." Another siren wailed in the darkness.

"Say who he was?"

"He said he was dying."

"He got that right. Somebody must've got tired of his face."

The comment struck Father John like a wrong note in a perfect aria. He said nothing as the siren grew louder. Abruptly it shut off, and another police car drew in alongside the Toyota. The red and blue flashing lights mingled with those from the other cars, projecting an eery, unreal quality to the road and the dark spaces beyond. Art Banner, the BIA police chief, hoisted himself from behind the steering wheel. He wore a dark blue uniform jacket and slacks. No slicker. Below the rim of his cap were the narrow black eyes and the prominent cheekbones of the Arapaho.

"What we got now?" The chief brought one gloved fist down on the hood of the Toyota as he came around the front.

Giving a little nod toward the cabin, the policeman said, "Some old guy got his face blown off. Father John found him."

Banner's black eyebrows shot up. "Hang around, will ya, John? I'm gonna want to talk to you." The chief started toward the cabin, shoulders rolled inside his jacket. The policeman drew a flashlight from under his slicker and hurried to catch up, shining the thin yellowish beam over the wet ground ahead. The other officers followed the pair inside the cabin. For a long moment, Father John watched the figures move past the opened door, silhouetted against the flickering light, his thoughts full of the dead man: the worn blue jeans, the hard-used boots, the weathered hands. A cowboy. A cowboy with something on his conscience who had wanted to talk to a priest.

The rain had begun to seep through Father John's jacket, past his flannel shirt, into his skin. His hands felt numb with cold; exhaustion and sadness were beginning to overtake him. He got back into the Toyota. It smelled as dank and musty as the inside of a cave. He started the engine and nudged up the heat lever, watching Banner make his way back over the muddy ground. The chief crossed in front of the pickup and climbed in the passenger door, slamming it hard behind him. "Damn miserable weather." He stared straight ahead at the wetness scrawled across the hood. "You know the victim?"

Father John shook his head. "He called the mission tonight."

"How'd you know it was him?"

Silence hung in the cab a moment, broken by the scratchy hum of the engine, the *brrr* noise of the heater. Father John had no proof, nothing that would lead to that conclusion. He drew in a long breath. "It was him."

The chief shrugged. "He give you a name?"

"No."

Banner was quiet a moment, considering. "Cabin belongs to the Hooshie family," he said finally. "I think it was Michael Hooshie built it back in the twenties. He was the grandson of Bull Bear—"

"Hold on," Father John interrupted. He didn't need an excursion into Arapaho genealogy right now. Every family had a story; every Arapaho was related in unexpected ways to some other Arapaho. "You think the dead man is a Hooshie?"

"Maybe. 'Cept none of them Hooshies been around for years. Cabin's been deserted long as I can remember. More'n likely he's just some old cowboy movin' around, pickin' up ranch jobs. Decided to squat here awhile. Pockets clean. No ID. Nothin' on him. Whoever pulled the trigger cleaned him out. Could be robbery. So, what exactly did he say?"

Father John related the brief conversation: how the caller wanted to talk to a priest; how something was bothering him—something about an old man getting hit in the head with a shovel.

"What old man?" Banner shifted in the seat, eyes narrowed in concentration.

"All he said was that today was the day."

The chief gave a quick shake to his head, a dismissing gesture. "Nothing like that reported on the rez today. Might've been some cowboy fight didn't amount to anything. What else he say?"

Father John began again, but the moment he mentioned the caller's coughing and rasping, Banner threw out one hand, as if he were directing a band. "Said he was dyin'. Right?"

Father John nodded. That was right.

"What the hell else he gonna say to get you out here? He probably got drunk in some bar, started feelin' sorry for himself, wanted somebody to talk to. So he called a priest. Who else is gonna drive out here at midnight? Trouble is, somebody followed him from the bar and robbed him. You're damn lucky you didn't show up while it was happenin' or you'd be dead, too."

Father John rolled his window partway down and drew in a long breath of cool air tinged with rain. Outside, the dark figures of the other officers darted about, stretching yellow tape around spikes set into the ground. He turned back. "The cowboy was scared, Banner. He had something he wanted to tell me. What are the chances somebody would rob him while he was waiting for me to show up?"

Banner blew out a long puff of air. "Trust me, John. Things are usually pretty much what they seem." He shrugged, as if the matter were settled. "In any case, this is one for that new agent the FBI sent us, Ted Gianelli. My boys'll do the preliminary investigation, but it's gonna be up to him to figure out what happened."

Father John nodded. He understood that murder on an Indian reservation fell into the FBI's jurisdiction, as did burglary and robbery and other major crimes. All placed in federal jurisdiction a hundred years ago when the government realized the Indians were more interested in rehabilitating criminals than in punishing them.

"Gianelli's welcome to this sucker," Banner was saying. "I got my hands full just keepin' the Indians and them nuclear activist screwballs from tearing each other's guts out. We probably got a couple hundred outsiders on the rez tyin' up traffic and makin' nuisances out of themselves with a lot of protesting and demonstrating."

"That explains the traffic," Father John said, more to himself than to the police chief. Outsiders here to protest plans to store nuclear waste on the reservation. The tribal council—the business council, as the Arapahos called it—wanted to build a storage facility on the Legeau ranch in an isolated valley in the middle of the reservation, between the Arapaho and Shoshone communities. Father John had just finished reading the environmental report tonight when the cowboy called.

"Either folks love the idea of storing nuclear waste here or they hate it." The chief shrugged again, as if nothing made sense. "Folks that love it see all the jobs and money it's gonna bring in. Millions of dollars, they say. Other folks don't think it's somethin' Arapahos oughtta be a party to, no matter how much money's involved. Jobs either. One thing's for sure, all them environmental protesters aren't gonna change the mind of any Indian. All they'll do is stir things up. Could get real interesting at the public hearing tomorrow night." Banner slid back the cuff of his jacket and glanced at the luminescent face of his watch. "Make that tonight."

Pushing open the door, the chief started to lift himself out into the drizzle. Then he leaned back inside, a look of fatherly concern on his face. "Why don't you go on home, John. Get yourself a couple hours' sleep. I guarantee Gianelli's gonna be on your doorstep first thing in the morning."

❮ 3 ❯

Father John awoke to a loud growling noise like the
sound of a truck bearing down a mountain. It took
him a moment to realize it was a chain saw. Leonard
Bizzel, the caretaker, was probably pruning dead
branches from the cottonwoods that sheltered the
grounds of St. Francis Mission.

Sunshine burst past the half-drawn blinds at the bedroom window and washed over the yellow walls, the
faded brown carpet. The sunshine surprised him. He'd
been dreaming of rain. Rain pattering on the tin roof of
the old log cabin as the cowboy struggled to sit up,
struggled to tell him something.

He'd slept badly, and a dull ache crept across his
shoulders and made its way up the back of his neck into
his head. It had been close to four o'clock before he'd
dropped into bed, every bone in his body screaming for
sleep. But his mind had kept rerunning the telephone
conversation, like a cassette player replaying the same
tape, trying to fix the caller's words, to understand how
a man—a drifter, perhaps, a drunk, it didn't matter—
how he had ended up shot to death in a deserted log
cabin. And hovering in the background, like some silent
witness, was his own sense of failure.

Now the hands on the alarm clock on the bedside
table stood at 8:27. The day had started without him.
Leonard was already tackling the spring cleanup on the

mission grounds; Father Geoff would have said the early Mass and put in a half hour at the office; and, judging by the sound of water swishing through the pipes, Elena, the housekeeper at St. Francis for more years than anyone could remember, was in the basement carrying out her self-imposed task of making sure no washable items in the priests' residence escaped a frequent encounter with the washing machine.

He swung out of bed. In twenty minutes he was showered and dressed in a clean, stiff pair of blue jeans and a long-sleeved plaid shirt worn into comfort. He shaved quickly, hardly noticing the gray hair mixing with the red at his temples, the little lines at the edges of his eyes. He would be forty-eight in a couple of weeks, but he still stood close to six feet four and was as trim as in his pitching days at Boston College. He could still hurl a ball dead center over home plate.

Downstairs in the kitchen, he stared through the window over the sink as he washed down bites of buttered toast with gulps of stale coffee, his sense of failure and guilt as sharp as the pain coursing through his head.

Out in the yard, Walks-on-Three-Legs, the golden retriever who had stumbled into his life—one of the unexpected gifts life sometimes offers—lay on his side in the buffalo grass, basking in the sunshine. The dog had been on his side that day last fall when Father John had caught a glimpse of something in the barrow pit along Seventeen-Mile Road and stopped to check, fearing it might be a child. He'd scooped up the animal and laid him on the front seat of the Toyota. Then he'd broken the speed limit all the way to Riverton. The vet had saved the dog's life, but at the cost of his mangled back leg.

Risen out of a ditch, Father John often thought, much as he himself had risen out of Grace House after his treatment for alcoholism and had come to an Indian reservation, the last place on earth he had ever thought to find himself. Had come here, like Walks-on, to begin a new life.

A few feet from the dog, a cluster of cottonwoods marked the boundary of the back yard. Leonard perched halfway up a ladder, maneuvering a chain saw among the branches. The saw sputtered into life, a loud, intermittent growl. Beyond the trees was the baseball field, matted and soggy-looking in the morning air. No telling when the field would dry out enough for the Eagles to practice. This would be the eighth season he coached the Indian kids, the eighth season they would show the teams in Lander and Riverton what baseball was all about. But spring was slow in arriving: a few mornings of sunshine, followed by afternoons and nights of pelting rain. Dark clouds drifted over the mountains. The rain would come again today.

Father John took another gulp of coffee. He forced his thoughts to the work awaiting his attention in the office. The minutiae of running a mission: Ladies' Sodality and men's meetings; religious education and adult literacy classes, Alcoholics Anonymous meetings, liturgy services—all to schedule and preside over. There were messages to answer, calls to return, bills to pay.

Always the bills. At least this was one area in which his new assistant had some expertise. Along with a master's degree in finance, Father Geoff Schneider had the propensity of his German ancestors for order and precision. He'd arrived two weeks ago, and Father John had handed him the books. Since then, the mission's finances had moved to the back of his worries. There was always the chance his new assistant would hit upon some brilliant plan to keep St. Francis Mission solvent.

He rinsed out the mug and started across the kitchen just as Elena stepped into the doorway, blocking his path. She wore a blue, flower-printed dress under a yellow apron that hung from her neck. Part Arapaho and part Cheyenne, she barely reached his shoulder. She was in her sixties, though not even she knew exactly where in her sixties. He could see the pockets of pink scalp shining through her gray hair.

"You sit yourself right down," she ordered, turning her round face upward and fixing him with blue-black eyes. "You'll have your oatmeal in no time."

"The office beckons." He threw out both hands. The matter was beyond his control.

"Office can wait."

"There are bills to pay. . . ."

"You ain't got no money."

"Didn't you hear? We got a check for a million dollars."

"What I hear is the pastor's havin' some wild dreams." The old woman gestured toward the round table in the center of the kitchen. "Sit yourself down. You need your oatmeal after bein' out half the night."

He sensed the conversation lurch toward the real point of his sitting down and eating breakfast: The old woman could ply him with questions about last night, and, maybe even gather information to transmit over the moccasin telegraph. Most likely she had arrived at seven this morning, as usual, and Father Geoff had mentioned the late-night call. And she had clucked over the stubbornness—the Irish could be so stubborn—that had driven the pastor of St. Francis Mission out into a miserable, rainy night when anyone with good sense would know to stay home. It was only by the grace of the good spirits that looked after fools and stray animals that he'd gotten back safely, and now she wanted to know all the details.

He said, "I promise to eat two bowls of oatmeal tomorrow."

The old woman fixed both hands atop her hips and gave him a long look of exasperation. He was impossible. She did her best to take care of him and contribute to the flow of news on the reservation. What else could she do? After a long moment, she said, "Somebody's waitin' to see you in the study."

"What? Why didn't you tell me?"

"You're supposed to eat your oatmeal first."

Father John expected to find Ted Gianelli, the stocky, black-haired FBI agent and former cornerback for the Buffalo Bills. He hailed from Quincy, Massachusetts, practically Father John's old backyard, he sat in the front pew at the ten o'clock Mass every Sunday with his wife and four little girls, and, Father John had to admit, the agent probably loved opera even more than he did. In the couple of months Gianelli had been assigned to central Wyoming, they'd become friends.

But as Father John walked into the study, two men rose from the blue wingback chairs in front of his desk. One was a white man he'd never seen before. The other was Lionel Redbull, an Arapaho in his mid thirties, close to six feet tall and slender in a muscular way, with the high, smooth forehead, prominent cheeks, and hooked nose of his people. His black hair hung in two braids down the front of a black blazer, which rode on his shoulders with ease. He had been tapped by Matthew Bosse, one of the Arapaho councilmen, to oversee the plans for the nuclear waste facility. Redbull was one of the *Kuno'utose'i o,* Father John thought, the Indians without blankets, the progressives.

"Sorry to show up unexpected," Redbull said, stepping forward, a brown hand outstretched. Discomfort and embarrassment mingled in his dark eyes. There was almost no excuse for an Arapaho to breach the forms of politeness.

"The fault is mine," said the white man, leaning past the Indian to extend his hand. "Paul Bryant, president, United Power Company. I flew into Riverton about an hour ago and suggested to Lionel we take a chance on finding you in your office. Father Schneider—I believe he said he's your assistant—directed us to the residence. I hope you can spare a few minutes."

The man's grip was firm and full of purpose. Father John guessed he was close to his own age, medium height and broad shouldered, with neatly trimmed dark hair and an intelligent face. He wore a gray suit, the jacket unbuttoned, a red tie knotted smartly at the collar of his white shirt.

Father John waved both men to the wingbacks as he sank into the worn leather chair behind the desk. A shaft of sunlight broke through the window and splashed over the papers in front of him; the washing machine hummed from below the floorboards. His headache had receded into a dull throbbing. He wished he felt a little more up to what was sure to be a discussion about storing nuclear waste on the reservation. He said, "What brings you to St. Francis Mission, gentlemen?"

"We hope to gain your support, Father O'Malley." The white man crossed one gray-panted leg over the other, relaxed and confident.

"My support?"

"Let me explain. My company was formed by thirty utility companies in the East, all of which generate electricity through nuclear power. Specifically, the plants rely upon nuclear fuel rods that contain uranium dioxide. Bundling the rods together causes fission, which, of course, creates the heat necessary to generate steam and produce electric power. Unfortunately it also creates a by-product—nuclear waste." The man shrugged, as if the matter couldn't be helped. "The spent fuel rods contain unused uranium and some transuranic elements, such as plutonium. When handled correctly, however, these radioactive materials can be stored with absolute safety."

"I've read the report." Father John nodded toward the red-bound book still on his desk where he'd left it last night. "It didn't mention radioactive materials that might leak into the groundwater or plutonium dust that could escape through vents."

"You must understand, Father," Bryant continued, his tone unchanged. "We're proposing a state-of-the-art storage system that eliminates such problems. The spent fuel rods will be contained in casks made up of three layers: stainless steel cylinders, heavy metal shields, and steel shells. Engineered to withstand impact, puncture, fire, immersion in water. They should remain impermeable for at least a hundred years."

"Plutonium remains radioactive for thousands of years," Father John said. "What happens after the casks disintegrate?"

Lionel Redbull shifted in his chair, both hands gripping the armrests. The white man kept his eyes on Father John. "We must trust the science of the future to address that problem. In any case, plutonium is not the bugaboo everyone assumes. It emits alpha radiation, which, as you know, cannot even penetrate the human skin."

Father John said, "Plutonium can be deadly if it's inhaled. Or if it's swallowed, say, in water." The room went quiet a moment. He continued, "What about the other waste products—cesium and strontium? They emit gamma and beta radiation. Even more dangerous."

Paul Bryant cleared his throat. "Only if released into the atmosphere or into the water. Impossible with the facility we intend to build. The casks will be stored in air-cooled concrete buildings, set on pads twelve feet thick. The entire facility will resemble a lovely industrial park, fenced and guarded, of course. It will be licensed by the Nuclear Regulatory Commission. Every precaution will be taken."

Redbull leaned forward, clasping his hands together—a nervous gesture. "You gotta understand, Father. We're only gonna have the facility on the rez for thirty or forty years. Just until the federal government gets around to building a permanent storage place somewhere else. The Arapaho Business Council is behind this interim facility one hundred percent. So's the Shoshone council. Two weeks from now the proposal's gonna go before the joint Arapaho-Shoshone council for a final vote. It's gonna be approved."

The Indian drew in a long breath and hurried on: "This here's our chance to bring in ten million dollars every year as long as the power companies rent the facility. Sure, a couple million a year will go to the Legeaus. Hell, it's their ranch gonna be leased." He shrugged, resignation crossing his face. "But the rest is gonna build and operate the facility and pay for a lot of benefits. We're talkin' new houses, schools, clinics, roads. Not to mention some high-tech jobs Arapahos and Shoshones can count on. No more goin' begging in Lander and Riverton for some low-paying job sweepin' out a warehouse. . . ."

Bryant cleared his throat, an interruption. "My company has given the Arapahos a grant to determine the safest location for the facility. Lionel here hired the best consultants available, and they all agree the Legeau ranch is an ideal storage site. The water table is safely below the surface. The soil is stable. No evidence of slippage or erosion. No bentonite that could cause expansion. No underground faults to cause an earthquake. And no known oil or mineral deposits in the area, which eliminates any drilling that could upset the ground stability. So you can see, Father O'Malley, every indicator points to a safe and profitable facility."

Father John picked up a ballpoint and tapped it against the edge of the desk. "What exactly do you want from me?"

"I believe you could be of great help, Father," Bryant said.

"To your company?"

A slow smile spread across the white man's face, as

if he had just taken the full measure of an opponent. "Unfortunately we must contend with the professional activists, the alarmists who come out of the woods at the mention of the words 'plutonium' and 'radioactive.'" Bryant squared his shoulders, as if to accept an unpleasant reality that must be faced. "Alarmists influence a lot of people, especially if they're Arapaho themselves, like the attorney, Vicky Holden."

Father John flinched, as if this stranger had hurled an invisible stone at someone in his family. He and Vicky Holden had worked together for three years now, ever since she'd returned to the reservation. Arranging adoptions and divorces; keeping some juvenile out of jail; talking some alcoholic into treatment. Vicky handled the legal side; he, the counseling. They made a good team. He enjoyed working with her—he loved being with her—although he hadn't called her in almost three months. And she hadn't called him. It was as if they had reached an unspoken agreement not to spend so much time together.

It didn't surprise him, Bryant's singling out Vicky instead of the protesters—the outsiders. As Banner had said last night, the outsiders wouldn't change the mind of any Indian. But Vicky might. Father John knew she'd spoken against the facility at several meetings on the reservation; she'd written a number of pieces for the *Wind River Gazette*. He'd read them all. All variations of the same question: If a nuclear waste facility brought so many benefits, why did no one else want it?

He said, "Vicky Holden is not the only one who opposes the facility."

"That's the point, Father." This from Redbull. "We got outsiders crawling all over the rez, thanks to her articles. They'll be at the public hearing tonight. And they'll be causin' trouble 'til the final vote at the joint council meeting. Some folks are gonna listen to them outsiders. Then they're gonna demand the joint council turn down the opportunity of a lifetime."

Bryant said, "I've looked into St. Francis Mission and your work here, Father O'Malley. You have a great deal of influence with the people. You could allay any unfounded fears. All you would have to do is explain the data in the report."

"The Arapahos can read the report for themselves," Father John said, getting to his feet. He had no intention of becoming a spokesman for a nuclear waste facility. As far as he was concerned, the meeting was over. His own thoughts had already shifted to the office: the bills, the messages. Gianelli had probably called by now.

The two men raised themselves out of the wing-backs, reluctance in their movements. The white man reached long, manicured fingers into the inner pocket of his suit coat and extracted a small leather case. He slipped out a business card and, leaning over the desk, set it on the report. "I'll be at the Alpine Bed and Breakfast until the joint council meeting. You can reach me there if you have any questions."

Father John followed his visitors into the front hall and reached around to open the door. He shook hands with both men—a nod to convention—and Redbull stepped out into the sunshine.

Bryant hesitated in the doorway. "I always like to know my adversary," he said. "I understand Vicky Holden's quite intelligent, as well as beautiful. Is there anything else I should know about her?"

Father John felt the flush of anger in his face. Who was this man? What right did he have to pry into Vicky's life? He felt as if her privacy had been violated, and some part of his own. He said, "I'm not in the habit of discussing my friends."

Bryant broke into another slow, knowing smile. "I'm looking forward to meeting her," he said. Then he turned, crossed the stoop, and started down the short sidewalk. Redbull was already behind the wheel of the green pickup parked at the edge of Circle Drive, but Bryant took his time removing his suit coat, opening the passenger door, and smoothing the coat over the seat. Then he stretched his arms upward and rolled his shoulders in an isometric exercise before lowering himself inside.

Father John watched as the pickup swung around Circle Drive and disappeared behind the cottonwoods at the intersection with Seventeen-Mile Road. Slamming the door shut, he walked back into the study, the dull throbbing now a full-blown headache. He picked up the phone and punched in Vicky's number. She should know about this outsider—Paul Bryant. He knew about her.

The secretary at Vicky's office sounded tentative and nervous. It was not a voice he recognized. Ms. Holden had just left, an emergency. Would he care to leave a message?

He would. He asked her to have Vicky call him the minute she returned. Father John O'Malley. Yes, she had his number.

The phone rang as he replaced the receiver, and he answered quickly, half expecting Vicky to be on the other end. It was Gianelli. "Need to talk to you," the agent said. "My office in about an hour?"

That left thirty minutes to make a stab at the work in his own office, Father John was thinking. Thirty minutes to hear from Vicky.

‹ 4 ›

Vicky Holden saw the plain white sheet of paper with the strips of black type pasted on in irregular, horizontal rows before she had taken off her jacket or set down her purse and briefcase. She felt her heart jump. The paper hadn't been on her desk when she'd left the office last night, but now it floated on top of a stack of folders.

She should have been prepared for another threat, she thought. The dream had come to her again last night, the same frightening dream she'd had several nights now. She had awakened this morning feeling weak and shaky. She still didn't feel like herself, and here was another threat, like the three others she'd gotten in the last three weeks. She bent over it until the type came into focus. Her breath sounded like the gasps of a small bellows. YOU WANT TO LIVE? STAY OUT OF WHAT ISN'T YOUR BUSINESS. YOU HAVE BEEN WARNED.

She let her briefcase and floppy black purse drop onto the carpet beside the desk and crossed to the open door that led to the outer office. Hunched over a computer keyboard, eyes fixed on the green monitor, sat the white woman the temp service had sent over last week after Robin Levall left to follow her boyfriend on the rodeo circuit. "Mrs. Peters, who was here this morning?" Stay calm, Vicky told herself.

The white woman raised her eyes from the monitor

and turned in her chair, a tentativeness in the movement. She appeared to be on one side or the other of sixty, with a pale, round face, short hair dyed as black as coal, and bangs that crept down the top half of her forehead. She wore a prim white shirt buttoned to the neck, a black skirt, and sturdy shoes, the kind of business uniform she had probably worn to work forty years ago. "Here." She repeated the word in a flat tone, as if to make certain she had heard it correctly.

"Someone left a note on my desk."

"I came in promptly at 8:30, as you requested. . . ."

Vicky held up one hand. "Mrs. Peters, I'm simply wondering how a certain paper got on my desk."

The older woman stared at her a second. "I didn't go into your office, and nobody else has been here."

"The outer door was locked when you arrived?"

The woman nodded, worry and fear mingling in her expression. "I used the key the service gave me."

Vicky glanced at the closed door with the frosted glass panel and the dark letters marching backward that, from the outside corridor, spelled VICKY HOLDEN, ATTORNEY-AT-LAW. A few feet down the corridor was the flight of stairs leading to the sidewalk on Main Street in Lander. Someone had climbed the stairs between 8:00 last night, when she had finally packed her briefcase and left for home, and 8:30 this morning, when Mrs. Peters had arrived. Or someone had come up the stairway from the parking lot and entered her office through the back hall. Either way, whoever had left the threat had come through a locked door. A chill ran across her shoulders: Someone had a key to her office.

"Please call the locksmith, Mrs. Peters, and have the locks changed immediately," Vicky said before turning back into her private office. She opened the top drawer of the gray file cabinet and extracted the brown envelope in front. Lifting the latest threat from her desk with two fingers, as if it carried some type of fungus, she slipped it into the envelope. Now there were four. Variations on a theme: If she wanted to stay alive, she should mind her own business; she should stay out of matters that didn't concern her.

Of course the threats were about the nuclear waste facility. She opposed the plan to store radioactive materials on the reservation. It didn't matter that it would only be for forty years—forty years was a generation, a lifetime. She would do everything in her power to make her people realize the dangers. Speak out. Write articles. Just as she'd been doing.

The day after her first article had appeared in the *Wind River Gazette,* she got the first threat—wedged between her front door and the frame. The second threat showed up on her windshield in the parking lot at Safeway. The third on her windshield again, four days ago, in the parking lot behind her office.

She had meant to report the threats. Why hadn't she reported them? Why had she put it off, told herself it was just some crank getting his kicks trying to scare her? The world was full of cranks, and something like a nuclear storage facility was bound to smoke them out. She had convinced herself not to take the threats seriously. But now a fourth one had joined the others inside the envelope. It was as if her grandmother had grabbed her by the shoulders and begun shaking her. Four. There are four of everything important in the world. Four winds. Four directions. Four seasons. Four hills of life. Four quarters of creation. You must pay attention.

Vicky grabbed her purse and slung the strap over one shoulder. Tucking the brown envelope under her arm, she walked through the office. The secretary had gathered herself toward the monitor, as if to seek some kind of shelter from a storm that had suddenly burst around her.

"Call Detective Eberhart. Tell him I'm on the way over." Vicky slammed out the door, not waiting for any confirmation, and ran along the corridor and down the stairs. The clack of her heels echoed off the brick walls. From somewhere came the languorous sound of a ringing phone.

Sunshine washed over the sidewalk, but the coolness of early spring still hung in the air, with its ever-present hint of rain. A gust of wind whipped her gray wool skirt around her legs and flattened her suit jacket against her back. Pickups and four-wheel-drive vehicles lined the curb and streamed down the wide street. Two men came along the sidewalk—businessmen in cowboy boots and cowboy hats and suits, suit coats blown back in the wind. Vicky started around the building toward the parking lot where she had left the Bronco fifteen minutes ago, then hesitated. The police department was only a few blocks away.

The moment the light turned green, she struck out across the street behind the businessmen, clutching the brown envelope against her chest, annoyed at having to take the time to admit this intrusion into her life. She had a full day of appointments. Molly Red Cloud would be in this morning to see about adopting her granddaughter, Little Molly, the child she'd raised from the moment Little Molly had opened her eyes on the world six years ago. Jane Latter needed help with the new lease on her beauty shop in Fort Washakie. And this evening was the public hearing on the nuclear storage facility. Vicky wanted to reread the environmental report before she finished writing the speech she intended to give.

She heard the roar of an engine and the squeal of brakes in the same instant that she glimpsed the truck out of the corner of her eye—a blurred mass of black and silver metal bearing down on her, threatening to engulf her. She leapt sideways, stumbling over the curb, the draft sucking at her as the rear wheels screeched past. One of the businessmen gripped her arm; she realized he had stopped her from falling. The strap of her purse had slipped off her shoulder, wrenching her other arm. The brown envelope scuttled along the gutter in the wind.

The other man ran to retrieve it as a crowd began to gather: a couple of gray-haired women; a young woman with a baby stroller; a teenaged boy, the knees torn in his jeans; a man in work clothes with a tool belt slung around his waist. Was she okay? That fool in the truck, he could've killed her.

One of the businessmen handed her the brown envelope, while the other kept his hand on her elbow, steadying her, asking if she were hurt. She was aware of the red blur of his tie, the outsized blue eyes behind thick glasses, the smell of coffee on his breath.

"I think I'm okay," she managed, pulling herself upright and away from his grasp, stamping her feet to stop her legs from quivering.

"Anybody get the license?" the man asked, glancing around the crowd. Heads shook in unison.

"Oughtta lock that bastard up," somebody said.

"Probably a drunk Indian," someone else said. The words were met with silence. Vicky felt as if she could have sliced through the embarrassment, it was so thick, as the crowd realized *she* was an Indian.

"Thank you for your help," she said, anxious to be free of them. She started walking fast along the sidewalk, staying close to the shop windows. It had been an accident, that was all. Had she been killed, that's what they would've called it. An accident. The driver had taken the corner too fast and hadn't seen her. Still, it seemed as though the truck had been waiting for her, had come out of nowhere after her. She gripped the brown envelope. YOU WANT TO LIVE?

She stopped at the end of each block, making sure no cars or trucks were approaching before she stepped into the street. By the time she reached the squat, gray stone building that housed the Lander Police Department, her skin felt prickly and flushed from the brisk walk. An icy feeling crept inside her. She tried to assure herself the threats and the truck were a dreadful coincidence. But all of her instincts protested. She kept hearing her grandmother's words: Now there are four. Pay attention. Pay attention.

She swung open the glass door and stepped inside a lobby of whitewashed walls, tile floor the color of spring leaves, and dull red plastic chairs. Warm air wafted from a metal vent lodged below the ceiling. A policewoman sat in a small cubicle on the right behind a counter and a half wall of glass, staring at a blue computer monitor. The phone next to the monitor started to ring. She picked up the receiver and pointed it toward a side door. Her eyes on Vicky, she mouthed the word "office." Vicky felt a pinprick of relief; something was going right. Her new secretary had followed instructions.

A buzzing noise sounded just before she turned the handle on the door. She stepped into a narrow corridor, fighting back the claustrophobia that always caught up with her in confined spaces. She preferred the outdoors, the far distances, the wind on her skin. A bluish light from the fluorescent bulbs along the ceiling bounced off the white walls. The faint smell of detergent mingled with that of stale cigarette smoke. Her heels clicked against the tile as she walked past several glass-paneled doors. She stopped at the door bearing a plastic sign that read: DETECTIVE EBERHART.

Before she could rap, the door swung open, and Bob Eberhart stood in front of her. He was a couple of inches taller than she was, with a thin wiry build, rounded shoulders, and a sunken chest. He was dressed in dark slacks and a gray oxford shirt that seemed to match his skin and hair, which was cropped short, military style. His eyes were blue, his lips a deep pink color.

Vicky recalled he had caught a bullet in the chest a few years back. She'd heard other lawyers say he wasn't the same after that, but the police department was keeping him on until he reached retirement. It gave her a measure of comfort. Eberhart was a white policeman in a white town whom the Indian people could trust.

"What brings you, Vicky?" He motioned her into a small office even more crowded than her own. Stacks of papers and folders tumbled across the desk. More stacks slumped precariously toward the edges on top of two filing cabinets that flanked a rectangular window in the opposite wall. He lifted a handful of papers from a side chair and gestured for her to sit down.

She sank onto the cushion, a sense of doom pressing around her. Pieces of dust floated in the column of sunshine that lay over the desk. Eberhart settled into his chair, and she handed him the brown envelope.

The detective shook out the four sheets of paper and laid them over his cluttered desk like playing cards. He peered from one to the other, as if pondering the next move in a game.

"I think somebody just tried to kill me," Vicky blurted out, surprising herself. It sounded crazy.

The detective's head jerked upward. His eyes leveled on hers. "What're you talkin' about?"

"I was nearly run down by a truck a few minutes ago."

"Somebody tried to run you down?"

Vicky began shaking her head. "I don't want to think so. It's probably just a coincidence." She explained what had happened, how the truck had suddenly appeared, how a crowd had gathered, how no one had gotten the license. She couldn't even identify the make of the truck.

"You got the names of your good Samaritans?"

"No," she admitted, letting out a long breath. She was an attorney; she should have thought of that.

Eberhart looked back at the four sheets of paper, his eyes narrowed, as if he might have missed something the first time. "Where'd you get these?"

Vicky explained they had been arriving over the last three weeks. But this morning's threat had shaken her. It was on her desk. Whoever had left it must have used a key to get into her office.

The white man leaned back, rocking side to side in his chair. "It's been my experience that when somebody gets mad enough to start sendin' threats and mad enough to try runnin' somebody down, the victim has a fair idea where all that madness is comin' from. You think about it, Vicky, you'll probably come up with somebody you pissed off real bad. Maybe some ex-husband that got saddled with a whole lot of alimony and can't see his kids anymore."

Vicky regarded this officer of the law a moment. "I know what this is about, Bob. This is about turning Wind River Reservation into a radioactive dump, which just happens to mean jobs and a boost to the economy in the whole area. I'm on the wrong side, and somebody doesn't want me to warn people about the dangers." She stopped. The realization hit her, like a door slamming in her face. The public hearing was tonight. She was on the agenda. Someone didn't want her to speak, and whoever it was had tried to kill her. The fear she'd felt on the street corner coiled inside her, like a rattlesnake about to strike. She felt as if she were choking.

Eberhart was staring at her. "You okay?"

She swallowed hard and started to explain. The other speakers at the public hearing tonight were all in favor of the facility: Lionel Redbull, the project director; Matthew Bosse, the tribal council member who had first proposed the plan; Alexander and Lily Legeau, who owned the ranch where the facility would be built; and someone named Paul Bryant, the president of the company whose sole purpose was to find a site where utility companies could dump their nuclear waste. Everyone, it seemed, wanted to dump it on the reservation—except for her.

"Nothin' in these threats says anything about nuclear waste." The detective's gaze shifted among the four pieces of paper. "On the other hand . . ." He set both elbows on the desk, made a tent of his hands, and peered at her over the tops of long fingers. "I read those articles you wrote for the *Gazette*. You got yourself involved in some real controversial stuff. Everybody on the rez could use the money from this facility, and lots of Indians want steady jobs. One of 'em could be warnin' you off."

"How about one of the white people?" Vicky locked eyes with the white man across the desk. "A lot of people in Lander and Riverton would like to see the facility built, especially if it's stuck out on the Legeau ranch in the middle of the reservation, far from their homes and water supply. They could have the economic benefits without the hazards."

Eberhart leaned back and drew in his lower lip. After a moment he said, "Maybe you got somethin'. We'll see if we can lift some fingerprints. In the meantime, I want you to make up a list of folks on the other side of this nuclear waste business. Anybody, white or Indian, who might be wantin' you to back off. And while you're at it, put down anybody you might've pissed off for any other reason." The detective stood up and leaned over the desk. "While we're checkin' this out, I don't want you goin' anywhere by yourself." The detective's tone had become fatherly; concern shone in his eyes.

Vicky rose to her feet. "That's crazy, Bob. I can't lock myself up. Whoever's trying to scare me off will have succeeded."

"You own a gun, Vicky?"

"Of course not."

"I can get a permit processed."

"I'm not going to carry a gun." Vicky stepped over to the door and pulled it open.

"Hold up there." Eberhart laid one hand on her arm, a friendly gesture, yet firm. "I'm gonna send a report on this over to Chief Banner. And I'll have a talk with folks around your office. Somebody might've gotten a good look at that truck, and somebody might've seen somethin' unusual last night. We'll keep an eye on your office and house, Vicky, but you gotta take responsibility for your own safety. There's people out there capable of murder, you know. A cowboy got murdered on the rez last night."

"What?" Vicky backed against the doorjamb, freeing herself from the man's grip. She hadn't heard about any murder. If she lived on the reservation, she would have gotten the news on the moccasin telegraph first thing this morning. But she lived and worked in Lander. Lately she had begun to feel even more isolated. Her own people didn't trust what she was trying to tell them. Didn't trust her, because she wasn't among them. When they needed her services, they had to come to the white world to find her. And now this news from the reservation—filtered through a white man.

"Some drifter," the detective was saying. "Male. Indian. No ID yet. Found shot to death out in an abandoned cabin on Johnstown Road."

"Who found him?"

"Priest from St. Francis Mission. Got a call late last night and drove out to a deserted cabin owned by a family named Hooshie. You know Father O'Malley, don't you? Somebody's in trouble, he's gonna try and help 'em."

"Yes," she said. "He's a good priest."

Eberhart stepped back behind the desk, picked up the phone, and pushed in some numbers. "I'm gonna have an officer drive you back to your office. You're not gonna fight me on that, are ya?"

Vicky glanced down the empty hallway, her thoughts a jumble: the nuclear waste proposal, the black truck roaring down on her, the threats, the murdered Indian on Johnstown Road. None of it would make her crawl into a shell, frighten her away from what she believed in. She would not allow it. She had faced tougher things thirteen years ago—a lifetime ago—when she'd realized she had to leave her husband Ben before he went on another drunk and killed her. When she'd had to leave their two kids, Susan and Lucas, with her mother and drive down the road without her children. When she'd driven all the way to Denver to go to school although she didn't know anyone in the white world and didn't know how she would make it.

She locked eyes again with the detective. "Thanks, Bob, for taking this seriously, but—"

"Oh, I take it seriously, all right," he interrupted.

"I intend to walk back to my office."

"Yeah." He set the receiver in its cradle, a grim look in his eyes. "I was afraid of that."

She was partway down the hall when he called out: "Be careful, Vicky."

❮ 5 ❯

Father John followed the narrow path across the center of St. Francis Mission. Sunlight filtered through the branches of the old cottonwoods and glistened on the buffalo grass. He drew in a deep breath of air thick with the smells of sage and wet grass. His head was beginning to clear, the ache a half-remembered dream. The sun felt warm on his back, but a breeze plucked at his shirt, and black-lined clouds hovered below the peaks of the Wind River Mountains in the distance. It was one of those moments he'd come to love about spring on the plains—when the earth and the sky seemed to flow together, almost to exchange places, so that it appeared as if the mountains rose out of the clouds themselves.

Walks-on bounded across Circle Drive, a red Frisbee in his mouth, and Father John shifted the stack he was carrying into the crook of one arm: two books on the Plains Indians that he'd borrowed from the Riverton library, a folder of letters he meant to answer, and the environmental report on the waste facility. The report was the only thing he'd gotten to last night. He managed to grab the Frisbee without dropping everything else and sailed it through the air. The dog bounded across the grass, spun on his back leg, and grabbed the spinning disk. He trotted back, and Father John threw the Frisbee again before starting up the cement steps in front of the administration building. He let himself in through the heavy wooden door.

The corridor had the high, stuccoed ceilings of the nineteenth century. It felt stale and cool, like a museum. Light from the glass ceiling fixtures cast a pinkish glow over the framed portraits above the oak wainscoting. The Jesuits of St. Francis Mission, his predecessors, stared at him through their little, round, metal-framed glasses. From farther along the corridor came the *tap-tap* sound of Father Geoff at his keyboard.

Father John stepped into his office on the right and dropped the books and folder onto the papers already spread over his desk. He tossed his cowboy hat onto the top of the bookcase, aware the tapping noise had ceased. There was the *squish-squish* sound of footsteps in the corridor.

Suddenly the other priest stood in the doorway, looking much like a serious college student. He wore a blue polo shirt, khaki slacks, and sneakers. His blond hair was combed neatly to one side, his blue eyes outsized by pinkish, bone-framed glasses. He was thirty-eight, a priest for three years now—a responsibility, Father John knew, that this new assistant took seriously, like everything else.

Father Geoff advanced into the office, one hand gripping a file folder. "Telephone's been ringing all morning. Everybody wants to know who was killed last night. Seems to think you'd have the answer." The younger priest shook his head in a slow, deliberate motion. "I tried to tell you not to go out. Looks like I was right. It was even more dangerous than I'd suspected. This the usual routine around here—middle-of-the-night calls? Murders?"

"Not every night." Father John shuffled through a pile of phone messages. He didn't want to discuss the poor cowboy with half his face shot off. Anyway, his assistant probably already knew as much as he did. The moccasin telegraph was unpredictable; Elena hadn't heard the news this morning—that's why she'd made such a fuss, wanting all the fragments. He thought of news as always arriving in fragments, like a dream that had to be reconstructed. He preferred his news whole, which was why, he supposed, he'd chosen the field of history. The news had already happened in history. It was complete. It could be observed and analyzed, placed into context, with precedents and antecedents. It allowed the illusion that events were comprehensible.

He was aware of his assistant's eyes on him as the younger priest slapped a folder on top of the books and letters Father John had just added to the clutter on his desk. "St. Francis Mission," Father Geoff began, "cannot continue to spend more money than it takes in. Nothing, with the exception of the federal government, can operate that way."

Father John slid back in his chair, bracing himself for the lecture sure to follow. "So I've heard."

Turning abruptly, his assistant walked over to one of the side chairs along the wall and sat down. "This is serious, John. I've gone over the accounts closely. The mission is this close to bankruptcy." He held out one hand, rubbing the thumb and index finger together.

"We've been that close for years," Father John said. As long as he had been here, anyway. He'd never been good at schmoozing with the businessmen in Riverton and Lander. They had stopped inviting him to dinners and cocktail parties sometime during his first six months here . . . or had he just started turning down the invitations? He couldn't remember. In any case, he had come to depend upon the kindness of strangers, to hope for the little miracles, which he always believed were about to occur. It never surprised him to open the mail and find a check—sometimes large enough to cover that month's bills. Not a method of financial planning this new assistant was likely to endorse.

"The Provincial—" Father Geoff began.

"The Provincial?"

"—is concerned, and rightly so, in my opinion, about the financial status of St. Francis Mission."

Father John leaned back in his chair. This new assistant with a background in finance hadn't been sent here by chance. He had been sent to straighten out the mission finances and, in the process, to straighten out the way Father John managed things.

"I suggest two viable solutions."

Father John gave the other priest his full attention.

"First, we must cut back on certain programs."

"And what might those be? Al-Anon? Religious education? Adult literacy? Shall we put off the repairs, like fixing the church roof?" Now with the rainy season, the leaky roof had become a major concern. It had poured last Sunday, and the entire time he was saying the ten o'clock Mass, he'd watched the thin stream of water running down the wall next to the altar. Leonard's cousin, Ralph Fox, had patched the roof a couple years ago. He'd tried to call him, but Ralph no longer had a phone. He would have to find some other way to get ahold of him.

"If we can't support a program," Father Geoff was saying, "we should drop it. If we can't fix the roof, well . . ." He shrugged. "We have to curtail our expenses until we institute new forms of revenue. I suggest tithing."

Father John was quiet. This was worse than he'd suspected. After a moment he said, "How can we ask the Arapahos to give ten percent of what they have? They don't have that much."

"Many churches tithe. A perfectly respectable tradition. Biblical, I don't need to remind you." The other priest's tone implied he *did* need to remind him.

Father John shook his head. "It's the Arapaho Way to be generous," he said, thinking of the "feasts" he'd been invited to at Blue Sky Hall where the food often consisted of bologna sandwiches and coffee, all the people could provide. "They give what they can. I'm not going to ask them to make that kind of sacrifice."

"Life is a sacrifice." The younger priest tossed out the words as if they had no weight.

Father John looked away a moment, aware of the old building creaking and sighing, as if it had its own concerns. He was thinking of Edel Long, who had just lost his job with the state highway department, and Rosie Big Bear, who eked out a living for her three kids as a waitress in Lander.

"There is another option. Less painful, but effective," Father Geoff said.

"Let me guess." Father John turned back to the younger priest. "We could hold bingo games in Eagle Hall."

"Exactly."

"Not while I'm pastor here," he said, getting to his feet.

A look of acute disappointment came into the other priest's face. Two weeks of careful financial analysis for nothing. He stood up slowly. "The Provincial has instructed me to remedy the abysmal financial situation here. He has already approved these options." He pointed to the folder on the desk. "I suggest you take this up with him." He turned and strode through the doorway. The *squish-squish* noise of his sneakers receded down the corridor.

Father John picked up the folder and flung it across the office. It landed at the foot of the chair the other priest had just vacated, white pages splayed against the wooden legs. Then he grabbed his cowboy hat from the bookshelf and slammed out the front door.

‹ 6 ›

He strode back across the mission ignoring the path, his boots flattening the short, wet fronds of buffalo grass. The Toyota was still parked outside the priests' residence where he'd left it in the early morning hours, and he folded himself behind the wheel. Then he took a deep breath. St. Francis was sinking in red ink. Like any business, it had to be floated into the black if it was to continue operating. Logical. But how to do it? He knew his assistant's conclusions were also logical, but he didn't like them. "Dear Lord," he said under his breath. "Spare me from take-charge assistants with financial degrees and perfectly logical conclusions."

Father John jabbed the key into the ignition and gave it a quick turn. The engine coughed and belched just long enough to make him think this could be the day the Toyota decided to break down for all time. More proof for the priest back in the administration building that drastic financial measures were needed. Finally the motor came to life, shaky and tentative.

He wheeled around Circle Drive while yanking an opera tape from the glove compartment and inserting it into the player. *Faust* burst into the cab, flooding him with the emotions of last night. For an instant he was back in the dark cabin, rain plinking against the tin roof, the cowboy slumped in the corner, alone in death. He hit the Stop button, extracted the tape, and, glancing between the road and the other tapes, selected *Carmen*. As he turned right onto Seventeen-Mile Road, "Toreador en garde" rose around him, robust and certain, not unlike the attitude of his new assistant. Easier to handle, somehow, than the lonely, sad ending of a man's life.

He rolled down his window partway. The rush of air mingled with the voices of the chorus and filled the cab with the pungent odor of damp earth and wild, wet grasses, of rebirth and hope. The long drives across the reservation, his operas—usually any opera would do— always calmed him, brought him back to himself. Just past St. Francis cemetery, he saw the traffic slowing ahead as it approached the turn onto Highway 789. He let up on the accelerator and coasted behind a dark, mud-spattered pickup. In the rearview mirror, he watched another pickup roll close to his tailgate, a line of other vehicles slowing behind it. Ahead a crowd of demonstrators marched down the center of the road, jabbing signs into the air, shouting at the line of trucks and cars. Father John leaned toward the windshield, catching the black words on the signs: NUCLEAR WASTE KILLS CHILDREN AND OTHER LIVING THINGS. NOW IS THE HOUR. STOP NUCLEAR POWER.

The passenger in the pickup ahead was leaning out the window, shouting and banging on the door, as if it were a drum. One of the demonstrators whirled about and started toward the pickup. He looked to be in his forties, an aging hippie, T-shirt taut across a bulging stomach, long blond hair pulled back in a ponytail. He waved his sign side to side, eyes bulging, cheeks flushed.

The pickup's passenger door snapped open. An Indian jumped out and lurched toward the demonstrator. Father John leaned onto the horn. The noise came like the blast of a steam whistle. Both men froze, then turned toward the Toyota, a mixture of surprise and irritation on their faces. The demonstrator shrugged—a change of mind—and started back toward the others. He thrust the sign high overhead, shouting something Father John couldn't make out.

The Indian stumbled against the side of the pickup and braced himself before pushing off toward the Toyota. Father John recognized him. He'd asked him to leave the Al-Anon meeting at St. Francis a few weeks ago, after he'd tried to pick a fight with everybody in Eagle Hall. He was drunk then, and, judging by the way he lurched around the hood, he was drunk now.

Father John got out slowly and slammed the door. He kept one hand flat against the hard roll of metal below the half-opened window, sensing the vibration the motor sent through the pickup. The marching notes of *Carmen* mingled with the sound of honking horns, the shouts of the protesters, someone yelling, "Move it!"

"You with us?" the Indian asked, leaning toward him. The sharp, sour odor of whiskey passed like an invisible cloud between them, and Father John stopped himself from stepping back. He would not give the slightest hint of backing away. Drunks were bullies and cowards. He'd learned years ago as a kid in Boston that when you stood up to the bully, the coward usually appeared.

"You're holding up traffic." He kept his voice firm, neutral. His eyes still on the Indian, he gave a little nod toward the traffic stacking up behind.

The Indian blinked, as if trying to bring the situation into focus. "Them outsiders don't have no right comin' here tellin' us what to do." He spat out the words. The saliva flew in the air like tiny silver beads. "You gotta decide which side you're on, you wanna stay around here."

Other horns started to honk—a cacophonous chorus. Father John could feel the tension in the man in front of him, a warrior surrounded by enemies: demonstrators ahead, angry motorists behind.

"Look," he began, using the counseling voice, quiet and calm, "the public hearing's tonight at Blue Sky Hall. That's the time to talk about the facility."

The man blinked hard, as if he'd glimpsed a way out of the ambush but wasn't sure whether to take it. From Seventeen-Mile Road came the wail of sirens, and the traffic ahead started to move onto the highway. The driver of the pickup leaned out his door. "Come on," he shouted. "Let's get the hell outta here."

The Indian hesitated, his gaze traveling between the pickup and the sound of the siren. The scrunch of metal gears caught his attention as the pickup lurched forward.

"Wait." He whirled about and grabbed the tailgate, running alongside, finally yanking open the passenger door. Then he fell inside and pulled the door shut. The rear wheels ground against the asphalt as the pickup spurted into the highway traffic.

Father John got back in the Toyota and drove past the demonstrators drawing into a circle at the side of the road. He turned north. In the side mirror he saw the BIA police car pull past the line of traffic and stop next to the demonstrators.

Then they were out of sight—the police, the demonstrators, Seventeen-Mile Road. Lost behind the squat, frame buildings that lined the west side of Highway 789—the lumberyard and hardware store, the Cozy-U Motel and self-serve gas station, the package liquor store with its red-lettered sign: SIX-PACK SPECIAL. MALT LIQUOR. BEST PRICE IN TOWN.

Milky rays of sunshine slanted across the buildings and the asphalt ahead. The sky was the lightest of blues, like faded silk; the air cool as it whipped around the cab. He turned up the volume on *Carmen* and thought of what the Indian had said: *You wanna stay around here . . .*

Of course he wanted to stay. Everything he cared about was here. Not at the Jesuit schools where he'd taught American history, not in Boston where he'd grown up. He hardly had any family left in Boston, just his brother, and he hadn't seen Mike and Eileen and the kids in nine years. Not since Mike had made it clear—more by what he didn't say than by what he did—that he didn't want him around. They both knew that if Father John hadn't decided to become a Jesuit, he was the brother who would be married to Eileen.

He felt a familiar stab of sadness: These were not memories he wanted. This was home now, the people here his family. And he seemed to have landed in the middle of a family squabble—the idea made him uncomfortable. It looked like most of the people wanted the facility. But last week at the senior citizens meeting, the old women had leaned their heads together and talked in hushed, tense voices as they beaded moccasins and key chains—arthritic fingers working in quick, jerky motions, not the smooth rhythms they usually flowed in. The grandmothers opposed the facility, he was sure, but it wasn't their place to speak out in public. Vicky had become their spokeswoman. He smiled at the irony. They had ignored her when she came back to the reservation three years ago: a woman who had divorced her husband and become a lawyer. Like a white woman.

She hadn't returned his call, and he made a mental note to try her office again when he got to Gianelli's. He swallowed back the sense of longing at the thought of her. He didn't want to think of her. He'd had years of experience at keeping his thoughts in an orderly, logical, appropriate sequence, at blocking out inappropriate emotions.

He had expected temptations as a priest; he'd been

prepared for temptations. He knew he'd be tempted against the vow of obedience—he came from a long line of stubborn Irish men and women who ground in their heels and took a perverse pleasure in refusing to obey orders. He'd almost broken the vow when the Provincial had ordered him to an Indian mission. Thank God he'd kept it. Now he felt as if his coming here had been part of some unfathomable plan for his life that only he knew nothing about.

He'd even expected to be tempted by alcohol, but that was one temptation he'd believed himself strong enough to overcome. He wasn't his father, thwarted in his dreams and ambitions, a brilliant conductor reduced to coaxing symphonies out of the spoutings and hissings of the steam furnaces of Boston College. No, he'd had the chance to make his dreams come true, to become a Jesuit, to teach history—the subject he loved.

But he hadn't been strong enough. He hadn't taken close enough measure of the enemy, or realized how devious it was, how it would lie in wait to snag him at his lowest points, at his loneliest, just as it had his father.

But to be tempted by a woman—he had put the possibility out of his mind. There had been one woman for him, he'd convinced himself, and the day he had told Eileen of his decision to become a priest he had considered the matter closed forever. It was not a matter he wanted to reconsider.

He parked the Toyota next to the curb on Main Street across from the two-story, red-brick building that housed the local FBI offices. Ted Gianelli's office took up part of the second floor. The shades were raised, and Father John could see globes of light beaming off the ceiling inside. The agent would be waiting.

❮ 7 ❯

The first floor of the FBI offices cried out with efficiency—brown tweed carpeting, cream-colored walls with framed prints of horses, rivers, and mountains. A receptionist with short, stylish blond hair and wide-open blue eyes sat behind a wooden desk in the small office to the right of the entry. "Upstairs, Father," she said as he stepped through the oak-framed doorway.

He asked if he could make a telephone call, and she pushed the phone across the desk. He punched in Vicky's number. The same tentative voice, the same message: Ms. Holden was still out on an emergency. He said he would call later and replaced the receiver with a sense of uneasiness, wondering what emergency had kept her out all morning.

He started up the narrow flight of stairs that hugged the wall across from the entry. The carved oak railing felt warm and satiny under his hand, a relic of another, more leisurely time. The mournful notes of a soprano floated from the hallway above. He recognized the aria at once: "Vissi d'arte" from *Tosca*. On the landing stood Ted Gianelli, thick black eyebrows lifted in mock surprise, dark hair barbered close to his scalp, one fleshy hand resting on the knob of the bannister. "Saw the Toyota drive up," he said. "Heard it. Smelled it."

Father John laughed. Nobody appreciated the Toyota, it seemed. That, and the fact it got him where he wanted to go, made him extremely fond of it.

He followed the agent through the doorway on the right, directly above the receptionist's office, toward the voice of Kiri Te Kanawa. The office was small and as neat as his was cluttered: an oak desk with a green-shaded lamp on the polished top, a single file folder positioned squarely in the center. Behind the desk, a swivel chair and a window that framed the peaked roofs of the buildings across the street. On the left wall, a bank of gray metal file cabinets. On the right, a couple of straight-backed chairs in front of an audio system sheathed in black glass. The music was so clear, the soprano and the orchestra might have stepped from behind the glass at any moment.

Father John stifled a groan of envy. Poverty was another vow he'd never thought he'd be tempted against. Material things never meant much to him. But every once in a while . . .

Gianelli dropped into his leather chair with the gracefulness of an athlete, despite his six-foot height and 220-pound bulk. "Last act of *Tosca*, set where?" It was an ongoing game between them—opera trivia.

Father John took one of the straight-backed chairs. He removed his hat and dangled it over one knee. "Castel Saint d'Angelo. That the best you can come up with?"

"Second act?" Gianelli spread thick fingers on the polished desk top, the glint of competition in his eyes.

"That would be the Palazzo Farnese."

The agent let out a loud guffaw. "Should know better than to ask a priest about the landmarks of Rome." He opened the middle drawer of his desk and retrieved a small, black object which he aimed at the audio system. *Tosca* faded into the background, like the blinds stacked against the top of the window. From outside came the sound of a horn bleating.

The agent's expression turned serious. "Looks like last night's victim caught a bullet from across the cabin. Banner's had investigators there since dawn. Not happy about it. He's got the whole BIA force on overtime keeping the roads clear and traffic moving, with all the nuclear protesters on the reservation."

The agent flipped open the folder in front of him and began thumbing through a stack of papers. "Banner's boys got several casts of footprints," he continued. "Yours among them, most likely. Also lifted a couple of partial fingerprints that'll probably turn out to be the victim's, and vacuumed up some hairs and fibers. Slim evidence, except for this." He extracted what he seemed to be looking for—a plastic evidence bag—and tossed it across the desk.

Father John picked it up and turned it slowly in his hand, examining the sole content: a silver button about the size of a quarter, large enough to button a jacket or coat. One side shiny and clear, except for the tiny sterling silver mark. The other side etched in feathers and circles, an Indian design.

"Recognize it?"

Father John shook his head and handed the bag back across the desk. "I don't know many people who wear expensive jackets with silver buttons."

"Just wanted to make sure before I sent it to the lab. Maybe we'll get lucky and get a print off it." Gianelli bit in his lower lip as he stuffed the plastic bag back into the folder. "We'll know more soon's we get the autopsy and lab reports. So far, all we've got is an ID. We ran the victim's fingerprints this morning. Your murdered cowboy was Gabriel Many Horses, Arapaho, born sixty-two years ago in El Reno, Oklahoma."

So the murdered man is mine, Father John thought. *Fair enough.* He had found him, had prayed for him in his death, would see that he had a proper funeral, if no one else did. There was a bond between them now.

"Any family here?" Father John didn't recognize the cowboy's name, but he could have connections on the reservation. All the Arapahos were connected in one way or another, through blood, marriage, or some spiritual bond, not unlike this new bond between himself and the dead cowboy.

"Nobody by the name of Many Horses around here," Gianelli said, shifting his bulk in the chair. "Couple of families by that name in Oklahoma. We'll contact them. Looks like the victim was a drifter. String of DUIs in Arizona, New Mexico, Colorado. Last week, he was working on a ranch outside Grand Junction. Collected a paycheck on Friday—$1,130.18. Cashed it at a Grand Junction bank in the afternoon and, by the looks of things, decided to head north. No sign of any vehicle. Either he hitchhiked or hopped the bus. I'm checking both possibilities. In any case, he ended up robbed and dead."

Father John glanced out the window. Clouds scuttled through the blue sky and sunlight peeled off the metal trim on the roof across the street. Banner had also mentioned robbery, but robbery didn't explain the fear in the cowboy's voice—the sense of being in a race against time. *I'm dying.*

"I don't buy it," Father John said, locking eyes with the agent. The music of *Tosca* drifted softly around them. "He saw somebody hit an old man in the head with a shovel. He'd been dreaming about it. It weighed on his conscience. Somebody killed him before he could talk about it."

Gianelli shrugged. "Money's missing. Pockets cleaned out. No old cowboy is about to give up his wad gracefully, even at the point of a gun. So . . ." Gianelli threw out both arms, as if the conclusion were obvious. Then he opened the center desk drawer and extracted a yellow pad. He set it next to the folder and brought a ballpoint pen from the drawer. "I've gone over the statement you gave Banner last night. We don't know who actually called you—the cowboy, or somebody who wanted you to find the body."

"It was the cowboy." Father John heard the stubbornness in his voice.

"Okay, okay. Let's go over everything. Every detail. Anything you might remember. You never know what might be important."

Father John glanced out the window again. In his mind he saw the darkness of last night, like a bad dream in all its jumbled, senseless details. He was flipping off the light in the study, starting up the dark stairs with the phone in hand, sinking onto the step as the phone rang.

He began with the call, then stopped. He'd forgotten something earlier. "There was the sound of traffic in the background," he said, "a whooshing noise. The cowboy must have called from an outdoor phone."

The agent scribbled on the yellow pad. "Okay. What else?"

Father John began again, describing the drive through the rainy night. He paused, remembering. After he'd turned off Highway 132, he didn't meet another vehicle, except . . . "A pickup came toward me heading south on Johnstown Road."

Gianelli's pen made scratchy sounds on the paper. "Funny how little details creep back into memory. What kind of pickup?"

Father John tried to visualize the vehicle rushing past. "I didn't get the make. But it was a dark color. Blue or green. Black, maybe."

The agent set the pen down and leaned back in his chair, clasping both hands behind his head. "So, let's assume it was the victim that called, since you seem certain it was. In forty-five, fifty minutes, somebody picked him up, drove to the log cabin, robbed him, and shot him. Then got out of there just before you showed up. Pretty close timing, wouldn't you agree? Either the victim called you from a phone close by or somebody else called and sent you to the cabin. Since there aren't any phones close by, my bet is on the latter."

"It took me twenty minutes to get to the phone at Betty's Place in Ethete," Father John said. "He could've called from there. The phone's outside, close to the road."

"I'll check it out." Gianelli got to his feet. "You got that? I'll check everything out. You're a damn good priest, John. You run that Indian mission on thin air and a lot of good intentions. Far as I can tell, the Arapahos think you're great. But that doesn't make you a great investigator. So you stick to your mission work, and soon as I learn anything, I'll let you know." The agent's tone had begun to soften. "I know you feel, well, involved, since you're the one who found the body."

"Let me know if he has any family," Father John said, lifting himself off the hard wood chair and setting his cowboy hat on his head. "I'd like to see that the poor guy has a proper funeral."

Gianelli hauled himself around the desk and placed one hand firmly on Father John's shoulder as they stepped out into the hall. "Come to dinner Sunday night," he said. "Maria'll fix spaghetti with that home-made sausage of hers. You can play with the kids."

Father John said he would have to let him know. The men's Al-Anon group and the Social Concerns Committee met on Sunday night, and his assistant might balk at taking both. He was down the stairs and in the front entry when Gianelli called out: "You spend too much time alone out there on that reservation. And don't tell me that old housekeeper and that robotlike assistant of yours are family. You're alone, buddy."

He turned and waved at the FBI agent, who was leaning over the bannister. Then he let himself out the door.

◀ 8 ▶

Father John guided the Toyota down Main Street a few blocks, then turned left and headed toward the outskirts. Traffic was light, typical midday traffic in a small town. The sun poked through drifting clouds. Shadows spiraled across the stores and restaurants, the supermarket and parking lot, the pickups at the curbs. He thought about what Gianelli had said. To a man with a wife and four kids, a priest must look like the loneliest guy in the world. But the Jesuits had been sending men out alone to faraway places for four hundred years. He was part of a long tradition: the tradition of the shepherd. And the shepherd was always alone.

He wheeled the Toyota into the graveled parking lot in front of a gray metal building with black block letters superimposed against the flat edge of the roof: ROOFS AND GUTTERS. The end of the building looked like a large garage, its overhang door flung open. Two trucks blocked the opening. Several men were loading buckets of tar, long-handled brushes, and shovels into the truck beds.

Father John parked on the far side and got out just as a short, heavyset man in jeans and white T-shirt emerged from the garage carrying a tar-smeared canvas. "Help you?" he asked as he punched the canvas down around the tools and buckets in the bed of one truck. Blue snakes and dragons crawled up the knotted muscles of his arms.

"Where can I find the boss?"

Metal hinges screeched into the air as the man lifted the tailgate and nodded. "Office that way."

Father John walked alongside the building, gravel crackling under his boots. The sun bounced off the metal wall and created a corridor of warmth, a hint of summer to come. A few feet from the corner was an unpainted wood door. He let himself inside.

A woman with short, honey-colored hair and large shoulders glanced up from the stack of papers on her desk. She looked older than she probably was, her face mapped in lines, like furrows in a miniature field. Father John introduced himself, said he was the priest from St. Francis Mission, and asked for Ralph Fox.

The woman's forehead wrinkled into deeper lines; her whole body seemed to stiffen. "He don't work here no more, Father." She stopped a moment, then hurried on, as if she felt compelled to explain—he was, after all, the Indian priest. "It's not like he didn't do a good job, or nothin' like that. But this is a small business me and my husband, Ed, run. This winter . . ." She shrugged and looked away. Remembering. "All that snow, there just wasn't much call for roofers, so we had to let a couple crews go. Only started hirin' back last week." She nodded in the direction of the men loading the trucks outside.

"Do you know if Ralph's working somewhere else?"

The woman hesitated. "Well, me and Ed run the only roofing business in town." What might have passed for embarrassment flickered in her eyes, and she blinked it away. "Anything we can do for you?"

Father John turned the knob and pulled the door open, considering. He could ask her to send someone to give him an estimate on fixing the roof, but he decided against it. As he stepped outside, he touched one finger to the brim of his cowboy hat—a gesture he'd picked up living in the West, a shortcut for whatever needed to be said: "Thanks, but no thanks" or "Much obliged." Everyone understood its meaning at the moment.

He retraced his steps along the building, the sun warm on his shoulders and back. One truck had pulled out, but a couple of men were still piling supplies into the other truck. That's the way it was, he thought. An Arapaho like Ralph Fox was the last to land a job, the first to lose it, the last to be called back. No wonder the business council wanted to build the nuclear waste storage facility. It would mean jobs the people could depend upon.

He drove the Toyota back toward Main Street, then south to Seventeen-Mile Road. The demonstrators had disappeared; traffic moved as usual. Turning right, he headed toward the wall of mountains in the distance, peaks bathed in white clouds, slopes etched in snow. His stomach rumbled. He hadn't had anything to eat since the toast and coffee he'd wolfed down earlier. Elena would have sandwiches waiting, but he wasn't ready to face Father Geoff yet. They seemed destined to be at loggerheads, he and this new assistant. What was the Provincial thinking of? An Irishman and a German at the same mission? He drove on.

He caught up to the protesters, white signs bobbing in the air as they marched along the road near the senior citizens' center. He could see the rows of cars and trucks parked in the lot behind the red brick building. The number of outsiders surprised him—more than he'd ever seen on the reservation at one time. Vicky's articles in the *Gazette* must have been picked up by newspapers around the West, and somebody had made sure a large opposition would be on hand for the public hearing. The sound of chanting filtered into the cab and mixed with the music of *Carmen*.

At Given's Road, he swung right. All around, the land dipped into arroyos and rose into bluffs. The breeze ruffled the wild grasses; the sagebrush and cactus shivered as if the earth itself were moving. *The earth is alive,* the elders had told him many times. A creature, like other creatures, growing and changing and becoming: never showing the same face. On days like today, he understood.

He slowed around the curve as the road jogged west. Another mile, and he pulled up in the soft dirt next to a pink house hunched down in the middle of the open plains. Toward the back stood a green pickup, the hood propped up on a metal pole, a man curled over the engine. Ralph at home in the middle of the day meant he didn't have anyplace else to go. Father John slid out of the cab, giving the door a hard slam.

The Indian straightened upright, a startled look in his dark eyes. Then his face relaxed and broke into a grin as he stepped around the truck, wiping his hands on the grease-smeared towel he'd pulled from the back pocket of his jeans. "Howdy, Father," he said.

Father John reached out and shook the other man's hand. The smell of motor oil floated on the breeze. There was the usual exchange of pleasantries: It wasn't polite to get right to the purpose of the visit. He asked Ralph how things were going, how LuAnn and the kids were doing. Fine, everything was just fine. Neither was it polite to burden other people with your problems.

"LuAnn," Ralph called, "come on out here. We got us a visitor." As if he knew it would be a few moments before his wife prepared herself and the kids for company, he asked how things were going at the mission.

"Good," Father John said. A bit of a lie that, but they were still in the dance of pleasantries. The sun slid wholly behind a cloud, throwing the house and trucks into shadow. A coolness spiked the breeze.

Ralph said, "Figured you might be comin' round."

"You did?"

"Yeah. Soon's I heard about the leakin' roof, I says to LuAnn, Father John's gonna be payin' a visit."

Father John laughed. "What else did you hear on the moccasin telegraph?"

"You gonna want me to fix it."

"You hear how I'm going to pay for it?"

"Oh, yeah. You been praying for some kind of miracle."

"I'm expecting one at any moment."

Ralph threw a light punch to Father John's arm. "Tell you what. I'll come by and fix the roof. You pay me soon's that miracle shows up. Anyway, once that nuclear facility gets approved, I'm gonna have some good, steady work. That's if them outsiders don't blow up the whole deal. Wouldn't surprise me none if one of them got himself shot last night."

"He was an Arapaho," Father John said, his thoughts abruptly pulled from the ordinary problems— the leaking roof, the chronically depleted finances—to the dead cowboy. The cowboy would be there, he realized, at the edge of his thoughts, until he knew what had happened to the man. "He was from Oklahoma," he heard himself explaining. "He'd been working on a ranch in Colorado. His name was Gabriel Many Horses."

The screen door slapped against its wood frame, and LuAnn stood on the cement stoop, a baby slung on one jeans-clad hip. Peering around her was a little boy with eyes as black and shiny as river stones and wide with curiosity. It wasn't every day a red truck drove into the driveway.

"Stay for lunch, Father?" LuAnn called. "I got us some bologna sandwiches and lemonade." She looked like a schoolgirl, with black hair trailing over her shoulders and down the front of her red-print blouse. Her face was scrubbed clean, no trace of makeup. Light glinted in her eyes, which were dark and oval. She was a beautiful woman, Father John thought, and in that instant he understood what the elders meant when they said that in the Old Time, the warriors from other tribes tried to steal Arapaho women, so that beautiful children would be born into their tribes.

He started to decline her invitation. He hadn't come here to take food from the family of an out-of-work man. But the elders also said something else: The world is full of good things. Sometimes they will be offered to you. Never turn down the good that someone brings. He smiled at the young woman and said he'd be glad to stay for lunch.

Ralph hoisted the baby onto his shoulders and clasped the chubby brown legs, swinging from side to side. The child giggled out loud and pulled at his father's hair. Within moments LuAnn had spread a blanket over the bare dirt in front of the stoop. A plate of sandwiches, a pitcher of lemonade, and a stack of red plastic glasses materialized in the center. Another moment, and Father John found himself sitting cross-legged on the edge of the blanket along with the family, biting into a bologna sandwich, washing it down with the sour-sweet lemonade.

"That business last night," Ralph began, glancing from his wife to his little boy—it wasn't good to be too specific—"Father John says the guy's from Oklahoma."

"I was born in Oklahoma," LuAnn said. "What's his name?"

Father John repeated the name he'd learned an hour ago. It already had a familiar sound, like the refrain of a sad melody.

LuAnn was silent a moment. Finally she said, "Some Many Horses lived over by El Reno. Ran a big ranch. I always heard they was stuck up. Thought they was better'n everybody else 'cause they'd held onto their land back when a lotta Oklahoma Indians sold out to the white settlers. Like my great-grandfather. He sold his land." She shrugged and looked into the distance. "He didn't have no choice. He needed the money real bad."

The opening of Oklahoma—Father John had taught the subject in his American history classes. Suddenly the story seemed real, as if it had happened yesterday and still mattered. Odd how history had a way of coming alive for him here, among the Arapahos. More alive than it had ever seemed in the classroom. He finished the sandwich and drained the last of his lemonade.

"Don't matter how stuck up people get," LuAnn was saying. "Nobody deserves . . ." She stopped, looked down at the little boy, and ran her fingers through his black hair.

Ralph said, "Heard the police arrested a couple of protesters this morning for blockin' traffic over at Ethete. They can get real mean for peace-lovin' folks. Wouldn't surprise me none if one of 'em followed that Indian out to that old cabin and robbed him and . . ." Now it was his turn to glance at the boy, who sat sipping lemonade, eyes wide above the brim of the glass.

"It's possible," Father John said. Gianelli and Banner thought so. He might even believe it if he hadn't spoken with the cowboy.

The wind picked up, curling the edges of the blanket; the sun had slipped behind a bank of clouds as heavy and gray as metal. Thunder rumbled over the mountains in the west, and LuAnn jumped up and pulled the little boy with her. Both Father John and Ralph got to their feet, the Indian hoisting the baby under one arm.

"I just wish all them outsiders would stay away from here and tend to their own business," LuAnn said, scooping up the empty glasses in the blanket. They clacked together as she threw the blanket over one shoulder, and, holding onto the boy's hand, stepped onto the front stoop. "They got jobs where they live. We got a right to jobs here."

Father John let the remark pass. It wasn't something he could argue against. He thanked the couple and patted the baby wriggling in the crook of his father's arm. He'd enjoyed being here. He liked the sense, if only for a moment, of being part of a family.

Thunder cracked overhead. Out of nowhere came a gust of wind that slammed the screen door back against the house—the kind of gust that meant rain was close. Father John dipped his head into the wind, holding onto his cowboy hat as he walked to the Toyota.

By the time he backed past the stoop, the family had disappeared inside the house. Suddenly LuAnn burst past the screen door and ran toward the pickup, the wind steering her sideways, her black hair blowing in her face. He hit the brake and reached over to roll down the passenger window. She leaned inside, pushing back her hair with one hand, gripping the rim of the door with the other, as if to stop herself from blowing away. "I just thought of somethin'. Ain't that woman that runs the big ranch south of Lander one of them Many Horses?"

"What woman?"

"The one married that white man." The wind crashed against her, muffling her voice. She shouted, "I hear she's a widow now. Never comes on the reservation. None of them Many Horses ever mixed with the People. Just stays out on her ranch."

"What's it called?"

LuAnn shook her head. "That big place west of the highway, rammed up there against the foothills. You can't miss it."

◄ 9 ►

Big drops of rain splattered against the windshield as Father John drove south on Given's Road. If what LuAnn said was true, the cowboy could have come home—home being where he had some family. And that meant Banner and Gianelli could be right. The cowboy could've flashed his cash in the wrong bar, and somebody could've offered him a ride, intending to rob him. It made sense, except . . . He thumped the edge of the steering wheel with his fist. Except for the phone call.

He turned east on Seventeen-Mile Road, which shimmered in the rain like an Impressionist's painting. Still the rain. The Eagles wouldn't be practicing this afternoon, he realized with an acute sense of disappointment. But the other teams in the league wouldn't be practicing either. That was some consolation.

He was anxious for baseball to start. He loved the practices, the games, the sun streaming over fields that changed from green to brown as the season wore on, the Indian kids connecting with the ball, racing around the bases, sliding into home, uniforms smudged with dirt, brown faces laughing. The shouts and cheers. The unbearable tension when the count was full, the bases loaded, and the best hitter up at bat. Even the errors and fumbled balls and strikeouts—he loved it all.

There was a part of himself he recognized in baseball. Recognized in the Arapaho kids. He hadn't been a whole lot different from them, back when he'd played on the sandlots of Boston. He'd believed in possibilities then. He still did. Just like the kids here. No matter what happened in the past, with each new season came new possibilities, a new beginning.

"It can't rain forever," he said out loud, the sound of his own voice surprising him. Now he was talking to himself. The season had better get underway soon, he thought.

As he turned right into the mission, he spotted the cars and pickups blocking Circle Drive. People were milling about, sweatshirts and jackets flattened against their backs by the rain. Two BIA police cars had drawn in behind the other vehicles, and several policemen, dark slickers snapped over their uniforms, stomped back and forth, like traffic cops, directing the crowd. Father Geoff was sheltering under an umbrella at the top of the stairs, intent on the scene unfolding below.

Father John stopped the pickup and jumped out. Rain lashed at his shirt; the wetness crept across his shoulders. Spotting Chief Banner at the edge of the crowd, he started toward him. "What's going on?" he called.

Banner swung around, anger and determination in his eyes. Thin strands of water ran off the beak of his blue cap. "They're leavin'," he said. An ultimatum. "Real peaceful-like. If the whole lot of 'em isn't off the mission grounds in two minutes, I'm arrestin' 'em for trespassing and disturbing the peace. They'll be guests over at the county jail tonight."

Thunder ripped overhead and, seconds later, lightning flashed around them. One of the protesters turned toward Father John. "You in charge here?" He had a round, fleshy face. Water dripped off the end of his nose, and clumps of blond hair lay flattened against his forehead. His gray sweatshirt had turned wet-black. "Randolph March," he said, "professor of literature,

University of Colorado. It is immoral and outrageous to establish a nuclear waste facility among the indigenous peoples. We are here to ask the priests of St. Francis Mission to stand with us for what is right."

"They've been chanting and shouting for an hour." This from Father Geoff, now planted next to the police chief.

"Because you refused to meet with us," the professor said, turning his gaze on Father Geoff. "A sad day, indeed, when even priests refuse to face the serious moral consequences of storing nuclear waste."

"I informed them they had to leave," Father Geoff shouted, as if to affirm he'd taken the correct action. Water dripped off the black bulge of his umbrella and onto Banner's shoulder. Another clap of thunder, then lightning split the sky, but farther away now, out on the plains.

"Everybody's leavin'," Banner said, stepping forward, as if to herd the professor toward the dispersing crowd.

"I'd like to discuss this with you," Father John said.

A mixture of surprise and wariness crossed the professor's face.

"Come back after the public hearing. I want to hear what the speakers have to say first." Most of the crowd had disappeared amid a chorus of slamming car doors.

March let out a long guffaw. "You'll hear rave reviews. You'll hear how the facility will be the safest scientific experiment since Marconi transmitted a message across the Atlantic. Nobody who opposes the facility will have the chance to speak. The opposition won't be on the agenda."

"Vicky Holden will be speaking." Father John assumed it would be true.

Randolph March was shaking his head. "I'm afraid you are misinformed, Father. Some of the indigenous people, misguided as they may be, intend to build the facility here. Believe me, they have no intention of allowing that attorney to speak, not with the articles she's written." He stepped past them and headed toward one of the remaining pickups. A line of cars and pickups had begun moving around Circle Drive, water splattering in the wake of the tires.

Father John turned back to the police chief, who raised both shoulders in a long, deliberate shrug. Father Geoff moved in closer, hoisting the umbrella a little higher. "He could be right," Banner said. "It's lookin' like that nuclear facility business is decided. Folks wantin' to bring it here don't want any opposition. Vicky's steppin' around land mines. Somebody tried to kill her this morning."

"What?" The sound of his voice startled Father John, as if it had come from someone else. Everything seemed to stop, even time itself.

Banner said, "Didn't she tell you? I thought you two were friends. Somebody tried to run her down in Lander. Detective Eberhart called me about it. Seems she's been getting some threats the last couple weeks." The chief kept his gaze on Father John. "Didn't tell you about any of it, huh?"

Father John looked away. This was the emergency. This was why she hadn't called back. Somebody had tried to kill her. He was aware of his assistant watching him, and he struggled to keep his voice calm. "Is she all right?"

"Scared," Banner said. "Takes a lot to scare that woman. We don't know for sure it has to do with this nuclear waste business. Eberhart thinks it could be something else. Anybody that messes with families the way lawyers do—divorces and all that—well, they pile up enemies. Lander police'll keep a close watch on her. And my boys'll be all over the public hearing in case there's any trouble." The chief placed a gloved hand on

Father John's arm. "Don't worry about her. She did the smart thing takin' it to the police."

The chief removed his hand and started toward the remaining police car, where a lone officer waited in the passenger seat. The other police car had followed the last of the protesters' vehicles out of the mission.

"Come to think of it, John," Banner said, starting to get behind the wheel, one booted foot still set on the ground. "You might wanna reconsider gettin' involved with this nuclear waste business. Father Geoff there"—he nodded toward the younger priest—"was right callin' us. This is volatile stuff. A lot of money ridin' on the outcome. You never know what folks'll do if somebody gets in the way of their gettin' some big money. And another thing, if I was you I'd stay away from the public hearing. No use lookin' for trouble."

Father John started toward the car. "I have no intention of staying away, Banner."

"Why doesn't that surprise me?" The chief lowered himself onto the seat. "You're just like Vicky—way too stubborn for your own good. Neither one of you knows when to back off. Well, this nuclear facility's somethin' you oughtta think about backin' away from. Let the experts make the decisions. Look where her meddling has got Vicky. Somebody warnin' her off, tryin' to scare her. Some screwball even tryin' to run her down. Neither of you gets paid for takin' those kinds of risks, you know. We're the ones getting paid for that." He pulled the door shut, and the police car started around Circle Drive.

Father John walked past the other priest toward the rain-washed steps of the administration building, his shirt soaked against his back. As he passed Father Geoff, he saw the judgment in the man's eyes.

❮ 10 ❯

Headlights streamed across the parking lot in front of Blue Sky Hall as pickups and 4x4s rolled between rows of parked vehicles searching for empty spaces. A crowd gathered at the front door, holding signs overhead—white flags shimmering in the glow of the lights. Vicky stared past the rain on the Bronco's windshield, her stomach tightening into a knot: Her articles had brought the protesters here. Her own people had to dodge past them to enter the hall.

She punched down on the accelerator and swerved around a couple of cars waiting to turn into the lot. A little farther, and she wheeled to the right, sending the Bronco bumping through a shallow ditch. Water spurted over the windshield, and suddenly she was rolling across the graveled lot toward the west side.

Just as her grandfather used to do, with the whole family packed into the pickup, four adults up front, kids on the hard, ridged floor in back, bundled in scratchy wool blankets. He would pull around the traffic on Ethete Road and plunge downward across the ditch—a shallow ditch, any good quarter horse could bound across—and park on the west side for the powwows, the wakes, the meetings, all the excuses for the People to come together, just as they did in the Old Time. She felt a momentary surge of satisfaction: She wouldn't have to walk past the outsiders.

She set the Bronco close to the building. The headlights washed over the red paint faded to the color of dried raspberries. Hers was the only vehicle in the side lot, which gave way to the open spaces beyond, the wide expanse of darkness. She flipped off the headlights. Except for the thin splotches of moonlight falling through the clouds, darkness crept around her. She grabbed her purse from the seat and leaned over to retrieve the briefcase that had slipped to the floor.

As she stepped out into the rain, she saw a small group approaching, blurred, bulky shapes moving in and out of the moonlight. She couldn't tell whether they were men or women. They walked with assurance, as if they intended to overtake her, to place themselves between her and the side entrance.

She drew in her breath, slung the strap of her purse over her shoulder, set the briefcase against the Bronco's door, and slammed it hard. A sharp whack in the darkness. Then she started toward the hall, her high heels tapping the gravel. She ignored the shadowy figures drawing so close she could sense the moist heat of their bodies. "Vicky, wait." A woman's voice.

She swung around, facing five women in parkas and slickers, hoods pulled low over their foreheads against the prickly rain. One of the women stepped forward. She recognized Liz Abel; they'd gone to St. Francis Mission School together until the eighth grade, when Liz had dropped out. She'd had a son that year. Now deep creases ran at the edge of her cheeks; her lips looked chapped. There was tiredness in her eyes, and a blend of fear and confusion. "Maybe you don't wanna go in there," Liz said.

Vicky was quiet, waiting. The sounds of tires crunching gravel floated from the front; a headlight bounced into the side lot and caught the faces of the women in a brief glow.

"A lot of folks are real mad about you writin' those

articles," Liz continued, moving closer. Vicky could smell the cigarettes on her breath. The other women moved hooded heads, up and down, up and down, like balls bouncing on their shoulders. "They got the place packed. Nobody who ain't for the facility is gonna get to talk. They ain't even lettin' in them protesters. They got people at the front door tellin' 'em they gotta wait 'til all the Indians get here."

"I'm on the agenda."

"No, you ain't." This from another woman, stepping around Liz. Vicky didn't know her. So many changes in the ten years she'd been away, people marrying Arapahos and moving to the reservation. Even if she were to move back on the rez, she wondered if she would ever feel at home again. She forced herself to focus on what the woman had said.

"How do you know?"

Liz dug into one of the pockets of her parka and thrust a white paper at Vicky. "You ain't listed on the agenda. Only people gonna get to talk are gonna tell us how great it'll be havin' that nuclear waste here."

Vicky glanced at the paper. It was too dark to make out what it said. Then she stepped to the building's side door and attempted to yank it open. It shuddered and creaked, resisting her effort. Most people used the main entrance. Finally the door gave about an inch. A thin sliver of light escaped from inside, illuminating the faces around her, the moisture on the women's cheeks, the dropped glances.

"You shouldn't go in there." Liz again.

"Did someone send you here to tell me that?" Vicky saw by the blend of embarrassment and shame in their expressions she had hit upon the truth. "Your husbands?"

Liz said, "Larry's been out of work now a couple years. Just puttin' up the buildings is gonna mean a lot of work. He does construction, you know."

"Are you saying it's okay to have radioactive materials on the reservation?"

The women were quiet, eyes turned toward the front, toward the sound of doors slamming, footsteps scattering the gravel. Toward the sky. Rain fell softly on their parkas.

Vicky decided to plunge on: "You have children. Doesn't it concern you how radioactive waste will affect the air they breathe? The water they drink? The earth they play on?"

"It's not about that," Liz said, raising a hand to wipe the moisture from her face. Vicky saw the slight tremble in the motion.

"What is it about?"

"Our gettin' back somethin'. Our gettin' somethin' of our own, Larry says."

"What do you say?"

"Maybe it ain't for us to say." Liz glanced quickly at the other women, all nodding in agreement. "It's like this, Vicky. We can't talk against our men. I mean, they come here tonight 'cause they need work. So what're we supposed to do? Stand up and say don't bring no jobs here?"

Vicky drew in a long breath. "I think you're as worried about the facility as I am. It's not that we don't want jobs, but there has to be another way. A lot of people feel the same."

"Maybe so." A third woman joined in, another face Vicky didn't recognize. "But nobody's gonna say nothin'. They're scared."

"Scared," Vicky repeated. The word hung in the air like a fist of moisture.

"Some people been gettin' threats," Liz said.

"Who?" Vicky heard the change in her tone, the insistence she usually reserved for the courtroom. This was more serious even than she had feared. She was not the only one being threatened.

Liz shrugged. The other women's eyes were on the ground. "Some people was talkin' against the facility, sayin' there wasn't no guarantees it was gonna be safe, like you wrote in them articles. Then they got these notes tellin' 'em to shut up, and everybody heard somebody tried to kill you this morning. So now folks are scared to say anything."

The moccasin telegraph, Vicky thought. Eberhart had called Banner, and the news had flashed past the receptionist and secretaries, past the police officers, and across the reservation.

"The people who've been threatened, did they go to the police?"

"Oh, God, Vicky," Liz said, the words weighted with exasperation. "You was away too long. You forget Indians ain't gonna talk to the police. It don't matter the police are Indian. They ain't gonna do it. Maybe you might call the police 'cause that's how it's done where you live, in the white world."

Vicky was quiet, stung by the woman's words. After a moment she said, "Somebody wants the facility badly enough to threaten people's lives. Why is that person, whoever it is, afraid of what we're saying? Don't you see? We can't let someone like that stop us from speaking out."

"You don't get it, Vicky." Liz began stepping backwards, shaking her head. The other women had started to walk away.

Vicky stretched one hand toward them. "You don't have to say anything. Just come inside. Just be there. We have to stand together."

Liz continued moving backwards, sneakers snapping at the gravel. The other women had already struck out in a diagonal direction toward the front.

Sensing Liz's eyes still on her in the darkness, Vicky let the briefcase fall at her feet and gripped the edge of the door with both hands, pulling with all her strength until the door cracked halfway open.

"You better not go in there," Liz hollered as Vicky retrieved the briefcase and slipped inside.

❮ 11 ❯

L ights shone down like spotlights, creating pockets of shadow around the crowded hall. Arapaho families shifted on the folding chairs arranged in long, tight rows. Groups of men crowded against the walls. People were still pouring through the front entrance, including whites who thrust white signs upright the minute they were inside. BIA police officers stood around the hall, hands on hips, eyes following the crowd. The musty smells of perspiration and wet wool filled the hall, the sounds of coughing and clearing of throats.

On the stage two long tables with metal legs flanked a podium. The six tribal councilmen sat at one table. Wilson Lee, the elderly chairman, occupied the middle chair, with Matthew Bosse on his right, surveying the audience, amusement and confidence mingling in his expression. It was Bosse, Vicky knew, who had proposed building a nuclear waste facility on the reservation. The councilman was in his sixties, the age of reverence, a good man, she knew, even though she found herself working against him now. It struck her she had become one of the upstarts, the younger generation, who challenged the elders, the kind of person her grandfather had always warned her about. The realization made her sad and uncomfortable.

She stole a glance at her watch. The hearing wasn't

scheduled to begin for another twenty minutes, but she knew it would begin soon—according to Indian time, the time when everyone had arrived and was ready. It had nothing to do with the clock.

Two men, Lionel Redbull and a white man she didn't know, broke from a knot of people standing along the wall and started up the side stairs to the stage. She followed them, her heels clacking against the wood steps. The white man strolled to the vacant table, pulled out a chair and sat down, but Redbull turned around, as if he'd just realized someone was behind him. A tall man, half a head taller than she was in her heels. He had on blue jeans and a black wool blazer over a white shirt. The silver medallion of a bolo tie held the collar closed. His black hair hung in thick braids down the lapels of his blazer. He had the golden-brown skin of her people, the prominent cheekbones and hooked nose, the jutting jaw. He might have been a warrior staring out of an old photograph.

"There's been a change in plans, Vicky," he said, hooking both thumbs into the side pockets of his jeans, elbows swinging free. He assessed her with a flat expression that concealed whatever he may have been thinking.

"I'm on the agenda." Vicky moved forward, forcing him to step back.

The Indian squared his shoulders. "We don't wanna stir up the enviromaniacs." He nodded toward the crowd still coming through the door—the outsiders. "All we're gonna do tonight is present the facts. Quick and simple."

"Matthew Bosse gave me his word." Vicky took another step sideways trying to get past the Indian, her eyes on the councilman at the far table. He was talking with the chairman, his back toward her. Redbull stepped into her view.

"You've already made your point in those talks and

articles. Thanks to you we got crazy people runnin' all over the rez tryin' to shoot down our plans. The business council decided no sense in givin' them any ammunition. There might be a meeting comin' up where folks that don't like progress can state their views, but this isn't the time."

Vicky exhaled a long breath. There would be no other meeting. "I intend to speak tonight. If Matthew Bosse is going to break his word, I want to hear it from him."

Suddenly the councilman was beside them, as if he'd heard his name over the scrape of metal chairs on the linoleum floor and the crescendo of voices. He looked like an old cowboy in fancy dress—the light blue Western suit, the plaid shirt with the collar smoothed over his jacket collar.

"You said I would be on the agenda, Grandfather," Vicky said, addressing him with respect.

"I've been tryin' to explain to this lawyer lady . . ." Lionel began.

The councilman made a slicing motion with one hand, a sign Vicky had seen her grandfather use, the Arapaho sign for silence. The buzz in the audience died back.

"She can speak," Bosse said.

"But you agreed. . . ."

"That was before." The councilman shifted slightly to face the younger man. "Now I say she can speak her piece like I told her."

"It's a mistake. We got all them outsiders here. We could have a riot on our hands."

"Get her a chair," Bosse ordered. Abruptly he turned around and walked back to his seat. Vicky avoided Redbull's eyes as she started for the other table. The white man who had preceded her up the stairs jumped up, grabbed his metal folding chair by the top rung and swung it next to his place. "Please take my chair," he said.

The name Paul Bryant came to mind as Vicky set her briefcase and purse on the table, then slipped out of her slicker and laid it over the back of the chair. She'd seen the name on the environmental reports—Paul Bryant, president of United Power Company. Not quite six feet tall, with brown hair, gray eyes shot with light and a smile breaking at the corners of his well-defined mouth. Dressed in a tailored gray suit, with a light blue shirt and burgundy tie, he was a handsome man, the enemy.

She realized she was about to be wedged between him and Redbull, who had retrieved a couple of chairs from somewhere. The Indian slid one toward Bryant and placed the second next to her.

"And you are Vicky Holden," Bryant said, holding the back of her chair as she sat down. "I've been looking forward to meeting you."

"I can't imagine why." Vicky snapped open her briefcase and extracted the stapled pages of her speech, a yellow notebook, a ballpoint. She lined them in front of her, just as she did in the courtroom as a case was about to begin. Then she let her eyes roam over the hall.

The quiet drone of conversation was as soft as the wind blowing in the pines, but the tension was so thick she could feel it on her skin. Where were they, the other people opposed to the nuclear waste facility? Scattered through the crowd, too scared to speak out? She couldn't spot Liz or the other women. All the opposition had grouped around the entrance—outsiders. She swallowed back the sickening realization she had aligned herself with the outsiders. It was not what she had intended.

Gradually Vicky found the grandmothers. Several near the front, a couple partway back, others scattered through the hall, children on their laps. The eyes of the grandmothers, she realized, were on her. She felt a renewed sense of strength and determination. The grandmothers were with her.

And then her eyes found John O'Malley. Not with the other white people, but seated at the end of a row near the front entrance, in a blue-plaid shirt, arms clasped across his chest. *Where have you been?* she thought. *How has your life gone these last three months? What took you to the cabin last night, to the murdered cowboy?* There was so much she didn't know about this man, this familiar stranger. Suddenly he caught her eye and smiled, and she knew he was also with her.

A loud rapping sounded, and Vicky turned in her chair, glancing past Bryant. Chairman Wilson, frail-looking with pink, watery eyes, gripped the podium with one hand. He was in his eighties, an old warrior honored with the title of chairman. He would believe whatever Matthew Bosse and Lionel Redbull told him about the facility, but forty years ago, Wilson Lee would have torn out the hearts of anyone who backed a plan that might bring harm to the People. He raised the gavel with his other hand and brought it down again. A hard knock. Quiet enveloped the hall like a heavy blanket.

"We all come here," the chairman said, " 'cause we wanna know more about storin' nuclear waste on our reservation. We're gonna hear all the facts tonight and see why it's gonna be a good thing for us." The old man threw back his shoulders, glanced about the audience, as if to make sure everyone understood the purpose of the hearing, then shuffled back to his seat.

Matthew Bosse strode to the podium next, the chairman in fact, if not in name, the public hearing now in his hands. He began talking about how the nuclear business had been going on for fifty years, how white people had gotten all the benefits—the money and jobs—how Indian people got atomic bombs tested close to their lands, got uranium mines and tailings; how maybe it was now time Indian people got some of the benefits. He said the nuclear waste facility would store 10,000 metric tons of spent fuel rods—he called them "ghost bullets."

"Ghost bullets can be deadly." The councilman paused and raised one hand to his forehead, as if this were a matter for consideration. Then he went on, "Maybe that's why Indian people oughtta handle them, 'cause we're gonna do what's right by the earth."

Maybe. Vicky scratched the word on the yellow tablet. What was going on? It was Bosse who had sought the grant from the United Power Company to conduct the environmental studies; Bosse who had handpicked Lionel Redbull to direct the project. And now Bosse was saying "maybe"?

Vicky drew a slash under the word as the councilman introduced Paul Bryant. The white man rose from his chair and moved to the podium, thoughtfulness in his expression. He carried a file folder, which he flipped open. He pulled the microphone forward. "United Power Company and the Arapahos," he began with a quick glance at the notes spread before him, "have the same goal: a facility that offers jobs and prosperity without posing any danger to the people or the environment. We have the scientific knowledge and technology to build such a facility."

Hissing noises erupted from the far end of the hall, and Wilson Lee began pounding the table. "I'm warnin' ya," the old man shouted with surprising vigor. "Any more outbursts and Chief Banner's gonna clear all you outsiders from the hall."

Bryant began again, his tone calm, reassuring. Yes, the spent fuel rods contained radioactive materials, but the materials could not escape their specially engineered containers. Such containers had been used in Europe for years. None had ever leaked. He paused, glancing around the audience, allowing time for people to wrap their minds around the information.

On he went, his tone still measured and calm: The casks would be transported to Casper on dedicated trains with special rights-of-way, past other trains in the sidings. Then trucked north across the reservation on haul roads, specially constructed for safe passage. Handled remotely on site, with heavy equipment, hydraulic lifts. Every precaution taken to insure workers were not exposed, in case the unthinkable, the impossible . . . The white man stared across the audience toward the outsiders grouped around the entrance, as if to defy anyone to finish the thought. "You have my word," he said, closing the folder in front of him. "The facility will not harm anyone on this reservation."

Lionel Redbull was at the podium almost before Bryant could step away. "Advantages." The project director's voice boomed across the hall. "Let's not forget the advantages." Vicky saw the wonder and anticipation in the upturned faces as Redbull hammered out the familiar list, all the material goods the money would buy, the new homes and schools and clinics, the new lives. Such good fortune, it was beyond imagining.

Vicky wrote the word FORTUNE at the top of a clean page. Next to it, she wrote REDBULL. Underneath, she put SALARY, PROJECT DIRECTOR, FACILITY MANAGER. Then she wrote POWER over and over down the page until the word resembled a utility pole supporting the other words. She glanced at the man still at the podium. How much did he want that kind of power? Enough to threaten anyone opposing the facility? Enough to run her down in the streets of Lander?

Redbull slid both hands into the pockets of his jeans, pulling the black blazer away from his shirt. The silver bolo gleamed in the light shining over the stage. A relaxed man, the crowd in the palm of his hand, except for the protesters waving signs overhead.

"Soon's the joint council approves the facility," Redbull was saying, "we're gonna file the safety analysis report with the Nuclear Regulatory Commission. That report's gonna contain all the facts that make the Legeau ranch the perfect site for this facility. After we get our license from the commission, we'll start construction. Then we're gonna be in charge of operations. It's about time, I say, Indians take charge of our own destiny."

People jumped from the chairs, cheering and clapping. Groups of men whirled about, fists raised toward the white protesters. Somebody shouted, "Get 'em out of here!" The words rang through the hall like a gong.

Suddenly the crowd around the entrance began to shuffle sideways, and Vicky realized the door had swung open. Someone moved through the protesters and started up the center aisle.

◀ 12 ▶

Lionel shouted into the microphone: "Let's hear from the man that's gonna lease out his own ranch for the facility so the rest of us can get the advantages. Alexander Legeau and his beautiful wife, Lily, come up here and say a few words."

A murmur ran through the hall, like an underground current, as the couple came up the center aisle, Alexander reaching along the rows, shaking hands, patting kids on the head, his black Stetson bobbing above the crowd. Lily matched his pace, glancing about, smiling, hands occasionally reaching out to touch an outstretched hand.

As if they were the king and queen of Wind River Reservation, Vicky thought. She hadn't seen the couple in years. Once they'd loomed large in her mind: when she and Ben had struggled to raise a small herd of Herefords that never brought in enough money, calves that didn't make it through the winter, alfalfa and hay that lay flattened under blankets of hail. Everything on the Legeau ranch had been beautiful—the house and barns and stock. An example to the world, the Legeaus, that Indians could be prosperous.

Alexander bounded up the stairs and across the stage to the far table. He stopped near the chairman, who sat quietly and waited. It was the rancher who first extended his hand—a proper sign of respect. Then

Alexander greeted the other councilmen. Lily followed, slipping her hand momentarily into theirs, smiling. Gracious and dignified, with black hair pulled into a knot at the nape of her neck. Her skin was dark and clear, her eyes shiny. The deep red lipstick had been carefully applied. Her black raincoat hung open over a red dress with a wide ruffle at the bottom of the full skirt, another ruffle around the neck. A silver and turquoise squash blossom necklace rested in the crevice of her breasts. She wore silver bracelets on both wrists, a large silver band on her wedding-ring finger. If Vicky hadn't known the woman was in her sixties, she would have guessed her twenty years younger.

Alexander shook hands with Redbull and stepped to the podium, grabbing the microphone as if it were a tool he used every day. He was also in his sixties, with the slender, toughened build of a cowboy. Gray hair hung below his Stetson and trailed around the collar of his green slicker. He had the cheekbones, the narrow eyes—like slivers of charred wood—of the Arapaho. But the light complexion, the long, straight nose, the tight-lipped mouth must have come from one of the French traders in the Old Time who had given his name to the children an Arapaho woman had bore him.

"You people that've worked for me over the years know all about our ranch," Alexander began, his tone exuberant. "A real stable piece of earth, them expert consultants tell us. That's 'cause the Creator didn't see fit to give us any oil or gas." Laughter rippled through the hall: The Legeaus didn't have everything.

Vicky found herself doodling in the margins of the yellow tablet, anger mingling with impatience. Legeau wasn't on the agenda, yet he'd been welcomed to the podium. She'd had to insist upon her right to speak, and hadn't yet had the chance. She looked up, her gaze traveling along the rows until she found John O'Malley. She saw the impatience in his expression—like her own. It was a kind of consolation.

She forced her mind onto what Legeau was saying: The dream had come to him when he was seventeen. It was in the summer, and he had gone into the mountains seeking a vision to help him know how to live his life. He had fasted and prayed for four days. And on the fourth day, weak with hunger, he'd fallen asleep in the midday sun. A black bull with horns like ivory, fire snorting from its nostrils, haunches as hard as steel, appeared before him. The bull reared up on its hind legs and turned into a man—an untrue man. Look around you, the untrue man instructed. Alexander had looked about. It was then he saw the herds of cattle rolling across the land, like waves of a brown ocean.

He awoke and made his way back to the reservation, weak but filled with joy. He didn't understand the dream, of course. No one can understand his own dream. He went to his grandfather, who was his dream guide. His grandfather explained that the Dream Maker had breathed life into the spirits to enter his mind. The bull was the symbol of his dream spirit. The dream spirit would give him power, and he should trust his power to lead him through life. He should always use his power for the good of his people. If he used it for harm, it would bring destruction to him.

Ten years later, Legeau said, his uncle Tinzant had died and left him the ranch. He then understood his destiny. He had tried to run the ranch for the good of his people. Always hired on a dozen cowboys. Always Arapahos. Always paid them a good portion of his own profits. The audience burst into a rhythmic, appreciative applause.

Legeau smiled and nodded, then went on: "Soon's Lily and I heard about the nuclear power plants back East lookin' for stable ground to store spent fuel rods, we started thinkin' the ranch might be the place. So I went to Matthew Bosse." He turned toward the tribal officials. "And he hired this fine young man, Lionel Redbull." A nod toward the man next to him. "Next thing I know, consultants are all over the ranch fixin' to write up their environmental reports."

Legeau stopped, gazed about the hall a moment. "Like my grandfather said, I gotta trust my dream power. Well, my power's led me to a way for my people to have real good jobs and a lot of benefits. We're gonna get us a real strong economy on the rez." Legeau threw both arms into the air, fists clenched, as if his horse had just crossed the finish line.

People were out of their chairs, stamping their feet, shouting, cheering. Beyond the crowd, Vicky could see the white protesters crowding around the opened door, pushing to get out. She felt a strange ambivalence: She hadn't intended to bring them here, but she didn't want them to leave. At least they weren't afraid to oppose the facility.

Alexander Legeau swung around and took his wife's arm. The couple marched down the stairs and along the center aisle—smiling, grasping the offered hands—and disappeared through the opened door with the knots of protesters.

Vicky got up and stepped to the podium. "It's my turn," she said to Redbull. The mike picked up her words; they echoed back on her.

"Make it short." The Indian stood at her elbow. Vicky realized she'd left the speech she'd intended to give on the table. It didn't matter. Most of the people were still on their feet, gathering jackets and bags. Some had begun herding children down the aisles toward the door. She could sense the tension in the hall—the restless motion of cramped legs and made-up minds. She had only a moment.

She leaned into the mike. "This is about trust," she said. Her voice rang across the hall. People stopped moving and turned toward the stage. Groups of people began sitting down. She could feel the eyes on her.

"My great-grandfather, Chief Black Night, brought the *Hinono eino* to the Middle Earth." It was a risk, she knew, speaking the name of an honored leader. The people might not think her worthy of it, even if he was her own ancestor.

She hurried on, "Chief Black Night trusted us to protect this sacred place, enclosed by the four sacred shrines—the Wind River, the Little Wind River, the mountains, and the sky. Now the experts tell us to trust them. They have written a report that says the facility will be safe. But forty years ago, experts assured us a uranium mill would be safe, and the people allowed the mill to be built. How many members of your families got cancer from the radon gas?"

Out of the corner of her eye, Vicky saw Redbull reach for the mike. She held onto it. "The experts tell us not to worry, to trust them. But what if, as Mr. Bryant says, the unthinkable occurs? If some disaster strikes the facility? a tornado? a plane crash? What if one of the missiles the Air Force fires over Wyoming goes astray? If anything like that happens, the casks could be thrown together with enough force to cause the fuel rods to break free. And that could cause a chain reaction—a meltdown. Radioactive materials would escape into the air and water. How would we handle that kind of emergency?"

Redbull yanked the microphone away with a sharp violence. He stepped into her, forcing her to move aside. "We all know this woman's been tryin' to scare people," he said. "Chances of some disaster happening are"—he gave a quick snort—"one chance in more than a billion. It's not gonna happen, folks." He glanced toward the tribal officials. "Chairman Lee just gave me the sign to close this hearing, so I declare it officially closed."

Vicky walked back to the table and began stuffing the pages of the speech and the yellow pad into her briefcase. She was aware of Redbull and the tribal councilmen filing down the stairs, Matthew Bosse in the lead. Aware of the crowd jamming the aisles and pushing toward the front door. She was thinking that if Redbull were behind the threats, he hadn't succeeded. She had made her point. This was about trust. It gave her a small sense of satisfaction.

She snapped the briefcase closed and glanced at where Father John had been sitting. The chair was empty. Her eyes searched the crowd pouring through the door. He must have already gone outside. She felt a stab of disappointment. He hadn't waited for her. She wanted to find out what he thought about the hearing, the facility. She might catch him, she realized, if she hurried.

She nearly stumbled into Paul Bryant standing behind her chair. It took her by surprise; she had thought he'd left the stage with the others.

"I'm very interested in what you had to say," Bryant said. "I wonder if we might discuss it further."

Vicky stepped around him. Father John could be in the Toyota pickup by now, heading out of the parking lot. She started down the stairs, Bryant behind her, saying they weren't as far apart as she may think. He kept pace beside her, weaving past the men and women in the center aisle, talking about the importance of trusting the right people. Suddenly he stepped in front of her. "What I'm trying to say, Vicky, is would you have dinner with me tomorrow?"

"What?" Vicky said, her attention now on the roar of angry voices, the sounds of shouting and scuffling that burst past the front door, coming from the parking lot. The crowd surged forward, jostling them, trying to get through the door. Two policemen came running down a side aisle and pushed their way outside.

"Something's going on," Vicky said, shouldering past the white man, past the crowd pressing around.

"Wait, Vicky," Bryant called. "Don't go outside. It sounds like a riot."

She was already squeezing through the doorway into the rainy night, the blurred headlights splashing over the parking lot, the mass of bodies surging around her. Signs waved in the rain, black ink streaming across the white poster boards. People were shouting and yelling. A woman screamed, a high, piercing wail. Another woman called out a name—a child's name—panic in her voice. There was the hard thudding sound of fists against bone and flesh.

She was in the middle of a nightmare, caught in frantic, grappling arms, holding up her briefcase to shield her face, darting toward an opening in the crowd only to be pulled into another gulf of bodies. Someone slammed into her, nearly knocking her off her feet. She stumbled sideways, groping for balance. Gravel jabbed and stung her right foot. She realized in a dazed, half awareness that she'd lost a shoe.

Then she felt a hard grip on her forearm and tried to glance back, but in the blur of moving bodies she couldn't make out who was pulling her through the angry crowd, steering her toward the darkness at the far edges.

◀ 13 ▶

"Where are you parked?"

A wave of relief flowed over Vicky at the sound of Father John's voice. He slipped his arm around her shoulder, propelling her through the shouting, scrambling crowd, past several men wrestling across the ground, their boots shooting up hard sprays of gravel.

"The west side," Vicky shouted. She was aware for the first time of the rain stinging her face. They pushed toward the edge of the crowd and hurried past a group of men jabbing at one another. A couple of policemen attempted to hold them apart. Vicky felt Father John's arm tightening around her. She gripped the briefcase, the purse, the slicker, hobbling in one shoe, her right foot scraping against the wet gravel. They dodged around the west corner of the building, threading their way among the pickups and cars parked there since she'd arrived, past another knot of people shouting into the night, past the group of men standing around her Bronco.

Vicky dug into the black bag for her key, feeling the men's eyes on her. Finally she found the key and began jabbing it at the notch: She couldn't locate it. Then Father John's hand was on hers, and the key was turning. She pulled the door open, threw in her purse and briefcase and the slicker, and slipped in behind, pushing them along the seat. "Lock the door," he said, leaning into a narrow opening. "I'll follow you home."

"You don't have to do that."

"Just lock your door." The door slammed shut—a loud clap against the shouts in the front parking lot.

The engine flicked into life. Pinpricks of rain danced in the beam. A couple of the men ducked their heads and turned away as Vicky started backing out. The others walked along the side of the Bronco: belt buckles, bulging jacket pockets, clenched fists slipping by the window. She couldn't see John O'Malley; she was leaving him in the darkness with the men who had been waiting for her. She hit the brake pedal as hard as she could with her stockinged foot and peered through the windshield at the dark figures moving about. He wasn't among them. No one as tall; no one who walked the same way.

She slammed the gear into drive and took a sharp turn to the right, tires harrowing the gravel. The Bronco barreled across the ditch, up the incline onto Ethete Road. In the rearview mirror, she saw the wavy line of trucks and cars pulling out of the lot. Sirens screamed as four police cars swung past her, red and blue lights flashing on the roofs. She wheeled onto Highway 132 and pressed down on the accelerator, aware of the hard grooves biting into her foot. The wipers waved across the windshield as she sped south, the moon a blurred silver disc in the sky ahead, shadows of cottonwoods passing outside her window, the dark bulk of the foothills riding on the right.

"My God, my God." Her voice rose over the growl of the motor. The highway took an abrupt jog, and she tried to concentrate on driving, her mind back at Blue Sky Hall. What was happening to her people? So much money tied to the facility, more than anyone could imagine, as plentiful as the rain that fell from the sky. And people willing to tear apart anyone who stood in the way. She felt sick to her stomach. She had brought the outsiders here, had stirred up the emotions that burst into a riot. She had never intended, had never imagined . . .

She swallowed back the bile rising in her throat and glanced again at the rearview mirror. One vehicle behind her now, coming out of a curve, far enough back she couldn't tell if it was the Toyota. What if John O'Malley hadn't gotten away? What if the men waiting for her had turned on him because he was her friend? She felt numb with the realization she had placed him in danger. She slowed down, considering whether to go back. But how would she find him in the angry, brawling crowd he'd just pulled her out of? It would be foolish. The police had called in reinforcements. She had to trust he was okay, that he was behind her, as he'd said.

The headlights were still in the rearview mirror as Highway 132 joined Highway 287, still behind her in the northern reaches of Lander. As she turned left into the neighborhood she had called home for almost three years, the vehicle drew close, passing under a street light. She saw it was larger than the Toyota and so black that, outside the scallop of light, it faded into the darkness behind its own headlights.

She jerked the steering wheel to the right, spun around the corner, and pressed on the accelerator. She sped down the street before making a quick turn at the next corner.

Out again on 287, she drove south through Lander, passing a 4x4, a couple of pickups, trying to put as much metal between her and the black truck as possible. She was close to the edge of town when she realized that, in another minute, she and the truck would be on a deserted patch of highway. She wheeled right, past a strip mall, a darkened gas station, and into another quiet neighborhood. Then another quick turn, unsure of whether she'd lost the truck or was just staying ahead of it. On she wove through the neighborhood, making one turn after the other, her breath coming hard and fast, as if she were running.

Only darkness lay behind her now, and she could feel her breathing begin to slow, the naked panic subside. She drove back across 287 and headed north through the side streets. She was almost home when it hit her that the black truck could be waiting there. Whoever was following her would find John O'Malley. He'd said he would follow her home, and she knew he would do whatever he said.

She drove faster, her heart beginning its familiar race. At the intersection close to her house, she slowed the Bronco and scanned the vehicles parked along the street. The usual neighborhood cars stood at the curbs and in the driveways, except for one—the truck in the shadows of the trees in front of her house.

◀ 14 ▶

For a moment Vicky's breath stopped in her throat, a hard lump she couldn't expel. Then she realized the truck was smaller, lighter colored. It was the Toyota.

She turned down the street and pulled into her driveway. John O'Malley was beside her door as she stepped out. "I've been worried about you," he said.

She pulled the briefcase, purse, and slicker out of the Bronco, jamming them into the crook of one arm, and shut the door with her body. Then she kicked off the remaining shoe, reached down, and picked it up before hurrying across the yard, her stockinged feet squishing the wet grass, the rain cool on her face. In a moment she had the front door unlocked and they were inside. She flipped on the wall switch. The lamp on the table across the room sent a flood of soft light over the gray carpet, the flowered sofa, the worn cushions of the easy chair, the books on the shelves against the far wall, the desk beneath the shelves.

She leaned against the door a moment, grasping her pile of things, her eyes on the man in front of her. She felt overwhelmed with gratitude to *Nih'a ca,* who holds all creatures in his hand, who makes all things possible. Gratitude that she had made it home safely, that John O'Malley was with her.

"What happened to you?"

"Someone followed me. A black truck." She saw the

little nerve pulsing at the side of his temple, the color rising in his cheeks.

"Damn," he said, slamming one fist into the other. "I got caught behind the police cars. It was a couple of minutes before I could get out of the lot." He drew in a long breath, then said, "The same truck that tried to run you down?"

Vicky nodded. She wasn't surprised he knew. The moccasin telegraph was efficient. He'd probably heard about the threatening notes, too.

"You'd better call the police," Father John said, but she'd already dropped her things onto the sofa and crossed to the desk. She lifted the receiver and tapped 911. While she explained to the operator what had happened, she watched the tall, redheaded white man shrug out of his jacket, lay it across the back of the sofa, and set his cowboy hat on top, as if he were at home. She set the receiver back in its cradle. "They'll notify the patrol cars to stop any black trucks. And Detective Eberhart left orders for the patrol to swing by here every twenty minutes or so."

Father John's eyes held hers. After a moment he said, "Perhaps you ought to go away for a while, Vicky. Go to Denver and stay with friends until things calm down around here."

"You think so? Would an Irishman walk away from a fight?"

He exhaled a long breath. "Not likely."

"Not likely for an Arapaho either." Vicky strode into the dining alcove. Threads of rain ran down the sliding glass doors that gave out onto the little brick patio. A counter with a wooden stool on either side divided the alcove from the kitchen. She stepped past the counter and flipped the wall switch. Light burst over the wood cabinets, the white countertop, the gleaming steel sink, the window gaping black behind the yellow curtains tied at the sides.

She extracted a can of coffee and a white filter from one of the cabinets while Father John perched on a stool. She placed the filter into the Mr. Coffee, measured out the grounds, and poured in the water before taking the stool across from him.

"I'm not the only one who's been threatened." She saw by the expression on his face this was something new. "The others are too scared to go to the police."

Father John was quiet. She could sense him marshaling his arguments into the most logical order. From the counter behind them came the rhythmic *drip, drip, drip* of liquid into the glass pot. The kitchen smelled of fresh coffee.

"Look, Vicky," he said after a moment, "somebody's trying to kill you. You've got to leave for a while. The reservation's torn apart. There's already been one murder."

"Some poor Indian alone in a deserted cabin. What does that have to do with the nuclear waste facility?" Vicky stood up and pulled two mugs from a cabinet and filled them with the fresh coffee. Little curls of steam rose toward her smelling of wild berries. She placed the mugs on the counter and sat back down.

Father John took a short draw from his mug. He kept his eyes focused somewhere beyond her shoulder, and Vicky regretted the sharpness in her tone, the precipitance. It couldn't have been easy to find the body.

"Was he a friend?" she asked, a consoling tone. There was so much she didn't know about this man—a whole lifetime of people he'd befriended, places he'd been.

Father John shook his head and brought his eyes back to hers. "He was just a cowboy. A drifter, I guess. He called the mission and said he wanted to talk to a priest. His name was Gabriel Many Horses."

It had a familiar ring; all Arapaho names had a familiar ring, but Vicky had never known anyone by that name on the reservation. "Oklahoma Indians," she said. "Why was he at the Hooshie cabin? It's been abandoned for years."

Father John gave a quick shrug to his shoulders, but Vicky could sense the bond he'd formed with the murdered man. This priest wouldn't rest until he had the answers. Until he knew why Gabriel Many Horses had called him. She said, "I went to St. Francis with a girl named Hooshie. Tina Hooshie. I heard she married a Lakota and lives in Casper now. Maybe she would know why the murdered man had gone to the cabin. I can try to locate her. . . ."

He gave her a lingering smile, as if he understood that she understood. Then he said, "It can wait, Vicky. You need to worry about yourself now."

"I'm not leaving here, John." She exhaled a slow breath. This was a stubborn man sitting across from her.

"For God's sake, Vicky. If you won't go to Denver, think about coming to the mission. You can stay in the guest house. No one will know you're there. Whoever is trying to kill you won't give up. You're fighting a facility that could be worth hundreds of millions of dollars. People have been killed for a lot less."

"It's not about money, John," she said. "It's about power. If the facility is built, Redbull will be the director. He'll decide who gets the jobs. And Matthew Bosse will have a big say in who gets the houses and where the schools and roads and clinics will be built. He and Redbull will be like the chiefs in the Old Time, distributing the goods. They will be the most powerful men on the reservation."

Vicky took another sip of coffee, then continued. "As for Legeau, he'll be heaped with honors at every powwow and celebration for having sacrificed the ranch he loved for the facility. It's the most any man could hope for—to be thought of as a good man. Don't you see, John? Power and prestige and dignity. Very important to Arapaho warriors."

Vicky saw by the way he smiled over the rim of his mug that he understood: The days of the warrior had ended—they belonged to the Old Time—but the warrior spirit lived on. Abruptly his smile disappeared. "Important enough to take your life?"

She set her mug down, spilling a black dribble of coffee onto the white counter. "If one of them is crazy enough . . ."

"All of them."

"What?"

"All of them, Vicky. Redbull, Bosse, Legeau. Even the president of the United Power Company, Paul Bryant. He and Redbull came to see me this morning. Bryant admitted he's been investigating you."

Vicky's hand tightened around her mug. Tonight, on the way out of Blue Sky Hall, Bryant had asked her to have dinner with him. And someone had followed her to Lander.

"I tried to tell you about Bryant."

Vicky nodded. "I got the message you'd called, but the afternoon was jammed with appointments. I didn't get the chance. . . ."

Father John stretched one hand toward her: It didn't matter. "They all have a lot at stake. They've been working for months to get the facility approved by the joint council. Maybe they want to make sure nobody gets in the way. You're only one woman, Vicky. You can't fight a conspiracy. My father used to say only a fool gets into a fight she can't win."

"Your father said that?"

His face broke into a smile. "A certain variation thereof."

Vicky took another sip of coffee, savoring the warmth that seeped inside her. "You're wrong about Bosse."

"I don't think so. It was Bosse's idea to build a nuclear waste facility on the rez in the first place. He convinced the other councilmen to hire Lionel Redbull. The two of them went after a grant from the United Power Company to hire the experts who conducted the environmental studies. Looks to me as if Bosse has been the prime mover."

"But something has changed." Vicky got to her feet, picked up the glass coffeepot and refilled both mugs. Settling back onto the stool, she said, "Oh, Bosse has backed the facility as if it were some kind of gift from the gods. But tonight . . ." She stopped, drew in a breath. "Tonight he kept saying 'maybe.' It puzzled me. He could be having second thoughts. Maybe he's starting to realize that nuclear waste is not our problem."

"What do you mean?"

"Just that, John. It's not our problem. There aren't any nuclear power reactors within a thousand miles of the reservation. Most of the nuclear reactors are back East. The people who use the power should store the waste. It's their problem."

"We all use the electricity." His tone surprised her, almost a reprimand. "We're using it right now." She followed his glance toward the glass globe on the ceiling. "Electricity is shifted in grids throughout the day from one part of the country to another," he explained, his tone patient now. "It doesn't matter where it's generated. Everybody in the country shares it."

"Then let everybody in the country share the dangers." Vicky could feel the anger rising inside her. "Or should the radioactive waste just be sent to Indian country, where nobody important lives? Isn't that how your people look at it?"

"Vicky," he began. She saw that he was struggling to maintain the patient, rational tone. "I've read the environmental reports. The scientists say . . ."

"Don't tell me what your scientists say." Vicky jumped off the stool and crossed the kitchen to the far counter, then whirled around, facing him. "Your scientists once said the world was flat. My people always knew that every sacred space is round."

She pushed herself off the counter and began pacing the small tiled floor, feeling as if an electrical charge had coursed through her, as if she'd been shot with one of the "ghost bullets." "Your scientists say the radioactive material can't leak out of the casks, but the casks may only last a hundred years. Then what? They say not to worry. The facility will only be on the rez for thirty or forty years. But where are the plans for a permanent facility? And why should one ever be built, once the nuclear waste is stored here?"

Vicky stopped pacing and gripped the edge of the counter in an effort to still her trembling as she leaned toward him. "How could I have been so wrong about you, John O'Malley? I always thought you were on the side of the People. On my side."

Father John got to his feet. "I am on your side, Vicky. But the potential benefits from this thing are so enormous. . . ."

She threw out both hands to stop him. "Nothing is worth the risk of destroying a sacred place."

He stared at her a long moment, and she thought she saw something change in his eyes. "No. Of course not," he said, suddenly reaching out and taking her hand. He pulled her along the counter to him.

She was so close. So close she could make out the lights in his blue eyes, the reds and oranges and golds in his hair—she had been twelve years old before she'd seen anyone with eyes and hair like that—so close she could breathe in the faint odors of wool and after-shave and sense the warmth of his body. She felt a change in herself, a sense of having come home, of belonging.

She placed her other hand over his and began examining the palm, the long fingers. She could feel the slight pulsing of blood beneath the skin. You could tell so much about a man by his hands. It was not the hand of a man who mended fences or tended to horses and cattle or baled hay, like the other men she had known. Yet there was a roughness in the creases, a man's roughness. She expected him to take his hand away, but he let it stay.

His other hand moved to the side of her face and touched it tenderly. She felt the nerves in her body quickening as he placed his arms around her—to comfort her, she thought, to calm her. She wanted to allow herself to melt into him, to give way to the emotions flooding through her, but she couldn't shake the awareness that they were crossing a line neither had wanted to cross. Once crossed, there would be no place for them—on this reservation, in this life.

She laid her hands on his chest and gently pushed him away. "You had better go," she said, her eyes locked on his, pleading for understanding.

Vicky stood near the sofa, forcing herself to stop trembling, forcing herself to breathe normally as she watched him pull on his jacket, set his cowboy hat on his head. He opened the door and was about to step outside when he turned back, one hand gripping the knob. "Vicky . . ." He hesitated. His eyes held hers a long moment. Finally he said, "You know I'll be there if you need me. Just call. . . ."

She closed the door after him and absentmindedly threw the lock and inserted the chain into the narrow brass ridge. Then she leaned her forehead into the hard wood, awash in feelings of sadness and anger and loss. Of course she needed him. He was the only man she had cared about in so long—so long, the feelings seemed strange and unbidden. She had never intended to love him. How had this happened? Why had such a man come into her life when there could be no life for them?

It seemed a long while before she heard the whine of the Toyota's engine, the slow, muffled thrum of the tires on the asphalt as he drove away.

❮ 15 ❯

Father John drove north through Lander, rain glistening in the headlights, the shadows of houses, evergreens, and box elders passing outside the windows. He hardly knew where he was until he was speeding down Highway 789, the Toyota swaying on its axles. At Hudson he turned left onto Rendezvous Road, the diagonal cut across the reservation.

On he plunged toward the darkness beyond the headlights, the music of *Don Giovanni* blaring through the cab. He could almost taste the whiskey in his mouth, the craving was so strong. This woman—he had lived a lifetime without even knowing she existed, and now she filled his thoughts. His body ached with the smells of her hair and skin, the memory of the softness of her body. She had been the one strong enough to fight the temptation, to pull away from his arms when he had wanted only to hold her.

He was disgusted by his weakness. It was so unfair to her. He wanted only for her to be happy, to be safe. Which was why he had waited outside Blue Sky Hall tonight—to make sure she got into the Bronco and arrived home safely. He had been worried about her. He had felt the tension building during the hearing, the kind of tension that could erupt into violence, and Vicky was the object of so much anger. She refused to take her own danger seriously. She was so damned stub-

born. He had thought his own people were stubborn—
they could take lessons from her.

That was what had drawn him to her, he realized,
her determination and dauntlessness, the way she gave
herself to what she believed in. Woman Alone, *Hi sei ci
nihi,* the grandmothers called her. So small and fragile,
she seemed to him, yet willing to wade into a den of
bears if she thought it necessary. It had transfixed him—
her passion for life, the force of her feelings. So unlike
his own feelings, marshaled into place and guarded, surrounded by the rules of order and logical thinking, and,
most of the time, controlled by sheer willpower.

At Seventeen-Mile Road, he wheeled right. His
whole being was dry with thirst. There was a time, he
knew, when he would have gone immediately to a bottle stashed in the back of a closet, in a drawer among
the clean shirts. When he'd believed no one knew. Not
his students at the Jesuit prep school in Boston who had
sat ramrod straight, foreheads creased in the effort to
understand what in heaven's name he was talking
about. Not his fellow Jesuits who'd gone wide-eyed and
slack-jawed and begun excusing themselves from the
dining table as he'd hammered home point after point,
until he was the only one left.

Dear God, he thought. What a mess he'd made of
his life. How he'd let down his students and superiors
and everyone who had believed in him. But he'd been
given the gift of another chance at St. Francis. Let there
be no more broken vows, he prayed. Let there be no
more pain to anyone who trusted him, to anyone he
loved.

The Toyota squealed through the turn into the mission. He slammed on the brakes in front of the priests'
residence, and the pickup skidded onto the wet grass. It
was time for him to go away for a while, he thought. He
would make a retreat somewhere else, sort out his

thoughts and feelings, pray for the direction his life should take.

But he couldn't leave yet. Not until he'd seen that the cowboy had a decent funeral. And he wouldn't be gone a week before his new assistant would begin preaching the value of tithing and calling bingo games in Eagle Hall. He had to get the mission's finances in better condition before he left. He decided he would write to some of the former benefactors, throw St. Francis on their generosity.

As he started up the sidewalk, he realized that either he or Vicky would have to leave. Was that the reason he'd tried to talk her into going to Denver? Was he concerned only about her safety? Or was he also worried about his own temptations? On the other hand, he'd also suggested she come to the guest house. What had he meant? These were the kinds of questions he might explore with someone he was counseling, not the kind he wanted to ask himself. He wasn't sure of the answers. But one thing was certain: Avoiding her these last months had made it harder to see her again.

The moment he walked up to the front stoop, before he'd touched the doorknob, he could sense the alcohol, as if it were reaching through the door for him. He let himself inside, a feeling of dread mixing with the other emotions of the night. A shaft of light floated down the hallway from the kitchen. His assistant was still awake. Awake and drinking.

Father John took his time hanging up his jacket on the coat tree, setting his cowboy hat on top. He was trying to settle himself, gain control over the anger pulsing inside him. Out of the corner of his eye, he saw the other priest swaying at the end of the hall, backlit by the kitchen light. "So you've returned." The words were slurred, belligerent.

The muscles in Father John's chest tightened. What the assistants at St. Francis did, how they conducted

their personal lives—it was their business. He demanded one thing: no alcohol at the mission. He started
down the hallway. The sweet, acrid, familiar smell of
Scotch washed over him, lodged in his nose and mouth,
in his pores.

"I know, I know," Geoff said, his eyes narrowing behind the bone-framed glasses, as if he were trying to
bring the room into focus. He stumbled backward as
Father John brushed past him into the kitchen. "The
no-alcohol rule. Well, I broke it tonight, but don't
worry. I'm not offering you any."

The man looked as if he'd been drinking all day:
When did he start? Father John wondered. This morning after their quarrel in the office? Was this the first
time? He decided it must be. Elena would've said something otherwise. Nothing got by the old woman.

"Sometimes, sometimes . . ." Father Geoff began,
the words drawn out, as if he were having trouble fitting his tongue into the right places. He dropped down
on the edge of a chair, groped for the glass on the table,
and took a quick drink of the pale yellow liquid. Father
John felt as if the fireball had slid down his own throat.
And then it was gone, a memory. His eyes fell on the
half-empty bottle on the floor next to the table leg. He
forced back the longing.

"It gets so damn lonely," the other priest said.

Father John held up one hand. He was in no mood
to deal with the maunderings of a drunk. "If you've got
something to say to me, say it. I don't want to hear
about how lonely it gets."

"You don't want to admit it." The other priest lifted
the glasses off the bridge of his nose and ran one hand
under his eyes. "All that collegiality and brotherhood
we're supposed to have. What a bunch of crap. You
know what? We're in god-awful places like this, alone."

"I'm going to bed," Father John said, starting for
the door.

"Wait. I'm trying to tell you for your own good."

Father John stopped, looked back. "What are you talking about?"

His assistant lifted the glass, took another drink. "I'm talking about women. We're out here on our own, by ourselves, and women know that." He jabbed the glass into the air. "It's been true for four hundred years."

"What's been true?"

"Women have been after us."

"For four hundred years? We must be very fast runners."

The other priest grabbed the edge of the table and propelled himself to his feet. "Joke. Joke!" he shouted. "You're good at that. Make a joke, then you don't have to face the truth."

In an instant Father John understood. Someone had called the mission, perhaps one of the men around Vicky's Bronco. Maybe he'd guessed Father John would follow her home. *You know where Father O'Malley is? He went home with a woman.* And his assistant, who was probably already in his cups when the call came through, had decided to confront him with the truth about himself, and he had made a joke. . . .

"Just say it."

Father Geoff shrugged. "I know, John. I know what it's like. You're lonely, and a woman makes herself available. I saw your face out there this afternoon." He swung the half-empty glass of Scotch in the direction of the administration building. "The minute Chief Banner said someone had tried to run down that woman, your face turned as red as the lights on the police car. This Vicky Holden, whoever she is, isn't just another parishioner. I got a call about you taking her home tonight. You've been with her since the hearing ended."

"I wanted to make sure she got home safely."

The other priest leaned down and grabbed the neck

of the bottle. He tipped it into the glass. Father John watched the yellow liquid accumulate, rise toward the rim. He forced himself to breathe through his mouth to avoid the smell as his assistant set the bottle on the table and lifted the glass in a toast, a grand gesture. "Have it your way."

Father John said nothing. Is this what people thought? Is this the gossip on the moccasin telegraph—the gossip that never reached the mission? The mission priest and the Arapaho woman who went away and became a white woman?

"We are not lovers," he said. The statement sounded hollow, half true.

Confusion crossed the other priest's face, as if he were trying to decide if he was wrong or if Father John was lying. "We're not lovers," he mimicked. "What does that mean? That you haven't taken her to bed yet?" His assistant leaned against the edge of the table, and Father John recognized the other man's effort to appear steady.

"The physical is only one level. What about the emotional and psychological? Can you say you're not lovers on those levels?"

Father John started down the hallway. "I'm not going to discuss this," he said over his shoulder.

"I know what I'm talking about. You're not the first priest . . ."

Father John turned and walked back into the kitchen. He'd been wrong. The other priest wasn't talking about him. The Scotch, the self-pity—why hadn't he seen it immediately?

Father Geoff stood at the table, balancing against the edge. "I met a woman," he said, a sobbing note in his voice.

"You don't have to tell me."

"I want to, damn it. Don't you understand? I need somebody to talk to."

Father John leaned against the kitchen counter and waited.

"Myra." The name burst into the air, as if it had made its way from some hidden place. "She was the mother of one of my students. She was divorced. Her kid was having trouble, and she needed somebody to talk to. A priest is better than a psychologist, you know. There's the confession aspect, especially when people are feeling guilty. They get a sense of forgiveness. But then . . ." The man stretched out both hands, a pleading gesture.

"Geoff," Father John began. He felt a surge of compassion for the other man; he understood the pain that comes from weakness. "This is hard for you. We can talk about it tomorrow." He stopped himself from saying, "When you're sober."

"We were lovers for six months," the other priest went on. "Somehow the superior found out. Somebody always finds out, and three days later, I was here. Three days."

Father John pushed himself away from the edge of the counter, his eyes still on the other priest. He'd gotten everything wrong. He'd thought this financial wizard had been sent to operate St. Francis Mission like a business, to total up the columns of profits and losses. But Father Geoff's assignment here had been a punishment, just as his had. A man involved with a woman, and an alcoholic. Two fallen priests, the priests at St. Francis. Were they supposed to save the Arapahos, he wondered, or were the Arapahos supposed to save them? "What happened to Myra?" he asked.

Father Geoff shook his head in a long, deliberative movement. "I didn't even tell her good-bye." His gaze traveled somewhere past Father John, toward the darkness in the hallway. "I pray for her every day."

A hellish trap, Father John was thinking, to fall in

love with a priest. He said, "You could have left the priesthood."

"No, I couldn't. I broke my vow, but I am still a priest."

"At what cost? When is the cost too high? The pain too much?"

The other priest backed along the table and lifted the bottle of Scotch. "If you can avoid . . ."

Father John nodded. "I understand." Why had he thought his own temptation so unusual? He stared at the other man a long moment, recognizing himself. The younger priest would drink until the bottle was empty, the pain obliterated, and then stumble upstairs to bed. "Will you be all right?" he asked.

His assistant waved the bottle, as if to wave away a question of no importance.

❮ 16 ❯

Vicky was climbing up the butte, hands clawing at the earth, feet scrambling for a solid purchase in the crevices. She had to reach the top where the spirits dwelled. She would be safe on top. The bear lumbered ahead, stopping and turning its massive head, eyes as sad as death urging her on. Finally the bear was on top, and Vicky saw it was no longer a bear. Now it was a person—an old man or an old woman, she couldn't tell which. The person beckoned for her to keep climbing, but the rocks were breaking away beneath her. She was slipping back, falling toward the green luminescent river that pounded below, falling, falling toward the swift current.

Vicky sat up in bed, her face and arms wet with perspiration. Her nightgown clung to her body. It was the dream that was real, not the moonlight at the edges of the curtains, the shadows falling over the dresser and nightstand, the white terrycloth robe at the foot of the bed. The clock on the stand glowed red in the darkness: 4:14. A moment passed before she was fully awake, before she realized the pounding noise in the dream was coming from somewhere in the house—the kitchen. Someone was in the kitchen.

Her hand reached for the telephone and struck the little clock, sending it clanking across the stand. Then she found the receiver. The cool plastic lay inert next to

her ear: Someone had cut the telephone line. A calculated calmness settled over her. She swung out of bed,
grabbed the robe, and slipped it on as she inched along
the hall and around the corner into the short hallway at
the back door. She stopped, listening. The pounding
was a rhythmic *chip, chip, chip.* She lifted the broom
from its metal holder on the wall. The handle felt light
in her grip, a twig against the prowler in her house.

Slowly she edged around the doorway into the kitchen. Moonlight glowed through the window and sent
shafts of light over the sink, the stove, the counters. No
one was there. Holding the broom out like a tomahawk,
she followed the pounding noise across the kitchen and
into the dining alcove. Someone was trying to break in
through the sliding glass doors.

Flattening herself against the edge of the counter,
Vicky moved toward the doors. She could make out the
dark figure crouched on the brick patio outside, jabbing
some kind of tool at the lock. She drew in her breath—
a sharp explosion in her lungs—as she groped for the
light switch next to the door frame. Her fingers found
the nub of plastic, and she pushed it upward. A milky
light flooded the patio. The figure jerked backward,
shock and anger in the movement. Vicky took in the
black jacket and pants, the black ski mask pulled down
over the face, and in the narrow slit, the eyes as wild as
those of a trapped bobcat. Then the figure ducked out
of the light toward the back door.

Had she remembered to lock the door? Vicky whirled
around, one hip crashing into the edge of the counter,
and ran back across the kitchen to the hallway. She
flung herself against the door, her breath making a small
cloud on the glass as one hand found the bolt. It was
locked. She flipped the switch on the side wall. Light
burst over the small backyard, but the figure in black
was gone. From inside a nearby closet, the furnace
hummed into the nighttime quiet.

Slowly Vicky made her way into the living room. Slivers of moonlight fell around the edges of the drapes. The room was filled with hulking shadows. She kept her eyes on the door, expecting it to fling open. Had she thrown the lock, snapped the chain into its channel after John O'Malley left? She couldn't remember. It seemed a lifetime ago. Her heart thudded against her chest as she moved around the sofa, still gripping the broom. Then she found the lock, the cold brass chain dangling from the channel. Her breath exploded in a kind of sob as she began jiggling the outdoor light switch. On. Off. On. Off. On. Off. "Please," her voice exploded around her, "someone please notice."

Suddenly she remembered opening the window in her bedroom about an inch before she'd gone to bed; she'd been so upset, she had yearned for the sound of the wind in the trees, the patter of the rain, the smell of wet leaves and grasses. What if the figure in black was already in the bedroom, waiting? She crossed the living room and started down the hallway, her heart still pounding like the wings of a trapped bird, fingers tightening into numbness around the broom handle.

She peered around the doorway. The bedroom lay in quiet shadow, white sheets and pillows on the bed gleaming in the moonlight. Her eyes moved to the window. The gauzy curtain billowed outward, a round puff of air, then sank back. She kept her back to the wall as she moved, barely breathing, expecting the dark figure to leap from some secret hiding place. Reaching for the window, she slid it into place and threw the lock. Then she saw the rip in the screen.

"Oh, God," she said out loud. The words startled her, as if someone else had spoken them. Whoever was outside had been trying to pry the screen off. Had intended to climb into her bedroom, attack her in her bed. Had heard her stirring and thrashing about in the dream and had gone to the patio doors. Her body felt clammy, as if she'd just stepped out of a sweat lodge. She longed for a piece of sage to hold to her mouth and nose to keep from being sick.

A loud whump sounded in the living room, like someone crashing against the door. She was halfway down the hall when she heard a man calling her name. She crossed the shadowy living room to the sound of pounding against the door. "Who's there?" she called.

"Police. You okay, Ms. Holden?"

Vicky moved to the window, shoved the drapes aside, and peered out. A white police car sat in front, its headlights shooting a long beam down the dark street. She stepped back, turned the lock, and pulled the door open the width of the guard chain. An officer appeared in the narrow opening, dressed in puffy jacket and dark trousers. She could see the black handle of a pistol in his hip holster. "Sergeant Larch, Lander police," he said. "Detective Eberhart gave orders to keep an eye on you. I saw the front light flashing. Everything okay?"

Vicky closed the door, snapped off the chain, then flung the door wide open. "Someone tried to break in. Out back."

"Lock your door," the policeman ordered. "I'll check it out." She saw him pull a little black radio off his belt and bring it to his mouth as he stepped off the porch and started around back. She shut the door and set the lock and chain back into place. In her mind's eye, she saw herself moving through the house, barefoot, wrapped in a white terrycloth robe, waving a broomstick into the darkness—a crazy woman. *Was that how it was in the Old Time?* she thought. The warriors out on a hunt; the enemy circling the camp; the women frantic to defend themselves.

She heard the low hum of a motor outside and pulled the drape back again. Another police car, the officer already running toward the opposite side of the house from where the first officer had headed. She waited, forcing herself to breathe slowly, to be calm.

After a few moments, another rap sounded at the front door. Soft, as if the officer knew she was just inside. He called her name. Still she left the chain in place as she cracked the door open. Two policemen stood outside, and she went through the whole exercise again before pulling the door toward her. "No sign of anybody," Sergeant Larch said. "You wanna tell us what happened?"

The officers stepped inside and stationed themselves near the sofa, rocking back on their heels, feet set apart. She told them about the pounding noise that had awakened her, the dead telephone line, the gouge in the bedroom screen, the figure dressed in black crouched outside the sliding glass doors. Then she told them about the black truck that had followed her home earlier, the same truck, she was sure, that had tried to run her down. Sergeant Larch had extracted a small notebook and a ballpoint pen from somewhere inside his bulky jacket and scribbled as she spoke.

"You got someplace you could stay for a while?" he asked, snapping the tablet closed.

Vicky was quiet, remembering John O'Malley's words: *You can stay at the guest house.* She said, "They are not going to drive me from my home."

"Who?" This from the second policeman.

Vicky shook her head. "Whoever wants me to stop opposing the nuclear storage facility on the reservation." She saw the policemen exchange a quick glance and read the message in their eyes. This was Indian business. Some Indian stalking an Indian woman. What business of theirs?

The second policeman cleared his throat. "The BIA police oughtta know about this. I suggest you take this problem to them first thing in the morning."

"Eberhart's gonna wanna know, too." Sergeant Larch turned toward the other man. "He gave the order to watch the house."

The second policeman gave a short nod. He accepted the order. He didn't have to approve.

"Officer Jackson here," the sergeant said, "is gonna keep circling the area and watching for a black truck. And I'm gonna stay in the neighborhood. If the prowler comes back, just flip that front light again." As if the matter were settled, he walked past her and stepped out onto the porch, the other officer following. Abruptly the sergeant swung around, facing her. "Make sure you keep everything locked up tight."

Vicky set the lock and chain into place and peered out the window, watching the officers slide inside the police cars. The faint red light of dawn outlined the roofs on the houses across the street as the cars pulled away from the curb.

She glanced around the living room, fighting down the sense of invasion and violation. The briefcase and purse, the slicker, her shoe, were still on the sofa where she'd dropped them. She sank down next to them, corkscrewing her legs under her and wrapping her bare feet into the folds of her robe. She snapped open the briefcase, withdrew the yellow pad. Flipping to a clear page, she began jotting down the names of people who might want to silence her: Lionel Redbull, Matthew Bosse, Alexander Legeau, Paul Bryant—the conspirators, John O'Malley called them. Maybe he was right. She would fax the list to Eberhart first thing this morning. The detective and Chief Banner could have a talk with everybody on it.

Vicky turned the pages back to the notes she'd made at the public hearing. Her eyes focused on the word *Maybe,* with the black slashes underneath. What had made Matthew Bosse begin to doubt the facility? Was the councilman having second thoughts about the issues she'd raised—the safety issues? She wondered if he'd learned something that wasn't in the environmental report.

She started scribbling down the margins—lines and circles, a mishmash of angry marks. Even if she were right, if Bosse had come across other information, why would he tell her? It was doubtful he'd even meet with her, after all she'd done to stop the facility. Nevertheless she made up her mind she had to talk to Bosse. When he arrived at his office this morning, she would be waiting.

‹ 17 ›

The first light of day shone through stained glass windows, casting a pink glow over the interior of St. Francis church as Father John said the ancient, familiar prayers of the Mass. At the Our Father, some of the old people in the front rows joined in softly, speaking Arapaho: *"Heesjeva hene Sunauneet: Heneseet vedenau . . ."* The solemnity of the words gave him a sense of comfort. There was only one God, and His Name was Wonderful. One God to whom the people brought themselves in all their poverty and richness; one God they petitioned in the Sun Dance and appealed to in the Sweat Lodge; one God they encountered in the Mass. Enough prayers could never rise into the heavens for the poor and forsaken and weak, all the lost and troubled creatures.

Leonard Bizzel, kneeling at the side of the altar, gave the little metal bell a jangle as Father John elevated the Host. Behold, the Lord with us. For an instant, in the stillness, he felt as if time had stopped, and he was at peace. He offered his prayers for the murdered cowboy, for all the people of the reservation, for Vicky, for himself. A prayer for peace and acceptance in all of their hearts.

"If it ain't rainin' today, Ralph says he's gonna stop by and see about fixin' that leakin' roof," Leonard said.

He was placing the Mass books and the chalice in one of the cabinets in the sacristy.

"He'll do a good job," Father John said as he fit his chasuble onto a wooden hanger. He hung the garment in the closet and set the door in place.

"You gonna pay him?"

"Absolutely." Father John was struck by the bravery of the statement. It was a good thing Father Geoff wasn't around to hear it.

"What you gonna use? Wampum?"

Father John laughed. He tried to keep the financial condition from the staff. They had their own worries; this was his. But there were no secrets from the moccasin telegraph. "Don't worry, Leonard," he said. "The Lord has taken care of St. Francis Mission for a long time now."

He was surprised to see the young woman in the foyer as he came down the center aisle. He hadn't noticed her at Mass. Everyone else had left, and the church was quiet, except for the wind whistling through a partially opened window. The faint smell of hot candle wax hung in the air.

"Hello," he said. She looked to be in her early twenties, slender, with a pretty face and long, black hair that hung around her shoulders. She wore a jeans jacket over a pinkish dress. Her legs were bare, and she had on flat, brown shoes.

"My grandfather said for me to stop by on my way to work this mornin'. He wants to know about Gabriel."

"Gabriel Many Horses?" The young woman had his full attention. "Was he a friend of yours?"

She shook her head in a slow, deliberate gesture. "Grandfather wants to know when the funeral's gonna be."

"Who's your grandfather?"

"Clarence Fast. You hearda him? He was a real

good cowboy. Used to call him Fast Clarence in the rodeos."

Father John didn't recognize the name. He said, "Tell your grandfather I'll let him know when the funeral has been set. Where can I find him?"

"He's been stayin' with me and my kid last couple months, ever since he give up wranglin'. He looks after Jamie while I go to work. I got me a job cleanin' rooms in a motel over in Riverton." She stopped, letting a smile play at her mouth. The job was an accomplishment. "Jamie and me and Grandfather live in the white house on Blue Cloud Road close by the river. You can find Grandfather there most anytime."

Father John opened the front door and followed the woman outside. The air was cool with a hint of rain, but the sun sparkled on the leaves unfolding in the cottonwoods. The woman hurried down the sidewalk and across Circle Drive to a parked yellow truck with a streak of rust along the side. He watched as she made a U-turn and sped around the drive toward Seventeen-Mile Road. He felt glad at the woman's news; the cowboy hadn't been alone in the world after all.

Elena had insisted he take a thermos of coffee, but he had tried to beg off, explaining she would have to brew another pot, and he didn't have time—an idea foreign to the old woman, he knew. People had nothing but time. Now the thermos wobbled on the seat next to the cassette player, and *Don Giovanni* filled the cab of the Toyota. He loved the music, the sense of space: the Wind River Mountains floating ahead in the haze, the sky an enormous blue bowl inverted over the earth, and the sun patterning the wild grasses and clumps of sagebrush on either side of Seventeen-Mile Road.

He swung left onto Rendezvous Road and drove south through Hudson into Lander. He slowed along Main Street, focusing on the asphalt ahead as he passed the red brick building where Vicky's office was. Then he was on the highway again, racing through land broken by buttes and arroyos, jammed against the foothills on the west. He passed one ranch after another, tapping on the brake, slowing to read the names on the mailboxes at the edge of the highway. What did he expect? What would identify an Arapaho woman with a white man's name?

A big ranch, LuAnn Fox had said. Runs up into the foothills. A good description of every ranch he'd passed so far. Suddenly he spotted the rock outcroppings ahead, as if the foothills had broken off and tumbled downward. An expanse of meadow disappeared into a canyon. He slowed past the mailbox with the name Cavanaugh and turned into a driveway lined with evergreens and cottonwoods. He parked next to the two-story ranch house with white board siding that gleamed in the morning sun. A porch extended across the front. As he walked up the steps, a gust of wind caught one of the webbed metal chairs stacked along the railing and sent it sprawling over the plank floor. He clacked the brass knocker against the door and waited.

The only sound was that of wind rustling in the evergreens and cottonwoods. He gave the knocker another clack before walking back down the steps. Around the corner of the house he could see the buildings out back—a series of sheds and barns. The door in the nearest barn stood open, and he started down the driveway through the shadows of the branches.

He could see two cowboys inside the barn, currying a couple of horses. Suddenly a woman emerged, leading two quarter horses—a sorrel with a black blaze on its face and a gray. She was probably in her thirties, with curly gold-red hair pulled into a thick bunch and tied with a yellow bandanna at the nape of her neck. She wore blue jeans that revealed the curve of her thighs and hips. Her jeans jacket hung over a white blouse. White ruffles flared along the lapels of the jacket and dangled around her wrists.

Father John set one boot on the lower rail of the fence and leaned onto the top, caught by the ease and fluidity with which she moved with the horses, as if the stroll across the bare yard were some kind of dance. They must be her best companions, he thought, the horses.

She glanced up and caught his eye.

"I'm sorry if I frightened you—" he began.

"You didn't."

She came toward him, not hurrying, bringing the horses along, the reins resting in each hand. He could see the green of her eyes, the sprinkling of freckles across her cheek and nose and in the plunging V of her blouse. She was the most beautiful woman he'd seen in a long time, a fact that gave him a momentary pang of homesickness. So like the Irish girls he'd grown up with in Boston, the striking women they had become. He introduced himself.

"A priest," she said, as if this piece of information held some fascination for her. She brought the horses close to the fence, light dancing in her green eyes.

"I'm trying to find a woman whose maiden name was Many Horses." He was aware of her perfume as she set one booted foot on the railing not far from his.

"My stepmother's in the upper pasture with most of the cowboys. They're moving the herd to higher ground." She allowed her smile to last a long moment. "Perhaps I can help you."

He said, "I believe your stepmother may know someone I'm trying to locate." A kind of Jesuitical evasion, he knew. In a way he was trying to locate a murdered man, place him in a context. But he didn't want to discuss the murdered cowboy with this beautiful, self-possessed woman who, he suspected, might decide her stepmother had nothing to say to him.

"I was just about to ride up to the pasture to give her a hand," she said. "Todd was coming with me"—she gave a little nod toward the barn—"but you can come instead. Take Beauty here." She raised the reins of the gray mare, which kept trying to nudge the sorrel stallion. "Think you can handle her?"

Father John was reminded of the first time he'd been asked if he could handle a horse. Jamie Little Bear and Dick Wooly had invited him on a four-day pack trip in the Wind River Mountains. It was his first summer at St. Francis; he'd never ridden before. He had learned by doing what they did. It was the way the Arapahos taught their children to ride. He'd gone on pack trips many times since. He and horses seemed to get along.

He climbed up to the middle railing, swung himself over the top, and jumped down on the other side. She was already leading the horses to a hitching post where she tied the halter reins. Then she walked toward a shed, and he followed. Swinging open the door, she stepped inside and pulled two blankets from the saddles straddled over a post. She handed one blanket to him—blue-and-red-striped wool, soft in his hands. They walked back to the horses, and he laid the blanket on top of the mare, pulling it along the spine just below the withers.

They walked back to the barn for the saddles. "Beauty likes that one," the woman said, nodding toward the saddle with the carved leather skirt. He lifted it off the post, walked outside, and gently set it on the mare. Then he shook it backward by the horn, making sure it fit comfortably before he cinched it up. After giving the mare a moment to get used to the straps under her belly, he tightened them. Another moment, another tightening.

The woman handed him a bridle. He removed the halter, dropped it on the ground, and slipped the bit in the mare's mouth. Then he swung into the saddle, settling his weight slowly. It took time to get used to a man's weight.

The woman was already mounted. "You learn how to saddle a horse in Boston?" she asked, amusement in her eyes.

"What makes you think I'm from Boston?" He crossed the reins behind the pommel, holding them loosely.

She smiled. "Dead giveaway, that accent of yours." Leaning toward him, she extended a slim hand, the back brushed with freckles. "Sheila Cavanaugh. I'm impressed."

"And do you ride every morning, Sheila Cavanaugh?"

"Every morning? Every morning I ride the Powell-Hyde Cable to Union Square. I'm an investment banker."

"Then I'm impressed."

"No, you're not." She switched the reins on both sides of the stallion's neck and made a little clicking sound. The horse started across the yard. He let the mare walk alongside.

Past the barn, she gave the stallion's rump a hard whack with one palm. The horse broke into a trot, and Beauty followed. In an instant they were galloping across the meadow, the breeze cool on Father John's face, the sun warm on his shoulders. They reached a path that started uphill through a clump of boulders and the overhanging branches of ponderosas. Sheila Cavanaugh reined in. He brought Beauty to a halt a few feet away.

The woman tossed her head back and laughed. After a moment she said, "I used to ride every day when I was growing up. But my mother died when I was fourteen, and Dad took a look at the ranch hands and at his nubile, adolescent daughter and said Off to boarding school with you. So you might say I'm from Boston, too. I spent the next eight years there. One Christmas I came back and found I had a stepmother. Alberta Many Horses. Arapaho. To say I was shocked wouldn't quite say it all. Dad died a couple years ago and left the ranch to both of us." She turned the stallion and started up the path, a slow walk, both horses picking their way through the ponderosas.

"Alberta runs the ranch," Sheila shouted over her shoulder. "I come here to regroup in between husbands."

Father John said nothing. He didn't think she expected a reply. She seemed so brittle and self-enclosed, so unlike Vicky. And the grandmothers called Vicky a white woman—he had to stifle a laugh. They hadn't met any white women like Sheila Cavanaugh.

On top of the ridge, the woman stopped in the shade, closed her eyes, and raised her face to the cool breeze. Father John reined in beside her. Sprawled below were the geometric squares of Lander, the peaked roofs, the leafing trees. The Wind River Reservation crept northward, brown earth and arroyos, isolated houses in the cottonwoods bunched along the river beds. This sacred space, Vicky called it.

On the other side of the ridge lay an open meadow, surrounded by mountains that shouldered into the sky. A herd of cattle rolled through the meadow, cowboys riding at the edges. He looked back at the woman. "I'm sorry," he said.

"Sorry?" She opened her eyes and gazed at him, blankness in her expression.

"That you seem so unhappy."

"Father O'Malley." She brought her chin down, her eyes leveled on his. "At this very moment, my husband is on a sailboat in the Virgin Islands fucking his secretary. What would a priest know about that, if somebody didn't tell you?"

The hissing of the wind in the ponderosas filled the

space around them. Finally Father John said, "It's got to be very tough."

"You're damned right," she said. "And you know what's the toughest? She's such a scrawny, washed-out bitch." The woman tossed her head toward the meadow. "You'll find my stepmother down there. I've decided I don't feel like helping out after all. I'll wait for you here."

◄ 18 ►

Father John yanked hard on the reins before Beauty turned away from the stallion and began picking her way down the steep path toward the meadow. Once there, he urged the mare into a gallop. One of the riders had turned from the herd and was riding toward him. "Help you?" a woman called over the thud of the hooves.

Father John reined in and waited until the rider drew alongside. She was dressed like every other working cowboy—boots and jeans smudged with mud, jeans jacket snapped to the collar, a brown felt cowboy hat pulled low over her forehead. He guessed she was close to sixty, with the leathery skin of a woman who had spent her life outdoors, the eyes and cheekbones of the Arapaho.

"John O'Malley," he introduced himself. "The pastor at St. Francis Mission. Your stepdaughter said I'd find you here." He glanced back to the ridge where the younger woman still sat on the sorrel.

"Gabriel." The word came like an exhalation. "This is about Gabriel."

"You knew him, then."

"He was my brother." The woman looked away, her expression unchanged.

"I'm very sorry," Father John said. A part of him felt the same relief he'd felt earlier, knowing now for certain the cowboy had not been alone. The meadow stillness was broken by the sound of mooing cattle, hooves pounding the earth, a cowboy shouting.

The woman brought her gaze back to him. "What happened?"

"Your brother was shot." He kept his voice low—the voice of hospital corridors and waiting rooms. It never got easier, telling this kind of truth.

"I saw the article in the *Gazette*," Alberta said, straightening her shoulders. "Some old Indian, no ID, found shot to death out on Johnstown Road. I knew . . ." She gulped in air. "I knew it was Gabriel. You're the priest that found him, right?"

Father John gave a little nod. "He called me. Said he had something he wanted to tell me. Do you have any idea what it was?"

"Father O'Malley," she began, lifting herself slightly in the saddle, and settling back, "until last Sunday, I hadn't seen my brother in thirty years. All of a sudden he was riding across the meadow on Beauty, like a ghost out of the past." She glanced around, as if expecting to see him yet. "When you rode up here, well, for a minute I thought he'd come back."

"What brought him to the reservation?"

"Some old business." The woman shrugged. "He wouldn't tell me. Said it was best I didn't know. I told him he could stay on the ranch—I could use a top hand. Gabriel was a good cowboy, the best. He said he'd like that a lot, except for one thing." She glanced away again. "He was dyin'. Lung cancer. The doctors only gave him a few months. Looks like he didn't even get that."

Father John leaned over the pommel, his eyes on the cattle moving farther up the meadow. So this was it, he thought, all he was ever likely to learn about the man with his face shot off on Johnstown Road. "I'd like to see him have a proper funeral," he said.

"Just bury him. Put him in the cemetery there at St. Francis. Send the bills to me."

"I'll let you know when . . ."

"Don't bother." She flicked the reins and turned her horse, which started trotting back toward the herd. Glancing around, she called, "My brother's been dead for thirty years."

Father John watched the woman ride through the meadow a moment, wondering about the ways that love dies. He allowed Beauty to turn and start back toward the ridge. Sheila Cavanaugh was no longer there. He kept the reins tight as the mare started after the stallion, hooves clacking against the rocks. Around an outcropping, Father John caught sight of the red hair and yellow bandanna.

And then the sorrel was galloping across the meadow below, the woman bent low along the stallion's neck. Beauty picked up speed, leaving the path in a burst of energy, and broke into a gallop. He let the horse have its head as it raced across the damp grass. He felt exhilarated and free, as if, for a moment, his feelings of loss and failure had fallen away.

By the time the mare trotted into the yard, Sheila Cavanaugh had dismounted and was handing the reins to a cowboy. "Todd will take care of the horses," she said as Father John dismounted. "Maybe I'll even give him a hand. What else do I have to do today?"

"Thanks for your help," Father John said as he started across the yard. He hoisted himself over the fence and dropped to the other side.

"Wait," Sheila called, walking to the fence. She laid both arms over the top rail, the ruffles of her blouse folding over the wood. "This is about Alberta's brother, isn't it? What happened? Did the old guy die?"

"He was murdered." Father John stepped back to the fence.

The woman flinched. "Bar fight?"

"He was shot in a deserted cabin on the reservation. Did you know him?"

She emitted a small laugh. "I didn't even know Alberta had a brother until an old Indian showed up in the rain Sunday morning, reeking of alcohol. Looked like he'd climbed out of a ditch. Said he was Alberta's brother. Well, you know, when your family marries up with the Indians, you're in for one surprise after another. Alberta was in the upper pasture. Rain never bothers her. Anyway, he said he'd find the way. I let him take Beauty."

"Look, Sheila," Father John began, "I'd like to know more about the man. Did he say why he'd come back?"

She was staring, as if he were some kind of a puzzle she couldn't quite fit together. "I didn't ask," she said finally. "I'm not in a particular hurry to get to know my extended family. But . . ." She glanced toward the barn a moment. "After he rode back from the pasture, he asked me to take care of Beauty. He seemed in a hurry. Said he had to get to Ethete to see some old friends. I think he said he was meeting them at Betty's Place."

Father John drew in a long breath. He'd gone to Betty's Place to call 911 after he'd found the cowboy's body. "How was he getting around?"

"Hitchhiking." Sheila shrugged. "That's why he was in a hurry. He probably figured it would take a while to catch a ride, the way he looked. And I didn't offer to give him a ride. I was glad to see him go."

He was about to turn away when she said, "I've been thinking, Father." She moved along the fence until she was directly across from him. "I could really use some counseling right now. My life is, well, pretty messed up."

He smiled at her. "I can give you the names of the best counselors in the area."

"Would John O'Malley be among them?"

"Among the best? I'm afraid not." He rattled off the names of three counselors in Lander, another in Riverton. "They're all good at helping people through transitions," he said.

"Transitions? Is that what this is?"

"A good question for your counselor," he said, starting down the driveway, aware of the soft shush of her footsteps as she kept pace along the other side of the fence.

"How about dinner, then? Sunday evening? Alberta will be here, so you would certainly be safe."

Sunday evening. Ted Gianelli had invited him to dinner. "Sorry, I have an invitation." He glanced sideways at her and smiled, relieved he didn't have to lie.

❮ 19 ❯

On the outskirts of Lander, Father John spotted the orange ball floating overhead and wheeled the Toyota onto the cement apron of the gas station. The gauge registered close to empty—an approximation, he knew, of the gas in the tank. With a little luck, he could make it to the reservation. He preferred to give his business to the Arapahos. He parked next to the telephone mounted on the brick wall and swung out, leaving the engine running, the voice of Pavarotti rising out of the cassette player like an invisible cloud.

After a quick check in the thin directory, he pushed a quarter into the slot and dialed Gianelli's office. The fed would want to know Gabriel Many Horses had a sister.

"Sorry, Father." It was the receptionist. "Mr. Gianelli left for the reservation first thing this morning. He hasn't returned yet." He thanked her, pressed the little metal bar, inserted another quarter, and dialed the BIA police department. The operator repeated nearly the same message: Chief Banner had been called out this morning and hadn't returned, but she would tell him . . . He set the receiver on the hook.

Inside the cab, he turned down the volume on *Don Giovanni,* twisted off the plastic cup of the thermos, and poured out some coffee, considering. Something must have happened—something important enough to demand the attention of both the FBI and the BIA police chief. The steam licked at his hand as he took a draw of the warm, black liquid. He felt a growing sense of unease. The riot last night at Blue Sky Hall, the threats against Vicky, an emergency this morning—what was going on? The nuclear waste facility had set the whole reservation on edge: Indians against Indians, Indians against whites. Sooner or later, somebody else might end up like the poor cowboy. He hoped it hadn't already happened.

He twisted the cup back onto the thermos and pulled onto Highway 287. Forty-five minutes later, he drew up next to the gas pump at Betty's Place, the gauge shuddering below Empty. He shut off the engine and pushed the Stop button on the player. "Deh vieni alla finestra" gave way to silence as he slammed out of the cab. After setting the nozzle into place, he watched the numbers tumble to ten dollars even—close to the last of the mission's petty cash.

Betty was waiting behind the counter inside. She was another of the women on the reservation who could be anywhere between thirty and fifty, short, with a light complexion, a helmet of black hair, and dark, hooded eyes. A half-breed. Her white blouse was missing a button, and something blue poked through the gaping hole. She had tied a purple-checked apron high above her waist, just below her ample bosom. "How about a tuna fish sandwich, Father?" she said as he slid a ten-dollar bill across the glass counter.

"I only just partook of a sumptuous feast." He laid one hand flat against his stomach. Not quite true. He hadn't eaten since breakfast this morning. "But a cup of coffee . . ."

She motioned him past the shelves stacked with potato chips, Fritos, candy bars, and cigarettes and into a small eating area in back. The air was filled with the smells of chili and strong coffee. There was a quiet buzz of conversation from the people at the tables: elders and grandmothers, a couple of young women with three children. He smiled at the women, patted one of the kids on the head, stopped to shake hands with the old people. Then he took one of the vacant stools at the counter. Betty flopped a white napkin in front of him before setting down a mug of steaming coffee.

"I'd like to ask you something, Betty," he began.

Her face froze. "Everybody's wantin' to ask me somethin' all of a sudden."

"Last Sunday," he pushed on, "an old man came here. A cowboy. An Arapaho, but not from the rez. He was meeting some friends."

"This about that murdered guy, ain't it?" Betty's voice was loud, as if she were addressing the tables. "I told the fed I didn't see that cowboy use the phone out front at midnight last Monday. God Almighty, I close up at nine and I'm a happy woman 'cause I get to go home. I ain't hangin' around here to see who's gonna use the phone. Now you show up wantin' to know if I seen him Sunday. I tell you same's I told the fed, Father. I don't know nothin' about him."

Father John sipped at the coffee, aware of the quiet seeping through the small area. The woman was lying, and she was scared. He'd counseled enough people to recognize deception and fear when they surfaced. Whatever Betty might know about the cowboy, she had no intention of telling him here. Whatever she said would make the rounds of the reservation within the hour.

Maybe the woman wouldn't talk at all, but he decided to take a chance. He slipped the ballpoint pen out of his shirt pocket and scribbled the mission's number on the corner of the napkin. Then he tore it off and folded it.

"I don't want no part of the trouble goin' on," Betty was saying, playing to the customers again. "That nuclear waste deal's got everybody crazy. Them white protesters runnin' all over the rez and causin' a riot last night. That cowboy got hisself shot. Now the councilman's gone and got killed. Well, I don't want no part of it."

"What councilman?" Father John held his breath.

"What councilman?" Incredulity edged the woman's voice. "Ain't you heard the news? Don't you got a radio in that old pickup?"

What he had was *Don Giovanni*. He said, "What are you talking about? Who was killed?"

A chair scraped over the floor, and boots shuffled on the linoleum. Then one of the elders was standing next to him. "Don't you know, Father? Somebody shot Matthew Bosse this morning."

Father John closed his eyes a moment. He'd been afraid something like this would happen. "Dear Lord," he said under his breath.

"Shot him in his truck." A man's voice came from one of the tables. "Yeah," said a young woman. "Must've been on his way to work." Another woman added: "I heard Lester Goodman come drivin' along and seen the councilman's truck in the ditch." Father John felt as if he'd stepped into the nerve center of the moccasin telegraph.

Betty leaned forward, her bosom resting on the counter. "I heard he got his face shot off."

The words hit him like a blast of icy wind. He jackknifed off the stool, dug two fingers into the small pocket of his blue jeans and set a couple of quarters on the counter. Then he held out his hand. "Thanks for the coffee, Betty." As he shook her hand, he slipped the small piece of folded napkin into her palm.

Outside, the sun splashed warmth over the pavement, but Father John was cold with apprehension. Matthew Bosse murdered, his face shot off, like the cowboy. Was it just random violence, or was there some pattern? Maybe Vicky was right. Maybe the councilman had changed his mind about the facility. An influential man like Bosse changing his mind about hundreds of millions of dollars—that could have gotten him killed. But what did Gabriel Many Horses, an old cowboy, have to do with the nuclear waste facility? It didn't make sense.

What did make sense was that Vicky was in grave danger. If the killer had stopped Bosse before he could explain his change of mind, sooner or later, the killer would stop an outspoken, determined woman like Vicky. He had to convince her to leave the area—at the very least, to come to the mission. There wasn't much time.

He strode along the building to the metal box that housed the telephone, fished another quarter—the last one—from his jeans pocket, and dialed Vicky's number. The same businesslike voice answered. No, Ms. Holden was not expected in the office today. She really couldn't say where Ms. Holden was. Would he like to leave a message?

Father John spoke slowly, distinctly: "Can you reach her?"

"Uh, I don't know."

"Well, try. And tell her she must do what we talked about last night. Immediately. Do you understand?"

Again hesitation. Then, "Yes, Father."

"Tell her I must talk with her," he said before hanging up.

He got back into the Toyota. The engine came to life the moment he turned the key, and he pulled onto Ethete Road, passing two semis. Fifteen minutes later he slowed through Fort Washakie and slid into the no-parking zone in front of the BIA police department, a two-story red brick structure with the impersonal look of authority. A group of policemen were about to enter through the double glass doors, Banner among them. The chief glanced around, then walked toward the Toyota. "I just heard about Matthew Bosse," Father John said as he slammed out.

Banner raised one hand and tilted the peak of his cap downward, his eyes narrow in the sunlight. "We got the call about eight this morning. Looks like somebody ran the poor bastard into the ditch and shot him."

"In the face, Banner. Just like Gabriel Many Horses."

The chief gave a little shake to his head, a dismissing gesture. "Just dumb luck they both took a bullet in the face. Somebody robbed that cowboy. But Bosse . . ." He stared into the parking lot a moment. "The councilman made himself some enemies over that nuclear waste facility. Folks're all riled up. You seen the riot last night. The councilman was right in the middle of it, swingin' with the best of 'em. We had to pull Randolph March off him."

In his mind Father John saw the heavyset blond professor with the other demonstrators at the mission. "Are you saying March might have shot him?"

The chief shook his head again. "March is one of the guys we know for sure didn't pull the trigger. My boys arrested him and about thirty others, Indians and whites both, for assault and disturbing the peace. Got the Indians over in the jail." He nodded toward the tribal buildings across the street. " 'Course the protesters aren't Indian, so I had to turn 'em over to the sheriff. They're still locked up in the Fremont County jail. County judge's gonna hold a hearing this afternoon. I suspect he's not gonna want any more riots around here. Probably give 'em about thirty minutes to get their tails out of the area."

"Look, Banner," Father John said, "I'm worried about Vicky. Whoever killed the councilman is trying to kill her, too."

"There you go again with your theories." The chief held up one hand. "Vicky and Bosse been on opposite sides of this nuclear deal. Why would somebody want both of 'em dead? Doesn't make sense."

"Vicky thinks Bosse had a change of heart. Maybe that's what got him killed. And Vicky may be next. Somebody's been sending her threatening notes, and somebody tried to run her down in Lander. Then, last night—"

"Yeah, I know." The chief raised one hand. "Somebody's stalking her. Lander PD sent over a report on the attempted break-in."

"What? What're you talking about?" Father John wanted to grab the other man, shake what he knew out of him.

"Somebody tried to break into her house before dawn this morning."

"Is she okay?" He heard himself shouting.

"Yeah, for now."

"For God's sake, Banner, you've got to give her some protection."

"I'd like to, John. Believe me, I don't wanna see anything happen to her. But she lives outside my jurisdiction. Police over in Lander say they're takin' care of it."

Father John whirled around and started for the Toyota. Vicky was alone; nobody was looking out for her.

"You oughtta talk her into gettin' out of here for a while," the chief called out.

"I've already tried that," Father John said as he got into the cab and slammed the door.

◀ 20 ▶

The asphalt shimmered in the late morning sun, the rain a memory as Vicky drove into the reservation. The turns in the road, the slim, green stalks of goldenrod and sunflowers spiking the ditches, the swales and dips of the earth seemed as familiar as the contours of her own body. She felt as if she could find her way across this land with her eyes closed, by the undulations beneath her feet, the set of the sun on her face.

She had intended to be at Matthew Bosse's office early, but she'd stopped at her own office first to rearrange the day's schedule. A crowd of Arapahos were waiting. They must have started out from the reservation at dawn, she'd realized, packed into a couple of pickups: two women, three grandmothers, and a couple of toddlers, all jabbering at once. Johnnie Macon and Kenneth Goodboy had been arrested at Blue Sky Hall last night and were still in jail at Fort Washakie. She had to do something.

It had taken several phone calls, the best part of an hour before she'd established they'd been arrested for disturbing the peace, and Goodboy was looking at an assault charge. A hearing had been scheduled before the tribal judge this afternoon. She had assured the families she would be there. Another thirty minutes of explanations and assurances had taken place before the crowd reluctantly filed out of her office.

She turned down the volume on the radio—Reba McIntyre singing about home and loss—and switched her thoughts to last night's prowler. It occurred to her the prowler could have been after something in the house. She'd brought her briefcase to the hearing—anybody at Blue Sky Hall would have seen her carrying it. The prowler had probably been at the hearing, and maybe he'd assumed it held something important. Something he didn't want made public. But what would it be?

The briefcase held the speech she'd planned to give, which simply restated the points she'd already made in public, and the yellow legal pad with her notes scribbled on a couple of pages. Nothing else. She'd left the environmental report in her office, and there was no sign that anyone had gotten into her office again. Besides, the report was free for the asking at the business council offices.

The Bronco wheeled through a wide curve, the body swaying sideways. The music stopped, and a woman announcer said something about another murder on the reservation. Vicky turned up the volume. "Councilman Bosse was found shot to death this morning in his Ford pickup at the edge of Yellow Calf Road, a short distance from his home. The BIA police estimate the murder occurred about 7:30 as the councilman was driving to his office at Ethete. This is the second murder this week on Wind River Reservation. Gabriel Many Horses—"

Vicky snapped off the radio and pushed hard on the brake pedal. The Bronco skidded in the gravel near the barrow pit before coming to a stop. She gripped the steering wheel, trying to still her trembling. "My God, my God." She kept repeating the words, a kind of incantation against some evil spirit.

Slowly the realization crept over her, like fog moving over the plains: Her hunch had been right. Bosse had started to have doubts about the facility. Why? What had he found? Nothing she had said or written had changed his mind, she was sure of that. After her articles had appeared, the councilman had sent letters to the editor of the *Gazette*, determined to refute every question she'd raised about long-term safety.

But what if whoever killed Bosse thought she had found something and turned it over to the councilman? Exactly what she would have done—had she found anything. The train of thought made her blood run cold: the threats, the black truck screaming down on her and following her, last night's prowler. She'd been kidding herself, pretending somebody was just trying to scare her off. Whoever had killed Bosse intended to kill her.

Vicky clamped her foot on the accelerator and whipped the Bronco into a tight turn across Highway 132, heading back the way she'd come. The sun-streaked plains flashed past her window. She had to get to Bosse's house. It was possible Bosse's wife, Agnes, knew whatever the councilman knew. She had to talk to the woman before the FBI agent cautioned Agnes against talking to anybody.

She wheeled the Bronco left onto Seventeen-Mile Road, then right on Yellow Calf Road, tires squealing into the morning stillness. Not far from the turn she saw the councilman's pickup, nose sloped toward the barrow pit, yellow police tape stretched around the periphery. She gasped, pressing harder on the accelerator. There was nothing else in sight, nothing to break up the sunshine on the endless plains.

She drove on, rounding one curve then another, until she spotted the trail of pickups and automobiles parked in front of a white frame house. She slowed. Maybe this wasn't a good idea, coming to pay condolences, to question the widow, when the house was filled with family and friends. Everybody knew she'd fought Bosse as hard as she could on the nuclear waste facility. They probably wouldn't even let her in.

Maybe she should turn around, drive to Ethete, and

call John O'Malley. No one would turn him away; he could talk to Agnes. Then the thought occurred to her he was probably here. She couldn't spot the red Toyota, but that didn't mean it wasn't parked up ahead somewhere. She drew in a deep breath and set the Bronco into a space behind a black truck.

She grabbed her purse and got out, eyes glued to the truck. It looked like the truck from last night, the truck that had come screaming down on her in Lander. But there were dozens of black trucks in the area—on every highway, every road crossing the reservation. It was ridiculous to think whoever was stalking her would show up at Bosse's house, especially if her theory was right and the same person trying to kill her had shot the councilman.

She threw her shoulders back and forced herself to walk past the truck. She had to think straight; this was no time to panic. It was just another black truck. Then it occurred to her the killer wouldn't expect her to show up at Bosse's house. She fished a pen and envelope out of her bag, turned back, and jotted down the license number before heading toward the house.

The knots of people around the cars in the driveway lapsed into silence as she moved through them. Before she reached the concrete stoop, the front door swung open. One of the grandmothers filled the doorway, the belt of her red-print housedress tied loosely around her middle, black bobby pins set at the temples of her gray hair. Vicky didn't remember the woman, but she saw in her eyes that the woman remembered her.

She expected the door to slam in her face. Instead the old woman reached out, grabbed her arm, and pulled her forward. "Agnes been hopin' you'd come," she said. "She wants to see you."

The name came in a flash: Goldie, Agnes Bosse's sister. Vicky stepped into the hushed living room: elders and grandmothers whispering to one another from chairs pulled into circles; knots of people standing around, heads bent together; kids dodging and giggling around the legs of the adults. Who drove the black truck? Vicky wondered. It could be anybody in the house.

The house felt warm and close, as if the air had been sucked out. The smell of fresh coffee mingled with the odors of perspiration and aftershave. Her eyes roamed the room again; John O'Malley was not here. But through the archway that led to the kitchen, she glimpsed a small group: Lionel Redbull, the Legeaus, Paul Bryant. She hurried past, following Goldie down the hallway.

"Agnes been restin'," the old woman said, rapping on a closed door. "She's real tired and confused. That fed showed up soon's they found poor Matthew out in his truck. Asked her all kinds of questions, actin' like she oughtta know why some bastard shot her husband."

Vicky felt her stomach muscles tighten. Gianelli had already been here; she wouldn't learn anything. She followed the other woman into the small bedroom. Agnes Bosse lay on the bed, eyes closed, her housedress bunched around puffy, arthritic knees. Two strands of gray hair spread over the pillow, like the clipped wings of a hawk. The room had the medicinal smell of cherry cough syrup.

"Agnes," Goldie said, stepping to the bed and touching her sister's arm. "Vicky Holden's come here."

The other woman opened her eyes, pushed herself up on her elbows with the quickness of a woman much younger. Then she swung her legs to the floor and patted the side of the bed.

Vicky sat down beside her. "I'm so sorry," she began.

Agnes Bosse laid a hand over hers. "I gotta know, Vicky. Else I ain't never gonna have no peace."

"I don't know who killed your husband."

The old woman shook her head so hard, the bed gave a little jiggle. "You gotta tell me what you told Mattie."

For a moment, Vicky said nothing. It struck her Agnes was in shock; she wasn't making sense. "What do you mean?"

"Matthew come home from that meeting real upset."

"The public hearing?"

"No. No." The woman's black eyes blazed with frustration. "That meeting last Sunday."

"Sunday? I didn't see Matthew last Sunday."

The old woman stared at Vicky a long moment, as if she couldn't believe what she'd just heard. Then she said, "It must've been you. Who else would've told him stuff about that nuclear place that got him so mad?"

"Told him what?"

Agnes squeezed Vicky's hand. "Matthew wouldn't tell me; said it was best I didn't know. Said it was dangerous, and he was just gonna handle it. All's he was tryin' to do was help the People. Then that riot started up outside Blue Sky Hall, and somebody bumped into him real hard, and he come home with this bruise on his chest, and he was too old for that. And now somebody's killed him." The old woman's voice broke.

Vicky clasped the woman's hand in hers. It felt lifeless and cool. "Did Matthew say he'd met with me?"

The old woman raised her eyes toward the dresser with a wood-framed photograph on top—a younger Agnes and Matthew, an anniversary perhaps. Vicky saw the grief and longing mingling in her expression. "Not exactly. I just thought . . ." She drew a tissue out of her dress pocket and dabbed at her eyes. "You was fightin' him so much, I thought it had to be you."

"I'm sorry, Agnes." Vicky patted the old woman's hand and got to her feet, fighting back her frustration and fear. She had thought Agnes might know something that would explain Matthew's death, but Agnes thought she was the one who knew.

Goldie slipped an arm around her sister's shoulders and laid her onto the pillow as Vicky backed toward the door. Suddenly Agnes raised herself again. "You better get away, Vicky," she said, a wildness in her tone. "They'll come lookin' for you, too, just like they did Mattie."

Vicky retraced her steps through the crowded living room, avoiding the eyes on her. The killer could be here—the thought sent an involuntary chill across her shoulders. But now she had a license number. She had something. She let herself out the front door and hurried past the Arapahos hovering in the driveway, aware of their quiet gasps of breath. No one spoke to her. She was the outsider here. As she slid into the Bronco, she checked her watch. Still two hours before the hearing at the tribal court in Fort Washakie. Time enough to seek the help she needed now.

Vicky drove to Highway 287 and stopped at a trading post and convenience store that drew mostly tourists. Inside, she selected a pouch of tobacco, three cans of beef hash, and a packet of cotton fabric with the blue, red, black, and yellow geometric designs of the Arapaho. After making her purchases, she drove into Fort Washakie and turned west on Trout Creek Road. After a few miles she wheeled right into a dirt yard, setting the Bronco in front of a small frame house painted the color of rosewood. White sheets and pink and blue towels danced in the breeze on lines next to the house. A white propane tank on metal legs shimmered in the sun. For a moment her mind switched back to other springs, when she and her cousins—brothers and sisters in the Arapaho way—would skip across the yard, darting through the sun and shadow.

Vicky forced her concentration to the present. Gathering her purse and the purchases, she let herself out of the Bronco and walked to the house. She rapped her knuckles against the front door. A hollow thwack. In an instant the door swung open, and Grandmother Ninni was hugging her close. The old woman was her mother's aunt. Only in the Arapaho world did that make Ninni her grandmother.

"We knew you was comin' by," the old woman said.

"How did you know? I didn't know if I could get by today."

"We seen you comin'."

Vicky understood. Perhaps Ninni had seen her coming in a dream. Or Grandfather Hedly, one of the guardians of the sacred truths, may have had a dream.

Vicky stepped into the small living room with the green linoleum floor, the round rug woven out of rags, the gray sofa sloping in the middle, the TV with rabbit ears sticking in the air. Grandfather Hedly sat in a green lounge chair against the far wall, and she walked over and took his hand. It felt rough against her palm. Then she offered him the plastic bag containing the tobacco, the cans of food, the fabric.

"Grandfather," Vicky began, in a tone of respect, "I have been having a hard dream. I don't understand what it means. I have come to ask you for guidance."

The old man nodded, his eyes ancient and blurry. Vicky knew he rose every day at dawn to pray for the People. He was the keeper of the sacred wheel, the *Hehotti*. He was also one of the Four Old Men—the *Bhe'uhoko*—who represented the spirits that guarded the four quarters of the world, the north and south, the east and west, and that controlled the directions of the wind so the creatures would have air to breathe. Only men with great composure and control ever became one of the Four Old Men. They had great self-discipline, even over their thoughts, since whatever they thought could become true. If they were to think bad thoughts, it could mean disaster for the People.

Grandfather Hedly indicated she should sit, and she sank down onto a chair near him. Grandmother Ninni's hand rested on her shoulder with a calming pressure as Vicky related her dream: She was struggling to climb up the butte; the thick, shiny green water swirled below her; the bear lumbered ahead and became a person, beckoning her onward and then disappearing.

Quiet fell over the little house, except for the sound of a clock ticking somewhere. After a moment, the old man pushed himself out of the lounge chair and said, "We must ask *Hehotti* for help."

Vicky and Grandmother Ninni followed him across the kitchen and out the back door. They crossed the soft dirt yard to a small shed. The old man fumbled with the combination lock on the metal bolt. The plastic bag she'd given him swung off one arm. After a moment, the door pulled open. A shaft of sunlight split the darkness as they stepped inside, moving to the right. Against the wall opposite the door, above a shelf, hung a large bundle wrapped in buffalo hide and tied with rope.

The old man approached the bundle, praying softly in Arapaho. *"In a sacred manner, I am walking."* Vicky realized with a kind of shock that she understood the words. She couldn't speak Arapaho, but sometimes, when she wasn't struggling to understand, the meaning of words floated into her mind. The old man was asking *Nih'a ca*—the Great Mystery Above—to come and live with the People, to hear them in their supplications. He set the cans of food in front of the bundle, the tobacco on the left, the fabric on the right.

The old man stepped back outside, passing to the left. After a moment, he reappeared carrying a large pan covered with a lid. Inside the pan, Vicky knew, were hot coals of cottonwood and chips of cedar. He carried the pan slowly by Vicky and Grandmother Ninni and set it on the shelf. Removing the lid, he allowed the cedar smoke to rise into the air. Then he passed his hands through the smoke and drew it toward him, blessing and cleansing himself in preparation to touch the sacred wheel.

Gently and reverently the elder reached up and removed the sacred bundle from its place against the wall. He laid it on the shelf next to the pan and began untying the rope and pulling back the buffalo hide. Again he placed his hands into the cedar smoke, then unwrapped the next layer of hide and fabric. He repeated the process until, finally, *Hehotti* lay open to the air.

A hush enveloped the little space. Vicky felt as if she had stopped breathing, as if all of time had folded into the moment as Grandfather Hedly lifted the wheel, circled it above his head, like the movement of the sun, and turned toward her.

She heard herself gasp. She'd seen the sacred wheel many times at the Sun Dance. It filled her with a wordless awe. It was round, formed of a single branch, with ends shaped like the head and tail of a snake—a harmless water snake, meek and gentle, like the snakes that lived in the buffalo wallows. Blue beads were wrapped around the top, and eagle feathers hung from four points around the wheel. Carved into the wood were the symbols of the Thunderbird, which represented the spirit guardians of creation; *Nahax,* the morning star; *He thon natha,* the Lone-Star of the evening; and the chain of stars, the Milky Way. All of creation, all of its harmony, was contained in the sacred wheel—a reminder through time to her people that *Nih'a ca* was always with them.

Still praying in Arapaho, Grandfather Hedly brought the wheel close to her. "May this woman, your daughter, accept what is given to her as it is given to her." Raising it to the right side of her head, he slowly brought it down along her body to her right foot. Still praying, he raised the wheel again and brought it down her left side. "May this woman, your daughter, find the direction you have given her without difficulty."

Then he repeated the blessing—four times in all—and said, "May this woman, your daughter, walk in balance to find the center of her life."

When he had finished, the old man returned the sacred wheel to the folds of the bundle and laid Vicky's fabric over it. Slowly he began folding the other layers into place—the fabrics, the buffalo hide. Then he turned around, his eyes on her. "*Nih'a ca* has allowed all creatures to share his power. Bear has come to show you how to use the power *Nih'a ca* gave to him. Bear is strong. His home is inside the earth, which he protects. The green river is the poison that will flood the earth if it is not protected. Bear has come to you in your dream to bring you the strength you need now. But your heart must be pure to accept the gift of strength. You must ask your heart: Do you wish to protect the earth and help the People, or do you wish only to become puffed up and proud so that people will say, 'How important this woman is.' You must think about these things. You must keep your heart pure. And then you must do what is right, and you will not become tired."

White clouds drifted across the sky, like waves foaming on an ocean, as Vicky climbed back into the Bronco. She felt calm, refreshed. Whatever happened to her, she knew she would have the strength to do what she must. She felt like a warrior in the Old Time, riding into battle with the *Hiiteni*—the symbol of the power given in a dream—painted on a battle shield. Confident in the dream power. Supremely confident, even as the warrior galloped toward death.

◀ 21 ▶

"You got the strike zone?" Father John called.

"Yeah, I got it, Father." Charlie Longbull did a little shuffle, concentrating on the space above the plate. His black eyes shone with anticipation as he gripped the bat.

Father John walked over and positioned the bat over the kid's shoulder. "Bat behind your hands, remember. Weight on back leg. Why is that?"

"So I get power, Father. When I connect."

"Okay. Let's see the power." Father John stepped out of the way. He motioned to the kid on the mound, who reared back, went into an exaggerated windup and unleashed a fastball. The pitch might come in anywhere, Father John knew, especially at the start of the season with the kids trying to remember everything they'd forgotten over the winter.

The ball curved over the outside edge of the plate, thigh-high, and Charlie stepped into it. The *thwack* sounded across the field as the ball spiraled out over second base. Jason Little back-pedaled after it, gloved it. Then dropped it.

Charlie loped to first. *Ah, well,* Father John thought. They would work on defense later. Today they were practicing hitting, renewing an acquaintance with the strike zone, making some progress on the basics: See ball, hit ball.

He'd nearly forgotten about practice this afternoon. He hadn't even realized it had stopped raining, he'd been so preoccupied when he got back to the office. He'd stopped by to see Agnes Bosse—poor woman, in shock and confusion. He'd have to go back later to discuss the funeral arrangements. This afternoon hadn't been the time. Only a few hours earlier, Matthew had kissed her good-bye and left for a normal day at the tribal offices.

Then somebody had forced him off the road and shot him. And Father John couldn't shake the feeling that Vicky could be next. The moment he'd gotten in the office, he'd tried to call her again, wanting to assure himself she was okay, ready to convince her to leave the area, and if that failed, which he expected, to insist she come to the guest house. She was stubborn, but so was he.

The secretary had answered. Ms. Holden was not in today, she'd announced once more. The same tone, but there was a hint of something new, he thought. Exasperation.

"Where can I reach her?"

"Sorry, Father O'Malley, but I'm really not at liberty—"

"Tell her I've got to speak with her."

He'd hung up and walked down the hallway to Father Geoff's office, a courtesy call to see how the other priest was feeling. He had a pretty good idea: head like a basketball, stomach lurching, walls spinning unexpectedly. He knew the feeling well. It was not a memory he wanted.

Father Geoff was on the phone. He glanced up, still intent on the conversation. Black circles rimmed his eyes behind the bone-framed glasses. His face was pale. It took a moment before Father John realized his assistant was discussing bingo equipment—the advantages of leasing versus buying.

"Absolutely not." Father John broke into the conversation.

The other priest hurried through the good-byes and hung up. "You're wrong, John. It's the only way." Earnestness filled his voice.

"I'm telling you, no bingo at St. Francis," Father John said. He swung around and strode down the corridor, aware of the sound of his boots clacking against the floor.

"We don't have any choice!" the other priest shouted just as Father John turned into his own office. He slammed the door, rattling the pane of glass.

For the next couple of hours, he had pitched himself into the work on his desk: returning phone calls, stacking and restacking bills in the order in which they should be paid, if and when they could ever be paid. Then he'd called the mortuary in Riverton and arranged for them to care for Gabriel Many Horses' body as soon as the coroner released it. The poor man had already been dead two days. He should be buried on the third day, his ghost shown the way to the spirit world. It was what the Arapahos believed, and Father John sensed it was what the murdered cowboy would have wanted.

He'd just finished the call and was making some notes to himself when Charlie Longbull had knocked on the door and edged it open, peeking inside, black eyes dancing with light. "Ready, Father?" the boy asked.

Father John set down his pen. Sunlight streaked through the window, making little patterns on the worn carpet and the stucco walls. He gave the kid his most serious attention, as if they were about to deliberate a matter of grave importance.

"Ready? For what?"

"You know." Charlie pushed the door wide open and thrust out his left hand. He had on a baseball glove.

"Oh, I get it," Father John said, leaning back in his chair. "You're ready to do some homework."

"No, Father. Practice."

"You want to practice homework?"

"Baseball practice, Father." It came out "Fad—der."

"Baseball!" Father John jumped out of his chair. "Well, why didn't you say so?" he said, tousling the kid's hair as he strode past him into the corridor.

Out in front, the other boys were waiting at the foot of the stairs, throwing balls into the air. One was throwing a glove. It landed on the gravel, and he ran after it, scooping it up as if it were a baseball.

"Where have you guys been?" Father John called as he hurried down the stairs. "I thought you were never going to show up."

"It finally stopped rainin', Father," one kid called out.

"That so? Then we better get going before it starts again."

The boys took off, racing across the center of the mission and out toward the baseball field. Father John ran after them, a sense of gladness washing over him. The ground was squishy, pocked with muddy puddles. It didn't matter. What mattered was that the season was about to get under way. They were going to play some ball.

He was working with the next hitter, repeating the same instructions—focus on the zone, relax your grip, easy does it—when, out of the corner of his eye, he saw Gianelli coming along the side of the field, hands thrust into the pockets of his tan raincoat. The batter connected. A grounder sped toward left field.

"Who's that, sweet-swinging Joe DiMaggio?" the fed asked, planting himself next to Father John.

"Looks a lot like Ted Williams to me." Father John motioned up the next kid.

The agent stomped both feet into the soft ground. Lowering his voice, he said, "You heard what happened? Reservation's starting to seem like goddamn

Tosca. Somebody ran Bosse off the road this morning. Shot him."

"I heard," Father John said. He didn't want to think about it right now. Now he just wanted to coach the Eagles.

Gianelli went on: "Must've rolled his window down, probably cussin' out the bastard for putting him into the pit. The killer put a bullet right in his face."

Father John motioned up the next batter. Then he turned toward the agent. "Just like the cowboy," he said, thrust back into the thoughts that had consumed him all day. He couldn't shake them. Not even baseball could completely banish them.

Gianelli shrugged. "Yeah, probably coincidence. We found a .38 bullet lodged in the wall of the cabin, but no fingerprints or hair, except for the cowboy's. Whoever the killer was, he didn't hang around very long. Should have a report from the lab tomorrow on what kind of gun Bosse was shot with. Then we'll know if there's a connection."

"Any leads?"

"Give me some time, John. Bosse was just killed this morning."

"I meant the cowboy."

Gianelli dug his hands deeper into his pockets. "Don't worry, I'll stay on it. But just now, with the murder of a tribal councilman, well, it's a lot like having a governor or senator assassinated in your district. I'm getting pressure to solve this one fast. The reservation's in enough of an uproar over that nuclear storage facility without somebody killing off the tribal officers."

Father John went into his batter's stance, knees slightly bent, weight on his back leg, holding an imaginary bat: "Like this," he hollered to the next kid up at bat.

"Got a message you called this morning," Gianelli said.

The kid took a wild swat, missing the ball by two feet. "Settle down, keep your eye on the ball." Keeping his own eyes on the hitter, Father John said, "I talked to Gabriel Many Horses' sister."

The agent drew in a quick breath. "Got a report from Oklahoma he had a relative living up here. How'd you find her?"

"Talking to people." A strikeout. The next kid grabbed the bat, eagerness and determination on his face.

"Yeah, well, I've been talking to people, too. Difference is, they talk back to you."

"Her name is Alberta Cavanaugh," Father John went on. "She lives on a ranch about fifteen miles south of Lander." The agent had pulled a small notebook and pen from inside his raincoat. He began scratching some notes on the paper.

"When can I hold the funeral?"

"Anytime you like. Coroner's made his report. Your cowboy only had a few weeks, turns out. Lung cancer."

Father John closed his eyes a moment, taking a deep breath. The dead man with no face was still his. Maybe that's why he was so anxious to hold the funeral—to put them both at peace.

"What if there's a conspiracy," Father John said, trying out the theory he'd come up with at Vicky's. "A group of people who want the nuclear storage facility badly enough to kill anybody who gets in the way."

The agent squared his shoulders. "You think I haven't thought about that? Doesn't make sense for a couple reasons. First, near as I can tell, a lot of people on this reservation want that facility, with all the jobs and money. That makes for a damn big conspiracy. Second, Bosse was doing everything he could to make sure it got approved."

The hitter sent a fly ball high into the air; the right-fielder was after it, looking up into the sun, shielding his eyes with his glove. He had the ball! He threw to second, but the kid who'd been on first had already turned around and was sprinting back. "Good catch." Father John threw one fist into the air. Then he motioned up the next batter.

"Not everybody wants the facility," he said, locking eyes with the agent again. "It's possible Bosse changed his mind."

Gianelli was quiet a moment. "What've you heard?"

"Just speculation."

"Yours?"

"Vicky's."

The agent raised both shoulders. "She's dreaming," he said. "She'd like to think the Arapaho councilmen will turn against the facility and convince the Shoshone council to do the same."

"It might be true in Bosse's case," Father John persisted. "And if it is, a group might have banded together to shut him up."

"Just who do you speculate is in this conspiracy?"

Father John turned toward the field. Another hit; the kid who'd gotten onto first was now rounding for home as the batter sprinted toward second. The conspiracy theory was something he and Vicky had come up with; there was no proof. Yet Bosse was dead, and Vicky was in danger. He took a deep breath and plunged on: "Who's got the most to gain?"

"Redbull," the agent said immediately. Then he added, "That rancher who owns the site where the facility will be built. He'll be pulling in millions in lease money."

"Alexander Legeau."

Gianelli nodded, his black brows knitted into thought. "I already checked on both men. They're responsible people. No criminal records. Nothing to throw suspicion on them."

"What about Paul Bryant?" Father John said. "His whole career could be riding on the facility."

"I ran a check on him, too. Comes from a prominent Chicago family. Already got all the money he could ever want. Seems intent on running his company. So why would any of these men take a chance on throwing away their lives?"

"Several hundred million dollars."

"Yeah, yeah," the agent shrugged. "Always a possibility, I guess. People can get greedy. But why would Bosse decide to turn against the facility?"

Father John shook his head. That was the hole in his logic—a hole big enough to march an army of warriors through. He had no evidence Bosse had changed his mind.

Gianelli frowned, his brows in a thick, black brush above his eyes. "Conspiracy or not, John, somebody wanted Bosse dead. Agnes says he had a meeting last Sunday, and when he got home, he was mad and scared. Could be that's why he changed his mind, but we don't know for certain. We're treading muddy waters at the moment."

Father John turned away from the field and faced the agent. "Bosse met with somebody last Sunday? Gabriel Many Horses' niece said he was meeting friends at Betty's Place last Sunday."

The agent snapped the notebook shut and stuffed it and the ballpoint into the inside pocket of his raincoat. He was shaking his head. "I talked to Betty. She says she never saw the cowboy."

"That's what she says." Father John let his eyes roam over the field again. There'd been a third out. He must've missed it. The fielders were running in to take their turn at bat; the other team slouched toward the field.

"You think she's lying?"

"I don't know for sure." Father John was thinking

he might know more later, if the woman called. "I'll let you know if I hear anything."

"Yeah," the agent said in a kind of snort. "I'd appreciate it."

As Gianelli turned to leave, Father John placed a hand on his arm. "I've been trying to reach Vicky all day," he said. "I'm very worried about her. The killer is after her."

The agent looked back, worry and distraction mingling in his expression. "I know," he said finally. "Maybe Vicky could—"

"I've tried to talk her into going somewhere else for a while. She's a stubborn woman."

"The worst kind." The agent shook his head. "There's nothing you can do with a woman like that. She's likely to keep on fighting that facility, even if it gets her—"

Father John thrust up one hand. "Don't say it."

It was almost dark by the time practice broke up. A line of pickups waited on Circle Drive, mothers come to haul the kids home. Father John let himself into the administration building and walked down the corridor, through the silvery shadows that flitted over the walls. The musty odor of old wood and plaster came toward him. The building was quiet, except for the groaning of a metal pipe somewhere. Geoff must have left for the residence.

Father John threw the switch inside the door to his office. Light blazed across the room and glanced off the papers on his desk, the beige telephone, the old leather chair. He picked up the phone and punched in Vicky's home number again. No answer. He hit the cutoff button and tried her office. This time he got the answering machine. He left the same message he'd been leaving all day.

He found the telephone directory under a stack of

papers, located *Cavanaugh*, and dialed the ranch. Alberta answered, and he explained he could hold Gabriel's funeral first thing Friday morning. "Whatever suits you," the woman said. "Send me the bills." The line went dead, and he set the receiver in place, haunted by the failures of love.

The phone jangled under his hand, and he lifted the receiver again, praying it was Vicky.

"That you, Father?" It was a different voice, but slightly familiar. "This here's Betty."

Father John walked around his desk, untangling the telephone cord as he went, and dropped into the chair. He groped for a pen, then flipped open a yellow notebook to a blank page. "I'm glad you called," he managed.

She had already begun talking. ". . . fed come around askin' all kinds of questions. And Chief Banner shows up. Just wants some coffee, he says, but he's askin' questions, too. It's lousy for business, cops all over the place. Scares people off. So I don't want no more cops around. What I'm gonna say, you can't tell nobody I told ya, okay?"

Father John hesitated. Then he laid down the pen. "Okay."

"That cowboy you was askin' about? I didn't wanna say nothin' when you was here 'cause the coffee shop was full up. Them tables got big ears."

"I understand."

"Soon's I heard about Councilman Bosse, well, I got to thinkin' it might've been that cowboy in here Sunday afternoon, but I don't know for sure. He looked like he'd been out on the range his whole life, you know what I mean? Clothes all dusty and boots fallin' apart. He sat over by the back wall kinda outta the way, like he wanted his privacy, 'cept he was glad enough for me to keep comin' over with the coffeepot. He was here about an hour. I figured he was waitin' for somebody 'cause every time the door opened and somebody come in out of the rain, he jerked his head around and took a long look. Then he'd go back to drinkin' coffee and coughin'. He had this really bad cough, like he was on his deathbed or somethin'. If he's the guy that got murdered, Jesus, he really was on his deathbed."

"Did you tell Gianelli or Banner about this?"

The line went quiet. Father John was afraid the woman had hung up. Then the voice came again, tentative: "They was askin' if I'd seen somebody usin' the phone out front Monday night. How could I see anybody from my house five miles away? I didn't connect the old cowboy with the guy that got murdered 'til I heard Bosse got murdered, too."

"Why is that?" Father John heard the edge in his tone. He felt as if some kind of pattern was beginning to emerge.

"After the cowboy drunk up most of my coffee, he goes into this real bad coughin' fit and stands up, all bent over like, you know, holdin' onto his chest. He throws some money on the table and goes out the door. Ten dollars, he leaves me. I mean, Jesus, for a pot of coffee? That's when I knew for sure he wasn't from around here."

"Betty, what's the connection to Bosse?"

She paused a moment. "Well, I seen the cowboy standin' out in the rain by the gas pump, shufflin' his feet like he was waitin' for somebody. After a while, this pickup drives up, and he gets in."

"Was Bosse in it?"

The line seemed to go dead. Finally the woman said, "You gotta promise, Father. You ain't gonna tell nobody I said they was together. They're murdered, the both of 'em. And if the cops think I seen 'em together, they're gonna hightail it back here and ask more questions and all my customers, well, they're just gonna disappear—"

Father John interrupted, "Are you saying the cow-boy got into a pickup with Matthew Bosse?"

The woman gasped. "I'm scared, Father. If the moc-casin telegraph starts sayin' they was both here, the killer's gonna think I might've heard 'em talkin'. I didn't hear nothin'. I don't even know for sure the old guy was the one got murdered."

Father John was quiet, weighing his words. After a second he said, "Gianelli's a friend of mine, Betty. You can talk to him about this, and nobody will know. He'll protect you. You can trust—"

"I'm not talkin' to the feds!" she shouted. "I'm tellin' you 'cause you was askin' about the cowboy. I feel sorry for the old guy. He had a good heart and give me ten dollars. And the cops'll turn this reservation upside-down lookin' for the councilman's killer, but maybe they'll just forget about the old cowboy. I just wanted somebody to know they was together, and soon's they find Bosse's killer, maybe they oughtta see what the killer knows about the old cowboy."

Father John thanked the woman, said he appreci-ated the information, said he also wanted to see justice done for the cowboy. Images flashed in his mind, not of the body slumped in the cabin with half its face shot off, but of the cowboy riding across the mountain meadow to see his sister, hitching a ride to the coffee shop, wait-ing at the back table—for Matthew Bosse.

The electronic buzz of disconnection sounded, and Father John replaced the receiver. He leaned back in the leather chair. Why would a dying cowboy come to Wind River Reservation to meet with one of the tribal coun-cilmen? Agnes Bosse might know. He made a mental note to ask her tomorrow when he went back out to the house to talk about the funeral arrangements. And there was someone else who might know—Clarence Fast, an-other cowboy from somewhere else who had sent his granddaughter to inquire about Gabriel's funeral.

He found the pen again and jotted down three names: Gabriel Many Horses, Matthew Bosse, Clarence Fast. Old cowboys, all of them. Maybe there was a pattern after all. But what was it? Two had been murdered, but only one was connected to the nuclear facility. And two weren't even from around here. He decided to pay a visit to Clarence Fast—he'd promised to let him know about Gabriel's funeral anyway.

He drew a black line across the page. It was possible the murders had nothing to do with the nuclear facility. But if that was true, why was somebody trying to kill Vicky? Another black slash across the page. Nothing was making sense.

He pushed in Vicky's numbers again—her home, her office. He waited a long while on each call, listening to the phone ring into the emptiness.

◀ 22 ▶

Vicky left the tribal court and drove south on Highway 287 as the sun disappeared behind the mountains. Plumes of red, orange, and scarlet shot across the faded blue sky. The ponderosas climbing into the foothills, the sagebrush and clumps of wild grass—all were tinged with pink. Long blue shadows lay over the rises and swales of the earth.

Myriad feelings bubbled inside her: confusion and frustration and sorrow, a sense of failure. She'd talked the tribal judge into dismissing the charges against one of the young men arrested at the riot. But the judge had ruled against her on Kenneth Goodboy. The assault charge would stand. Out in the hallway, she'd tried to explain to the young man's family, tried not to notice the way they'd glared at her. They had expected a miracle; well, she didn't work miracles.

She heard that she'd had more success than the lawyer for the white protesters in the county court, a small comfort. The judge had dismissed the charges on the condition they leave the area. That gave her a certain sense of hope. With most of the outsiders gone, maybe the People could settle down to a reasoned discussion of the nuclear storage facility.

She turned through the familiar streets of Lander, her thoughts on the facility. So much anger and dissension. And now a tribal councilman murdered. The fact sent a chill through her. What difference if Bosse had championed the facility or decided against it? Nobody deserved to die for what he believed in.

Leaving the Bronco at the curb on Main Street, Vicky climbed the shadowy stairway outside her office, briefcase in one hand, raincoat under her arm, purse hanging from one shoulder. The evening was beginning to settle in. From behind the parapet near the stairway came a dim light, but the corridor ahead was dark. Her heels snapped against the wood as she walked toward her office. She made a mental note to ask her secretary to have the bulb in the ceiling fixture replaced. Setting the briefcase on the floor outside her door, she rummaged through her bag for the key.

From inside came the muffled jangle of the phone. She stabbed the key into the lock, but the ringing stopped just as she opened the door into the dark interior. She was about to pick up her briefcase when she heard the scrape of footsteps on the stairs. She stood still, hardly breathing, staring down the corridor. Suddenly a large figure rose out of the stairway and started toward her, silhouetted by the light behind. It was a man in a dark raincoat, hands at his sides.

She stepped into the office and slammed the door. Her hand found the knob, and she jammed in the lock button. Then she realized she'd left her briefcase in the corridor.

She opened the door partway and reached down for the briefcase, a black hump on the floor. "Hello," the man said. She did not recognize his voice. He was standing over her—her eyes took in polished shoes, pant legs with crisp creases, the hem of a dark raincoat. She gripped the hard leather handle of the briefcase, aware of her heart pounding, and raised herself up, facing the intruder.

"Paul Bryant," he said. "I didn't mean to startle you."

Vicky swallowed hard as she groped for the switch next to the door inside her office. Light cascaded around them, flashing in the man's eyes. "I was hoping you'd return to your office," he said. "I've been waiting for you."

"What can I do for you, Mr. Bryant?" Vicky held her place in the doorway. She willed her heart to resume its normal pace.

He smiled, showing a row of white teeth, a dimple in his left cheek. "My question first. You ran out of Blue Sky Hall last night without answering my question."

"What question is that?" Vicky felt a surge of annoyance and impatience.

"Will you have dinner with me?"

"Mr. Bryant . . ." she began.

"Please"—he held up both hands—"my name is Paul. I'd like to call you Vicky, and I'd very much like for us to be friends. There's a lot we should talk about, especially now with Matthew Bosse's murder." He shook his head. "A terrible thing. I can hardly believe it."

Vicky drew in a breath and held it a moment. "I'm sorry, but I've work to do tonight."

"I'm interested in the points on safety you've been talking about," Bryant said, persistence in his tone. "I'm sure I can answer them to your satisfaction. And if I can't, well . . ." He squared both shoulders and jammed his hands into the pockets of his raincoat. "I'll have to reassess them. Believe me, Vicky, I'm interested in seeing that a safe storage facility is built here."

Vicky felt her defenses relax. Maybe this was a chance to discuss her concerns about safety with someone who could do something. She hated the idea of the nuclear facility, would fight it with everything she had. But if the joint council voted to approve it—and it looked more and more as if that would be the case—she wanted it to be the safest facility possible.

As if he'd read her mind, watched it switching gears,

Bryant suggested the steak house a couple of blocks down Main Street.

They sat in a booth next to a plate-glass window. A thin stream of cars and trucks lumbered past outside, as did an occasional pedestrian bundled in a jacket or raincoat. The restaurant was filled with the odors of steaming coffee and charred meat. Over the soup and salad, Bryant talked about the councilman's murder, how hard it must be for his wife. He'd stopped by the house to pay his condolences as soon as he'd heard. But he didn't believe Bosse had been killed over the nuclear storage facility.

"What makes you think so?" she asked, surprised.

"The majority of the Arapahos and Shoshones support the facility." He raised his fork, making the point. "I know you've tried to change that, and I respect your efforts, but the fact remains . . ." The unfinished thought floated between them a moment. "If it hadn't been for Councilman Bosse, my company wouldn't have considered the Wind River Reservation. He called our attention to the Legeau ranch as a suitable site. It seems to me he was doing what the majority of the people wanted. Why would someone kill him?"

Vicky said nothing. She had no intention of divulging the theories she and John O'Malley had come up with: Bosse's change of mind; the conspiracy to ram the facility through, even if it meant murder. This white man was a stranger. She knew nothing about him, and John O'Malley had a way of being right: Bryant could be part of the conspiracy.

She shifted the topic to the safety issues. The moment she mentioned the storage containers, Bryant smiled and began a familiar recital: layers of impermeable steel, the most reliable, the safest, tested and approved by the Nuclear Regulatory Commission. They'll last a hundred years.

As if he'd read her doubts, he said, "And future science will produce even better storage materials and technologies."

Vicky took a bite of lettuce soggy with oil, marveling at the faith white people placed in science, the offhand way they regarded the future. She told him the future was not an arrow shot into the distance. The future and the past, all of time, were part of the present.

Bryant was quiet, his eyes on her as a waitress with streaked blond hair, rouged cheeks, and thin red lips brought them each a plate filled with steak and baked potato. Butter and sour cream coursed through the potato. As the waitress backed away, Bryant began talking again, pointing out the strengths and quality of the materials enclosing the radioactive waste.

Vicky picked at the edges of the steak and thought about the work back in her office. She hadn't opened today's mail or returned her calls. There was sure to be a stack of messages on her desk. Suddenly Bryant's words caught her attention.

"Of course, even concrete structures aren't strong enough to contain radioactive materials in case of an earthquake or some other act of God," he said.

Vicky stared at the man across from her. He had made her point exactly. "There are no construction materials strong enough to contain such a disaster," she said, testing to see if she had heard him correctly.

Bryant gave a quick nod. "Fortunately the likelihood of an earthquake at the Legeau ranch is zero." He set down his fork and leaned toward her. "But let's just say, for the sake of argument, that some act of God occurs. A tornado, for example. With the facility at the Legeau ranch, the nuclear waste would melt down into the earth, where it would be contained. Radioactive exposure to the atmosphere or to underground water channels would be minimum." His eyes held hers a moment. "Believe me, Vicky, if that weren't the case, my company wouldn't even consider the Legeau ranch."

Vicky leaned back into the cushion of the booth and looked past the speckles of rain on the window at the sidewalk glistening with wetness. "How do you know the scientific reports on the ranch's stability are accurate?" she asked.

"Because the studies were done by licensed geologists and hydrologists. The reports have passed the scrutiny of the Environmental Protection Agency. They're accurate, Vicky."

But what if they aren't? she was thinking. She had never heard of the consultants who had prepared the reports. They weren't the usual experts the tribe hired from time to time. And everything depended upon the stability of the earth at that particular location—the Legeau ranch. Suddenly she understood what she must do. It had been so obvious. Why hadn't she seen it before?

The waitress appeared with a coffeepot and filled their cups. "You're not from around here, are you?" She bestowed a smile on Bryant.

"No," he said in a dismissing tone.

The waitress whirled about, carrying the pot to an adjacent table, and Bryant began talking about himself, as if the woman's question demanded an answer. A native-born Chicagoan, he called himself. Lived all his life there, Lake Michigan in the backyard. Graduated from Northwestern, but took his MBA at Chicago. Then a number of interesting jobs. But the United Power Company offered the challenge he'd always wanted. Challenge and opportunity. After all, the country was full of nuclear waste, more generated every day. He liked running a company that was in the business of making sure nuclear waste was safely stored.

Another sip of coffee. Personal life hadn't turned out so great. Divorced last year after fifteen years of marriage. You got used to the same woman, her likes and dislikes, knew what size to buy her. Rough, the breakup. No kids, though. Probably for the best, as things turned out. What about her?

Vicky drew in a long breath, wondering why she was drawn to divulge herself to this man. Before she knew it, she was telling him about her life: born on the reservation, married young, like most of the girls; two kids, Susan and Lucas, grown up and on their own now in Los Angeles. She hurried through the rest of it: the divorce thirteen years ago, the move to Denver for college and law school, the move back. It amazed her how deliberate it all sounded, like an arrow shot at a specific target, when in reality her life had been a series of adjustments to plans that didn't work out.

The man across from her never took his eyes away. He was very handsome, she thought, with cheekbones and strong chin visible beneath rugged-looking skin, gray eyes with little squint lines at the sides, as if he'd spent long days peering across the waters of Lake Michigan, and a full mouth that broke into easy smiles. He sat in a straight, relaxed manner, an aura of certainty about him that, she suspected, never left him, whether in the clubs of Chicago or a steak-and-potatoes diner in Lander. He seemed honest, with an open mind, a good heart. On the wrong side of the issue right now, but a good man nevertheless.

It struck her she'd never been attracted to white men until she'd met John O'Malley. She felt a stab of pain at the thought of him; she was a fool to think about a priest. She drained the last of her coffee and forced herself to smile at the white man on the other side of the table.

The waitress swung by with the coffeepot and refilled their cups before stepping reluctantly away. They lingered, chatting about his life in the city, hers on the reservation. He helped her into her raincoat, and they strolled outside into the drizzle. When he asked where she was parked, she gestured at a point down the street. "I'll walk with you," he said, placing one hand on her elbow. His touch was firm.

Vicky held her raincoat closed, set the strap of her purse into the wedge of her shoulder, and bowed her head against the pinpricks of rain as they hurried along the sidewalk. Halfway past the parking lot next to the restaurant, she wrenched her arm free and stopped, frozen with shock. Bryant turned toward her. "What is it?"

At the edge of the lot, in the circle of the overhead light, stood a large black truck, chrome bumpers gleaming in the drizzle. Vicky dug into her purse until she found the envelope with the license number she'd jotted down at Bosse's house. Hands trembling, she spread the paper open in the rain, glancing between it and the license on the truck. The numbers were the same.

Bryant followed her glance. "It's the truck I rented," he said.

Vicky reeled backward, as if he'd struck her. "You!" She shouted. "You tried to run me down. You followed me after the public hearing. You've been stalking me."

"Vicky, what are you talking about?" Bryant came closer, tried to take her arm again, but she was walking backward, stumbling over a crack in the sidewalk.

"You're trying to kill me."

"That's crazy!" he shouted. "I don't know what you're talking about."

Vicky kept her eyes on the man, the way his mouth worked around the words. A part of her wanted to believe him, but she had heard so many people lie on the witness stand. People lied with such ease. "Someone in a black truck tried to run me down yesterday morning," she said, forcing her voice into steadiness.

"Run you down?" A mixture of anger and concern crossed his face. He looked away, as if he needed a moment to absorb the information. Then he found her eyes again. "You must believe me, Vicky. I rented the truck yesterday afternoon. Lionel had been chauffeuring me around, but I wanted to drive myself. Just dumb luck the truck is black."

Vicky let him take her arm again, and they moved under the restaurant awning, out of the drizzle. "I would never do anything to harm you," he said. "I'm very attracted to you; I hope to get to know you better. There were moments in there"—he nodded toward the red-brick wall—"when I imagined you felt the same way."

Vicky said, "I've reported the incidents to the police. They'll want to talk to you."

Bryant seemed to hesitate before he said, "I welcome the chance to clear my name of any suspicion. Most of all, I want you to believe me." He moved closer to her, as if he were about to kiss her, and she stepped away.

"Let me see you home," he said, disappointment and anticipation mingling in his expression. "I'd like to know you're safe."

"I'll see myself home." Vicky turned and started down the wet sidewalk toward the Bronco.

❮ 23 ❯

Father John spent most of the morning arranging the
cowboy's funeral. He made a half dozen phone calls:
Fred Brush would make sure the grave was ready—
Fred and his brother always dug the graves at St. Francis Cemetery; the mortuary would bring the corpse to
the church; Max Ernie, one of the elders, would be the
orator and take care of the painting; Jonathan Razon
would bring the drum group. The cowboy deserved the
sacred paint Ernie would place on his body, deserved
the sound of drumbeats rising into heaven, conducting
his spirit to the ancestors.

With the funeral arrangements made, Father John
dialed Alberta Cavanaugh's number. He wanted to give
the woman another chance to say good-bye to her
brother. Sheila answered. The funeral at nine o'clock tomorrow would be fine, she assured him. Anytime was
probably fine; she doubted Alberta would be there.
Then she asked how his day was going. He excused
himself and rang off.

Next he tried Vicky's office. She had not come in
today. Even the secretary seemed perplexed. "She left a
message on the answering machine this morning to can-
cel her appointments," the woman explained, more
forthcoming than usual.

Father John pushed down on the bar and tried
Vicky's home number. Pressing the receiver to his ear, he

listened to the rhythmic buzzing noise, imagining the phone ringing on the desk in her living room. The answering machine came on, and he hung up. Maybe she had taken his advice after all and gone to Denver. He knew he was grasping for some logical explanation. It would be so unlike her to leave.

He forced his attention back to the mission. He'd asked Father Geoff for the financial records earlier, before his assistant had left for a meeting of the senior parishioners in Eagle Hall. Now Father John scanned the pages, searching the neat columns of numbers for some hidden asset, some deposit lost in the swelter of debits. His assistant had brought the accounts up to date. As of yesterday, debits exceeded assets, and nothing balanced. He pulled out some sheets of stationery from the side drawer and wrote several letters to people who had contributed to St. Francis in the past. *We're still here,* was the gist of the messages. *Still need your help.*

Just before noon, he tried Vicky's office again on the chance she'd picked up her messages. But the secretary said she hadn't called in. He heard the worry in the woman's voice as he struggled to keep his own anxiety in check, to keep his thoughts logical. He wanted to believe she had taken his advice and gone away for a while.

He slammed down the phone and strode out of the office. A few minutes later he was driving west on Seventeen-Mile Road, *Carmen* blaring from the player. He turned south onto Plunkett Road. The asphalt wound up an incline ahead, and Father John pressed on the accelerator. The engine roared with disapproval as it went into the climb. From the top, he spotted the small gray house in a cluster of cottonwoods, a creek loping along the periphery like a silver ribbon flung over the plains that were flushed with green from the rains.

Father John left the Toyota under one of the trees and walked across the soft dirt to the front of the house.

The screen door hung out over the stoop, its mesh curling downward. He stepped around it and rapped on the wood door. Out of the corner of his eye, he saw something move.

He glanced around. A boy, maybe four or five years old, stood at the edge of the house, brown face smudged with dirt, eyes wide in curiosity. Long black hair hung around the shoulders of a worn blue jacket, and one knee poked through the slit in his jeans. "Hello, there," Father John said. He didn't move, not wanting to frighten the child. "What's your name?"

The boy moved toward the corner of the house. "Jamie," he said, dropping his eyes. It was impolite for Arapaho children to make eye contact with adults.

"You know a man named Clarence Fast?"

"Yeah." A smile lit up the boy's face. "Grandfather."

"Do you know where I can find him?"

"Yeah." Jamie turned and disappeared beside the house.

By the time Father John rounded the corner, the boy was already in the back, waving for him to come on. He strode alongside the house. The gray paint crumpled in ridges on the boards. His boots sank in the moist, brown earth. When he reached Jamie, he saw the old man seated in a webbed folding chair in a sunny spot a few feet from the back door. He had pulled a white blanket over his shoulders. One leg was extended, the heel of his boot sunk into the dirt. The other leg was missing. A crutch lay alongside the chair. "You meet my grandson?" Clarence Fast asked.

The boy ran to a mound of dirt close to the chair and scrunched down. A pudgy hand reached out to gallop a tiny plastic horse over the imaginary plains.

Fast kept his eyes on the child. "I watch him while his mother's workin'. She's my brother's granddaughter."

Father John understood. In the Arapaho way, she was also his granddaughter, and her son, his great-grandson. He introduced himself and said he was from the mission.

"I figured that's who you was." The old man looked up, one hand shielding his eyes from the sun. He was in his sixties, with a rough, weathered face. He wore a jeans jacket over a dark plaid shirt, and blue jeans with one pant folded and pinned around the stump. "I sent my granddaughter over to the mission to find out about old Gab's funeral."

Crouching close to the chair, Father John took off his cowboy hat and began turning it between his hands. "I'm going to hold the funeral tomorrow at nine o'-clock. What can you tell me about him?"

The old man took his hand from his eyes and, squinting, seemed to assess him a moment.

"I found his body," Father John said.

The old man nodded, as if the explanation was satisfactory. "I ain't seen Gab in more'n thirty years. Two days ago, my granddaughter went to the post office and brung me home a postcard. Doggone if it wasn't from Gab. Wantin' to meet me Sunday afternoon over Betty's Place. Trouble is, Sunday'd come and went by the time I got the card, and old Gab was dead." The Indian slipped one hand past his jeans jacket into the pocket of his shirt, brought out a postcard, and held it toward Father John.

Father John took the card. A photo of a cowboy flying off a bucking bronco on one side, the loopy, hurried scrawl of a dying cowboy on the other. "Don't know where you is for sure. If this finds you meet me at Bettys you know the place Sunday in after noon. Gotta clear up some thing very important." The cowboy had underlined the last two words.

Father John handed the postcard back. Gabriel must have sent a similar message to Matthew Bosse. Who else had he tried to contact? And what was so important he wanted to clear it up before he died?

"We was the best wranglers there was by the time we wasn't much bigger'n Jamie here. Gab come up to the rez one summer with his grandfather. Liked it so much he stayed around." The old man turned his eyes to the child, who was making little snorting noises as the plastic horse leapt over a mound of dirt. "We probably worked every spread in Wyoming one time or another." He waved one arm overhead taking in all directions.

"You and Gabriel and who else?"

"Mattie Bosse." The Indian brought his eyes back to Father John. "Now he's dead, too. Who'd wanna shoot a couple of broken down old cowboys?"

Father John was quiet a moment. He hadn't realized Bosse had also been a cowboy, hadn't thought of him as other than one of the tribal councilmen. "What do you think Gabriel wanted to see you about?" he asked.

The old man shook his head. "Like I said, Father, I ain't seen Gabriel in more'n thirty years, not since I got hired on down at the KO Ranch in west Texas. Worked there up 'til a few months ago when my leg went and got gangrene and they had to cut it off. Wranglin's not much good with one leg, so I come back up here where I got family. Gab stayed around here for a while after I left, then he lit out for some ranch in Arizona. That's the last I heard 'til this." He waved the postcard before slipping it back inside his pocket.

Father John stood up and stamped his boots into the ground to work out the kinks in his legs. He wasn't getting anywhere; he didn't know much more than when he'd driven out here. The cowboy had a sister and two old friends. One of the friends was dead, and the sister and other friend knew nothing about him. Unless . . . "Did Gabriel have any other friends on the rez that you know about?"

The Indian shook his head slowly. "Nah. Gab left thirty years ago. Earth keeps turnin'." He looked at the child, eyes watchful. "Might've called on Mattie, I guess, 'cept he was on the tribal council. Doubt he would've remembered old Gab or me. Same with Alex, even though he used to cowboy with us."

"Alex? You mean Alexander Legeau?" Father John swallowed back the excitement. Maybe there was some kind of pattern after all.

The Indian let out a quick snort. "He only got to be Alexander after he got his uncle's ranch. He was always a lucky—" The Indian stopped himself, his eyes still on the child, who had produced another horse and was staging a kind of war in the mound of dirt. "Alex was a good cowboy, but I never thought he had it in him to run a big spread like that. Surprised the hell outta me."

"Do you think Gabriel went to see Legeau?"

Fast kicked the heel of his boot into the dirt, building up a miniature mound, then knocking it down. "How'd I know? I ain't seen nothin' of Alex in more'n thirty years either. You think he wants an old one-legged cowboy come callin' at his big, fancy ranch house? I 'spect he'd sic the dogs on me. Sic the dogs on Gab, too, most likely." The old man let his head wave back and forth. A faraway look came into his eyes. "The days we was friends is long gone by. Him and Mattie went their ways and got to be real important. Me and Gab just kept on cowboyin'."

The little boy had started running around the mound and hollering, as if he were now the horse. "Would've been real nice to see old Gab," Fast said over the sound of the child's voice. "Talk about the old times. I'm real sorry I didn't get down to the post office for my mail."

Maybe you were lucky, Father John thought. He patted the old man's shoulder, thanked him, said he hoped to see him tomorrow at Gabriel's funeral. Then he told him Matthew's funeral would probably be held in a couple of days. It depended on the coroner, on the family. He was thinking the coming days could be filled with funerals.

As the Toyota shuddered into life, Father John debated with himself whether to call Gianelli right away. All he had was another theory—the possibility of a connection between the two murdered men and a prominent rancher who may or may not have known that Gabriel Many Horses had returned to the reservation. He rammed the gear into drive and nudged the Toyota across the dirt yard and out onto the road. Before he mentioned the name of Alexander Legeau in the same sentence with murder, he wanted to have a talk with the man himself.

❮ 24 ❯

Father John drove north across the reservation, past the turn-off to Fort Washakie and on through Ethete. A few miles beyond Bighorn Flats, he took the jog around Riverside Dam and continued north on Maverick Springs Road, "Toreador en garde" filling the cab. The sun rode on his left, leaping over the buttes, draws, and arroyos. The farther north he went, the more isolated the land, with the only sign of human life an occasional wreck of an old cabin rising unexpectedly out of the bareness. Ahead lay the humpbacked hills of the Owl Creek Mountains.

As he came down the gradual slope into Wildhorse Flats, he saw the Legeau ranch before him. The barns and outbuildings, the pastures girdled with log fences, the white ranch house—all glowed in the sun, like a medieval village. He swung right into the driveway and parked near a bed of red and yellow tulips. A series of paving stones led across a stretch of lawn to the house.

The front door opened partway as he came up the steps to the porch. Peering around the door was an elderly Indian woman—Arapaho, he guessed by the quiet way her eyes stayed on him.

"I'm Father O'Malley, Grandmother," he said. The woman gave a little nod: She'd heard of him, the priest at St. Francis.

"Is Alexander Legeau in?"

The woman pulled the door back and motioned him to enter. He removed his cowboy hat as he stepped into the entry. Sunshine streamed through the two windows flanking the door. The floor was dark and polished, a handsome frame for the rug upon it, woven in reds, whites, blues, blacks, and yellows—the colors of the Arapaho. A staircase rose on the left, the railing and balustrade polished to the same hue as the floor.

The old woman ushered him through an archway on the right into a living room that resembled a lodge in some exclusive club, filled with overstuffed sofas and chairs, blue velvet drapes folded back at the windows, tables with tops as shiny as glass supporting stacks of old leather books and silver boxes, walls lined with oil paintings of horses and cattle in green mountain meadows. Over the stone fireplace that took up most of the far wall was a deerskin shield with a black bull painted on it. The *Hiiteni,* Father John realized. The symbol of Alexander Legeau's dream power.

"Please wait here, Father." The old woman turned back into the entry and disappeared. He could hear the quiet shuffle of her footsteps along a hallway.

He walked over to the bank of windows that looked out over the back: another stretch of lawn, more beds of tulips, a series of barns and, beyond, five or six quarter horses grazing in a pasture. A couple of cowboys in blue jeans and checkered shirts emerged from one of the barns, saddles slung over their shoulders. They strode toward the horses. Neither cowboy looked like Alexander Legeau.

"To what do we owe this unexpected pleasure?" a woman asked.

Father John turned toward the entry. Lily Legeau stood in the archway, framed by the sunshine. She was dressed in a pale yellow tunic and long pants made of some kind of gauzy material that clung to the curves of her slim body. Silver bracelets glistened at her wrists. A silver necklace fell among the folds of her tunic. Her black hair was parted in the middle and pulled back, shiny in the sun. He knew she was probably in her sixties, but she had the clear, dark complexion, red lips, and tapered eyebrows of a younger woman.

"This is a beautiful place, Lily," he said. "I'm surprised you want to give it up."

"The ranch is Alexander's dream." She came toward him, extending a slim hand tipped with red nails. Her hand felt cool and silky, like the petal of a rose. He could see the tiny crow's feet at the edges of her eyes, the quizzical furrow in her forehead, but her skin stretched taut across the high cheekbones and the delicate curve of her nose.

"My husband followed his dream to help Our People," she said, pulling her hand away. "Just as his dream spirit, the bull, instructed him. He is still following his dream. The nuclear storage facility will help the People even more. So, you see, his dream has come true. How many of us see our dreams come true, Father? Of course, some people believe the Dream Maker controls our dreams and determines whether they will come true." She shrugged, as if to dismiss the idea. "But it takes very hard work to make a dream come true, wouldn't you agree?"

"Even then it may not happen," Father John said. "I was hoping Alexander might be around."

"Please have a seat." She stepped back a little ways, let herself down into one of the overstuffed chairs, and crossed her legs, gracefulness in the movement. "I'm afraid Alexander's out on the ranch. Can I help you?"

Father John perched on one of the sofas and hung his hat over one knee. "I thought Alexander might like to know about the funeral arrangements for his friend."

"You came all the way out here for that, Father? Surely a phone call . . ."

"I was in the area," he said. A stretch of the truth. He wasn't in the area until after he'd determined to come to the ranch.

The woman lifted her face and seemed to study him, to weigh the information. After a moment she said, "A terrible blow for my husband, Matthew's death. They were boyhood friends, you know. Hadn't seen much of each other over the years, however." She glanced around the room a moment. "Of course, these last months, they've been working on the plans for the facility. Matthew understood the enormous opportunity. With him gone, well, I'm afraid my husband will have to carry both of their work loads. Not alone, of course. I'm always here to help him. And we mustn't let up. We must continue to make sure the People receive accurate information—the facts, Father, to counteract the scare tactics put out by Vicky Holden."

Suddenly Lily looked beyond him toward the entry. Father John could feel another presence in the room, and he glanced around. Alexander Legeau stood in the archway. "Father O'Malley? What brings you out this way?" the rancher asked.

Father John got to his feet and shook hands with the other man. He looked older than his wife: a working cowboy just in off the range in worn jeans and red print shirt, with a jeans jacket slung over one shoulder and a black Stetson cocked partway back on his head. He stood half a foot shorter than Father John; his build was slim and wiry, his grip that of a man still capable of throwing a calf.

"Darling, how fortunate you're here," Lily said. "Father O'Malley stopped by to tell us about the arrangements for Matthew's funeral."

Father John stepped back and took both the rancher and his wife into view. "Gabriel's funeral," he said.

Silence descended over the room, as if a windstorm had suddenly subsided. From outside came the sound of a horse whinnying, a man shouting. Lily seemed to withdraw into the overstuffed cushions of the chair. Father John couldn't decide whether she sought protection or just a solid position from which to launch an attack. The rancher remained still, a large, ropelike vein pulsing in his neck. "Old Gab," he said after a moment. "I seen in the newspaper that some drifter got shot. Then I seen another article that said it was Gab. First I heard of him in a good many years. Thirty, at least." He glanced at his wife, as if for confirmation.

"Didn't even know he was back on the rez," the rancher continued, warming to the subject now. "Friend of yours, was he?"

Father John drew in a long breath, then plunged on: "In a way. He called and arranged a meeting just before he was murdered." He watched the rancher for a reaction, a flicker of awareness that whatever information Gabriel Many Horses had given to Matthew Bosse, he might also have given to him. Silence seeped through the room, and Father John sensed that the rancher had taken in the information just as he had hoped he would.

Alexander Legeau crossed the room to the bank of windows and looked out, his jacket still slung over one shoulder. After a moment he said, "We used to ride together, Gab and Mattie and me and a couple other guys. Hell, we worked ranches all over this area. Got started when we wasn't much taller'n fence posts."

"Did Gabriel work here?" Father John made an effort to keep his expression unreadable.

"Gab? Sure, he worked here some of the time. So did Mattie. Old Tinzant—he was my father's brother—hired us on. Never had no kids himself, so he was good to me and the guys I cowboyed with after my dad died. Used to call me Breed. He'd say, 'Hey you, Mr. Breed,' even though he was probably a breed himself. Dad's family, they come from some French trader in the early days, and there wasn't too many white women wandering 'round these parts then. Anyway, I got a lot of Indian blood from my mother. She was all Arapaho, like my beautiful wife here." He gestured toward Lily, who was still pressing herself into the cushions, an earnestness about her.

The rancher went on: "Tinzant married a white woman, and she had some nephews. After she died, they showed up here, maybe thinkin' they was gonna get the ranch when the old man died. But he left the ranch to me, Mr. Breed, just like he said he was gonna." The rancher gave a short, dry laugh. "Surprised the hell outta them white relations of his wife's."

"Gabriel was trying to locate some old friends," Father John said, bringing the subject back to the murdered cowboy. "Did he come to see you?"

The rancher looked startled, as if he'd just been jabbed with an electrical wire. "Who told you that? I ain't seen Gab in thirty years."

Lily was on her feet now. She stepped to the side of her husband, linking one arm through his. "That old cowboy was part of the past, Father. He had nothing to do with us. I'm surprised you seem to think otherwise."

Father John kept his eyes on the rancher. "Two men who worked on your ranch have been murdered. I'm wondering why."

The rancher shrugged, patted his wife's hand. "Folks turn up dead on the rez from time to time. You been around long enough to know that, Father O'Malley. Everybody knows why Matthew Bosse got killed. He's been working on the nuclear waste facility, and there's a lot of white protesters don't wanna see that facility built. As for Gab, no tellin' what trouble he got himself into. He was always a hothead, doin' things the rest of us would say no thanks to."

"His funeral's tomorrow morning, nine o'clock," Father John said.

Alexander gave his wife's hand a kind of caress before releasing her arm. "I 'spect I'm gonna be busy." He backed into the entry, a signal the meeting was over, and Father John followed.

"By the way," the rancher said as he opened the front door. "How'd you happen to connect me to Gabriel Many Horses?"

"Just heard it around." Father John set his cowboy hat on his head and stepped onto the porch. His boots made a loud thwacking noise on the steps.

It was past dark before Father John finally got to his office. The kids were waiting when he drove into the mission, and he was glad to spend the next couple of hours practicing baseball. They worked on defense: the hows and whens, as he called the strategy. How to position the infield. When to guard against a stolen base. The Eagles were great at strategy. They'd brought home the trophy last season, in large part because of strategy, and they hadn't rusted out over the winter. He was the only one feeling a little rusty.

Now, with darkness settled outside, he saw his own reflection in the window next to the desk as he punched in Vicky's number. No answer. He pressed down on the lever and tried her office. When the answering machine picked up, he left another message for her to call him.

The same message he'd been leaving since yesterday. Still, she hadn't called back. He hung up and called Gianelli's office. Another answering machine: "You have reached the Federal Bureau of Investigation." He hit the lever again and tapped out the agent's home number. Someone answered on the first ring. In the background was the sound of kids jabbering and laughing. "Gianelli here," the agent said.

"I'm worried about Vicky." Father John passed up the customary greeting. The agent knew his voice.

"What's going on?"

"I haven't been able to reach her for a couple of days."

"Maybe she took your advice and left town. That would've been the smart thing to do. Vicky's very smart."

"She didn't leave town, Gianelli. I know her. Somebody's been trying to kill her, and now she's missing."

"You haven't talked to her in two days. That doesn't mean she's missing." Gianelli stopped. His breath came in sudden bursts. "Okay, I'll call Eberhart. He's supposed to be keeping a watch on her. He'll send a patrolman over to check her house and office. I'll get back to you if there's anything suspicious. Okay?"

"Thanks." Father John wished the offer made him feel a little better. "Something else," he began. Then he told the agent about the connection among a bunch of old cowboys: Many Horses, Bosse, Fast, Legeau.

"Who's Fast?" the agent wanted to know.

Father John related what he knew; it wasn't much—an old cowboy with one leg and probably a serious case of diabetes who'd returned to the reservation to finish out his life. He told the agent where Fast was living. Then he said that something must have happened years ago; something Gabriel had come back to clear up before he died. Whatever had happened, it involved Legeau. Just a theory, he said.

"Damn right, it's just a theory." Gianelli's voice came like a burst of thunder. "Not a shred of evidence to connect Alexander Legeau to murder. He's a respected man around here. A real example of how hard work pays off. Sure, I know, he inherited that ranch of his, but it was a small operation when he took over. Alexander built up the herd, made the ranch one of the best known in Fremont County."

"Look, Gianelli. I'm just pointing out that Legeau and the two murdered men go back a long time."

The line went quiet. Finally the agent said, "Okay.

I'll drive out to the ranch and have a chat with Mr. Legeau. And listen, John, stop worrying about Vicky. From what I've seen of that woman, she's capable of taking care of herself."

The electronic buzz followed the cutoff click, and Father John replaced the receiver. He strode out of the administration building, locking the door after himself, and got into the Toyota. He drove west on Seventeen-Mile Road, then south on Rendezvous Road, the shortest route to Lander.

◀ 25 ▶

Father John had passed the night in a kind of half-awake state, tossing about, waiting for the phone to ring. A couple of times he'd started out of bed, dreaming it had rung, that Vicky was calling, that she needed him. He'd stopped at both her office and her house last night. The doors were locked, the interiors dark. It had only increased his worry. She was nowhere, and he hadn't heard anything from Gianelli.

Morning had dawned in a gray haze with clouds rolling over the distant plains like fog. By nine o'clock, the sun still hadn't broken through. The inside of St. Francis church was enveloped in the hush of the clouds. Every sound seemed muffled: the drums, the mournful voices of the singers, the shuffling in the pews of the few people who had come to pay last respects to a forgotten cowboy—Gianelli, Clarence Fast, and the little boy, Jamie; Leonard Bizzel and Elena, three elders, a couple of grandmothers who came to Mass every morning.

Gabriel Many Horses' body lay in a closed pine casket in front of the altar, under an arched ceiling painted blue, like the sky world. Father John said the ancient, familiar words of the Mass. He prayed for the cowboy, that no matter where life had taken him, his soul would now go to God.

After the Mass, Father John took the chair on the opposite side of the altar as the three elders approached the casket. One removed a small leather pouch from his shirt pocket. He lifted the lid of the casket, then dipped two fingers into the pouch. Praying softly in Arapaho, he leaned over the corpse, tracing red circles, Father John knew, on what remained of the cowboy's face, on the head and hands, the skin of the chest. Ancestors, here he is, one of the People.

A small cavalcade—the gray hearse, the Toyota, Gianelli's Blazer, a couple of old trucks—drove to the cemetery out on the bluff adjacent to Seventeen-Mile Road. The air was hazy and cool. A sharp wind caught Father John's stole and blew it sideways across his jacket as he sprinkled holy water across the open grave, the casket suspended above. He prayed out loud: "May you go on your way to the ancestors, Gabriel Many Horses. May your spirit live in the Spirit of the kind and loving Lord Jesus who understands the human heart and accepts us as we are."

As the drums began beating, the casket cranked downward into the earth, and Father John felt a sense of peace as gentle as the clouds descend upon him. The cowboy had yearned to tell the truth, to unburden himself, to set something right. A sign in itself of redemption.

Afterward the little crowd started toward the vehicles parked on the dirt road at the edge of the cemetery. Father John fell into step beside Gianelli. "Did you hear from Eberhart?" he asked.

"No sign of any break-in at Vicky's house or office. Everything looks normal, like she just stepped away." Father John had already ascertained that much for himself. He saw the reflection of his own worry in the agent's eyes.

"She have any family around here?" Gianelli asked.

The grandmothers called her Woman Alone, Father John was thinking. He said, "An elderly aunt, Rose Left Hand. One of the Four Old Men, Hedly Yellowbird, and his wife. An ex-husband, Ben, who works up north on the Arapaho ranch." Almost no one.

"I'll make some calls."

The church was empty and still when Father John returned. He spent a few moments tidying up the sacristy, setting the Mass books in the cabinet, hanging his chasuble in the closet. He crossed in front of the altar and genuflected. As he turned, he saw Vicky in the last pew. He hurried down the aisle toward her, feeling as if some terrible weight had lifted from him. She wore a raincoat the color of pewter; her hair hung loose, brushing her shoulders, not gathered back with a clip the way she usually wore it. Her expression was a curious mixture of fatigue and exhilaration.

"Are you okay?"

She nodded. "I'm sorry I missed the funeral. I just got back from Casper. Do you have a minute?" Getting to her feet, she swung a black bag over her shoulder and picked up the briefcase leaning against the kneeler.

Outside the church, Father John placed a hand on her arm and guided her toward the priests' residence. They could talk in his study without the interruptions of the telephone in his office, of people dropping by.

They walked across the open space in the center of the mission grounds. The path was soft and dry, but little beads of moisture clung to the stalks of wild grass. The clouds seemed to close around them. Vicky hugged her coat to her—against the chill, he thought. He was filled with a sense of gladness and relief that she was alive.

The aroma of fresh coffee floated down the hallway as he held the front door and followed her inside. Elena must have guessed he would be ready for hot coffee following the funeral. After he showed Vicky through the doorway on the left, he walked into the kitchen and poured two mugs of coffee, which he carried to the study. Vicky had laid her raincoat over one of the wing-back chairs. She wore a silky blouse in blues and greens, and a dark wraparound skirt with a fringed edge. He handed her one of the mugs.

She sipped at the coffee a moment before she set the mug down near the edge of the desk. Flipping open her briefcase, she extracted a packet and shook out the folds before allowing it to float over the center of the desk. It was a map of Wind River Reservation. "I met with the geologists, Hunter and Bradshaw. They know every inch of the reservation. The Arapahos and Sho-shones usually hire their firm to conduct geological studies. Evidently Redbull decided a larger firm in Den-ver ought to do the studies for the facility. Anyway, we spent yesterday going over the report, sentence by sentence. They assured me it's accurate, as far as it goes."

Leaning over the map, Vicky placed an index finger in the center and made a little circle. "Oil wells are located here, five miles south of the Legeau ranch. And here, about eight miles north." He could make out clusters of black dots representing the wells.

Her finger was now on the Legeau ranch itself. "The perfect place for a nuclear storage facility," she said, glancing up at him. He could sense her excitement. "Except for one problem."

Father John walked around the desk and bent over the map. The ranch did seem perfect. In the center of the flat plains, miles from any other human activity. He must be missing something, he thought, and then he saw it: the squiggly red lines indicating the rise of the land toward the oil wells—a rise so gradual he hadn't noticed as he'd driven through.

"The ranch occupies the low ground," he said. He saw by her expression he had hit on the problem. "The report doesn't mention any danger of flooding."

"That's because there isn't any, not above ground," Vicky said. "What the report fails to mention is the dan-

ger of underground flooding in special circumstances."
She tapped the map again, a nervous gesture. "After
about two-thirds of the oil in an area has been taken, oil
companies sometimes pump water and detergent into
the wells. The remaining oil bonds with the detergent
and rises high enough so that it can be pumped out."

Father John took a long draw of coffee. "How much
water are we talking about?"

"Over time, it can be millions of gallons. Enough to
form a small underground lake at the lowest point in
the area."

"And that's happened?" He was beginning to catch
her excitement.

"These wells have been pumped for years. I figured
the chances were high. So I made a few phone calls to
the oil companies that hold the leases on the fields. They
confirmed that water has been pumped into the wells.
And they plan to pump even more water over the next
few years."

Father John set the mug down and took his chair,
lifting the front legs off the carpet. "And all that water
has to go somewhere."

"According to Hunter and Bradshaw, the natural
drainage routes would take the water below the Legeau
ranch." Vicky picked up her mug, took a sip, and began
tracing the rim with one finger. "In the case of some
horrible disaster, the storage casks could be thrown together with enough force to start a nuclear reaction,
and . . ."

Father John let out a low whistle. "Melt down into
an underground lake."

Vicky took another long sip of the coffee. Then she
said, "The explosion would release radioactive steam
that would blow Wyoming into Nebraska and Colorado. Let's not even think about how far the cloud of
steam would travel."

Father John was quiet. After a moment he said,

"What are the chances of that kind of disaster? One in ten million?"

"Much less." Vicky shook her head. "One to the minus six, the geologists say. An infinitesimal risk. But, don't you see, John, the result would be catastrophic. And a catastrophic result makes any risk unacceptable."

Father John got to his feet and crossed the room. Clouds lapped at the window, but toward the west they were beginning to break into jagged canyons with small corridors of sunshine. Turning back, he said, "Is there any evidence a lake actually exists?"

Vicky came across the room and stood next to him. "None." Her voice was low. "It's only conjecture, a possibility. The geologists in Denver relied on computer modeling. They did not factor in anything about the pumped water. If they had, all sorts of red flags would have gone up. It would have meant further studies—either seismic studies or bores into the earth to determine whether a lake actually exists. Very expensive studies," she said, keeping her eyes on his. "My guess is United Power Company might've decided it wasn't worth pursuing. Lionel Redbull and Alexander Legeau weren't about to take any chances on that happening. They made sure the report would not mention a possible underground lake."

"By paying off the consultants to leave out certain information," Father John said.

"I'd bet my life on it." Vicky swung around and walked back to the desk. "It would explain why Redbull didn't hire Hunter and Bradshaw—they couldn't be bought. He hired consultants who've never worked on the rez, who have no ties here. For enough money, they were willing to produce the kind of report Redbull and Legeau wanted. Who knows what other critical pieces of information they conveniently forgot to factor in?"

Father John strolled across the room and sat down in

his chair. The conspiracy theory was beginning to make sense. "Either Matthew Bosse was involved and got scared, or he wasn't involved and found out what Redbull and Legeau were up to. Either way, it got him killed."

"That's what doesn't make sense," Vicky said. "I can't imagine Bosse involved in something like this. He's been on the tribal council a long time. There's never been a hint of scandal about him. On the other hand, if he wasn't involved, I don't think he ever figured it out. If he'd suspected anything, I'm certain he would have gone to Hunter and Bradshaw, just as I did. He trusted them. I can't imagine how Lionel convinced him other consultants should conduct the study, but Lionel can be very persuasive. In any case, Hunter and Bradshaw told me Bosse never contacted them. Yet the way he acted at the public hearing—all those 'maybes'—something was bothering him."

Father John was quiet a moment, his thoughts on the other theory. Perhaps it wasn't too farfetched after all. Maybe Bosse's murder had nothing to do with the facility; maybe it had to do with something in the past, some secret the cowboys wanted to keep hidden. He told Vicky what he'd learned about Many Horses coming back to the reservation to contact old friends—Bosse, Fast, maybe Alexander Legeau.

"There's more of a connection than you know." Vicky sat down in one of the wingbacks and leaned forward. "I also found Tina Hooshie while I was in Casper. We had a long chat on the phone last night. She'd seen the notice in the newspaper about Gabriel's murder. It didn't bring any tears to her eyes. Her family hated the man, she said. Seems Gabriel Many Horses was responsible for putting her uncle, Anton, in Leavenworth. It was Gabriel's testimony that convicted Anton of murder. He died in prison two years ago, just before he was due to be released. Tina said her uncle died claiming he was innocent."

Father John leaned back in his chair. The pattern

he'd been looking for was beginning to emerge. "So Gabriel came back to tell the truth and clear Anton's name. He must have gone to the Hooshie cabin hoping to find him, not knowing the poor man had died in prison."

Vicky was shaking her head. "Tina wouldn't believe Gabriel Many Horses capable of that kind of remorse. He knew what he was doing. He deliberately sent an innocent man to prison. He was paid off."

"Who was murdered?" Father John was sure of the answer; he wanted only the confirmation.

"Tinzant Legeau," Vicky said.

Father John shook his head. "Gabriel wasn't sure where Anton was. That explains why he tried to contact two old friends who might have been able to help him. He connected with Bosse and told him the truth."

"Which got the councilman killed," Vicky interjected.

"And he must've called on Legeau, just when the man was about to sign a forty-year lease for two million dollars a year."

Vicky got out of her chair and crossed to the window again. She turned slowly around, backlit by the hazy daylight. "Gabriel Many Horses was a stalker," she said. "He would have destroyed Legeau's dream. Had he named Legeau as the real killer, the investigation into Tinzant's murder would have been reopened. Legeau would have stood trial, and that would have thrown the title to the ranch into question. You can't inherit from someone you've murdered, so all of Legeau's plans to lease the ranch would have come to a halt until the outcome of his trial. He couldn't allow that to happen, so he killed Gabriel. But the cowboy had already told Bosse, so he had to kill the councilman, too. He would've killed Fast if Gabriel had managed to meet him. And"—she broke off, gulped in some air—"he would've killed you, John, if Gabriel had told you."

Father John was quiet. He didn't want to tell her that he'd deliberately planted the notion in Legeau's mind that maybe Gabriel *had* told him. What had he been hoping for? he wondered. That Legeau might show his hand, come looking for him? And then what? Did he really believe he could snare the hunter when the hunter had the gun? He pushed the thought aside. He was more concerned about the woman across from him. The hunter had already come after her.

"So what now?" Vicky said. "You realize this is all just theory. We have no evidence Legeau killed his uncle. The only witness is dead, and the only person Gabriel told is dead. As far as that goes, we have no evidence Legeau and Redbull conspired to falsify the report. Let's face it, we don't have enough evidence for a jaywalking charge. If we took this to Gianelli, he'd laugh us out of his office."

Vicky walked back, stopping in front of the desk. "Redbull's the key," she said. "He's an ambitious and greedy man. I'm going to have a talk with him. It's just possible I can make him think I've found some evidence."

"No, Vicky." Father John jumped to his feet and walked around the desk. "Don't even think it. Redbull and Legeau are in this together."

"I won't do anything foolish."

"Don't do anything at all." The sternness in his tone surprised him. "We'll take this to Gianelli."

"But first we need some evidence, John. Even some hint that evidence exists."

"Stay away from Redbull," Father John said. "You're in enough danger. I don't want anything to happen to you." He took her hand, aware of its warmth. The longing for her engulfed him, the fear of something happening to her. He felt sick with worry at what she might decide to do. This was a stubborn woman; he'd never won an argument yet, and he was afraid he wouldn't win this one.

A muffled knocking sounded at the front door as Vicky said, "About the other night, John. I'm sorry if I led you to think that, well, that I expect something else from you than friendship."

The knocking came again, followed by the soft shush of Elena's footsteps in the hallway.

"I want you to know how much I value your friendship," Vicky hurried on. "It means everything to me. I wouldn't want anything to keep us from being friends."

"Vicky . . ." he began, still holding her hand. He searched for the words. He didn't want her to feel an explanation was necessary. He fought the temptation to take her into his arms.

She said, "There really isn't anything else for us, is there?"

The question surprised and disturbed him. He knew he'd been asking himself the same question in some wordless way. "I don't think so," he said.

She withdrew her hand and stepped back, leaving him with an acute sense of loss. "Well, in any case, it doesn't matter, does it?" she said. "We each have to go in the direction of our own lives. And that won't change." She looked away, somewhere beyond him. After a moment, she said, "About your conspiracy theory, I don't believe Paul Bryant is involved. I had dinner with him before I went to Casper. He seems like a good person."

"We don't know who may be involved," Father John said, trying to ignore an unfamiliar stab of jealousy. "We don't know anything for certain. At the very least, Bryant wants you to stop opposing the facility. He's interested in gaining your support."

"Strange," Vicky said. "I have the distinct impression he's interested in me, as a woman."

Of course Bryant was interested in her, Father John thought. What man wouldn't be? The sense of loss was pervasive now.

There was the click of the knob turning, and the door pushed open. It startled him. Sheila Cavanaugh walked in: the reddish gold hair, the flashing green eyes, a long blue coat that hung loosely from her shoulders, almost hiding the blue jeans, the white sweater. The study was filled with her perfume.

"Oh, sorry. I didn't realize you had a visitor. Your housekeeper . . ." The woman gestured toward the hallway, allowing her arm to float in the air a moment. Smiling at him, she said, "I really intended to come to the funeral. Had it been a little later in the morning, perhaps. But, never mind. It must've been difficult for you, John, after finding the body and all. Alberta has arranged a wonderful lunch at the ranch today, and I have come to fetch you."

Father John saw the stunned look of recognition and disbelief on Vicky's face. She kept her place a moment, staring at the woman, then suddenly twisted past him. "Please don't let me keep you, Father O'Malley," she said, grabbing her raincoat and flinging it over one arm. She picked up the briefcase, the black bag. In an instant, she was through the door.

Father John brushed past the other woman and caught up with Vicky just as she was about to step onto the front stoop. He took hold of her arm. "Wait, you don't understand."

"Oh, you're wrong." She pulled away from him. "I finally understand everything, Father O'Malley." Then she was marching down the sidewalk, the black bag slung over one shoulder bouncing against the raincoat still on her arm.

Father John could sense Sheila Cavanaugh behind him, could smell her perfume. He took a deep breath before he turned to face the most beautiful woman he wished he'd never met.

◀ 26 ▶

Vicky gripped the steering wheel, scarcely aware of her nails digging into the palms of her hands as the Bronco plunged down Seventeen-Mile Road. Thick clouds pressed downward, parting occasionally so that the Bronco seemed to dive in and out of a wet mist. "How could you be so stupid?" The sound of her own voice startled her.

For almost three years now, she had yearned for a man who had always seemed exactly as he appeared— a good man, a whole man. He was a priest, and she had respected that reality, had worked hard to keep her own feelings in check. When that had become difficult, she had stopped calling him, had gone out of the way not to see him, even though there had been many instances, many legitimate excuses, many times she had longed to pick up the phone and hear his voice.

She had scarcely acknowledged her own feelings. Except for the other evening in her kitchen, when they'd been so close, and for the first time she had allowed herself to dream that perhaps . . . things could change. Priests left the priesthood everyday. They married.

But not priests like John O'Malley. That was the truth of it, the reality she could never get around. How could he leave the priesthood? It was his dream, and the power of his dream made him who he was. What drew her to him, she had always thought, was the very thing that kept him from her. She had never thought it was something else.

She gripped the steering wheel tighter. Her knuckles blanched, her palms stung. How could she have been so wrong? All that time, there was another woman strolling into his study, just as she had this morning, perfectly at home. An everyday occurrence. His own housekeeper had told her to go right in. This woman with sun-gold red hair and green eyes and skin as clear and white as the china she probably kept stacked in one of her cabinets.

Sheila Cavanaugh. One of his own people. She was probably from Boston—the broad words, the swallowed *r*'s, just like his. How long had she been here? Had he brought her with him when he'd first come to St. Francis? It wasn't possible. She would have heard the rumors. The moccasin telegraph would have never stopped buzzing. When had this woman come? Where did he keep her? Vicky had heard about such women—the women who consorted with priests. She did not want to be one of them.

She swerved into the oncoming lane and passed a pickup. Another fast swerve, another pickup. The mist clung to the windshield, and she flipped on the wipers. They made a screeching noise, like that of a small, hungry animal. She had to think rationally, to bring her feelings under control. She could not allow the sense of loss to overtake her. She could not lose what she never had. "Do not cry for something you never had," Grandmother Ninni once told her. "It does not cry for you." She would be okay as she was. *Hisei ci nihi.* Woman Alone.

Vicky wheeled into the parking lot in front of the tribal offices at Ethete. She set the Bronco next to the cement curb, switched off the ignition, and waited, watching the tiny specks of rain accumulate on the windshield.

It was several minutes before she felt some semblance of control again.

She opened the glove compartment and removed the small tape recorder she used to take depositions. She checked to make sure the tape inside was new. One hundred and twenty minutes—more than enough, she thought. She checked the buttons. Everything worked. Pushing the On button, she clipped the recorder inside her purse near the top. If she didn't snap the purse closed, the recorder would pick up voices. She would only have to reach in and press the Dictate button to start the recording.

As she walked up to the double glass doors of the tribal office building, Vicky felt herself trembling, as if the cool mist had crept inside her. The lobby was deserted except for the receptionist and a young couple who occupied two of the metal chairs against one wall. The woman tossed back her black hair and thumbed through the pages of a magazine, ignoring the man leaning toward her, his voice earnest and low. The odor of stale cigarettes mingled with the chemical smells of floor wax.

Vicky walked past the couple to the desk against the far wall. The receptionist glanced up from a computer monitor, her fingers resting on the keyboard. One of the Bushy girls, Vicky thought. Iola Bushy, in her twenties now, pretty, with wide eyes that gave her a look of surprise.

"I'm here to see Lionel," Vicky said.

"You got an appointment?" Little furrows appeared in the young woman's forehead, as if she were trying to remember.

"Just tell him I'm here."

The receptionist raised both shoulders, a fierce gesture, like that of a bear rearing up to protect her cubs.

"Sorry. Not possible. Lionel's in a real important meeting with the tribal council right now."

It crossed Vicky's mind that Iola Bushy was sleeping with Lionel Redbull. She shook the notion away. Was this what she would think about every woman she met? That every woman had someone to love, while she had no one? She had to do better than that, she told herself, forcing her thoughts back to the moment. The receptionist's fingers had begun tapping the keys in a sharp clattering rhythm.

"Call Lionel out of the meeting, Iola."

"What?" The young woman stopped tapping and sat back, eyes wide with shock.

"You heard me. Call him out of the meeting."

"I can't do that, Vicky. Lionel will get real mad at me."

Vicky recognized the way Iola spoke the man's name. It was the way any woman spoke the name of the man she loved. She'd been right. She said, "Tell him I know what's missing."

The receptionist hesitated. Finally she gripped the edge of the desk and pulled herself toward the phone. Her fingers raced over the buttons. A moment passed. Iola stared past Vicky toward the glass front doors. Suddenly she started apologizing—"I'm so sorry, Lionel"—and delivered the message. Then she was quiet, surprise and hurt mingling in her eyes. Replacing the receiver, she said, "His office is on the right."

"I know where it is." Vicky started down the hallway past a procession of frosted glass doors. She reached inside her purse and fingered the cool plastic recorder, groping for the Dictate button. Just as she was about to press it, one of the doors opened. Lionel stepped out. He wore blue jeans and a white shirt, sleeves rolled up to the elbows. Beyond him, Vicky could see the tribal council members seated around a conference table. A voice drifting into the hallway was cut off as the project director slammed the door. "What the hell's this all about?" he asked. He moved in front of her.

Vicky yanked her hand out of the purse. She hadn't expected him to appear like this. She realized with a sinking feeling she hadn't managed to press the Dictate button.

"I've found some information you'll be interested in." Vicky locked eyes with the man in front of her. Was she mistaken, or did the smallest trace of fear come into his expression?

Lionel Redbull turned on his heel and started down the hallway. Vicky hurried to catch up and strode alongside, wondering if she dared reach into her purse and search again for the button. She decided against it. The man pushed open a door with black lettering on the frosted glass: TRIBAL PROJECT DIRECTOR. She followed him through the doorway.

The office was small, the walls lined with a desk, file cabinets, a couple of straight-backed chairs. The air was filled with the musty odor of stale smoke and perspiration.

"Make it quick, Vicky." Lionel stood in front of her again. She could smell the sourness of his breath.

She stepped past him and sat down in one of the chairs. Deliberately she opened the purse on her lap, aware of his eyes on her. With her left hand, she pushed through the jumble of contents until she located a small spiral notebook and a ballpoint. As she extracted them, her right hand found the recorder and one finger pressed down on the Dictate button. She set the purse down carefully at her feet, leaving the flaps open.

Lionel grabbed the other chair. The legs screeched

across the tile floor as he swung the chair around in front of her and straddled the seat. He set both arms across the back. "You've got one minute," he said.

Vicky opened the little notebook and glanced at the notes she'd scribbled to herself. Reminder notes that had nothing to do with this. She looked up. "I've been studying some old geologic reports."

"So?"

"So I understand why your consultants forgot to mention the great volume of water pumped into the oil wells north and south of the Legeau ranch."

Lionel drew back, a quick reflex. She thought his face actually took on a lighter shade. His eyes stayed on hers. "What are you talking about?"

"We know where the water pools, don't we, Lionel? An underground lake makes the Legeau ranch a highly risky site to store radioactive materials."

"You have no proof."

"Oh, you're wrong. I found the geologic reports, reports you obviously didn't know existed." She kept her face a mask, praying it wouldn't slip, that he wouldn't see she had nothing.

Lionel drew in a long breath and slowly let it out. "What do you want?"

"How much did you pay the consultants in Denver to forget about the water, as well as any other factors that might make the site unsuitable?"

"Other factors?"

"Come on, Lionel. We know they exist." Vicky shrugged. "It doesn't matter. I have proof the underground lake exists. I want the same amount you gave the consultants."

The man let out a loud snort. "If you think I'm going to give you $250,000, you've gone round the bend, lady."

"Two hundred fifty thousand dollars." Vicky let the words hang in the air a moment. The consultants could have asked for more. The information they'd agreed to withhold was critical; it determined whether the facility would be built. It always amazed her the way greedy people grasped at the first money they saw, rather than angling for more, as if they couldn't bear the risk of missing any of it, not the smallest part.

"You're playing a dangerous game, Vicky."

"Yes, I know. I got your threats." She was taking a chance. She hoped the recorder was working.

"You didn't heed them."

"You missed me."

"What do you mean?"

"When you tried to run me down in front of my office. When you tried to get into my house. When you followed me from the public hearing."

"You got me all wrong." Lionel was shaking his head.

"I know how desperate you are to get the facility," Vicky went on, prodding. "You've probably already stashed a large part of the grant money in some secret bank account. You hired consultants you could bribe. You threatened me. And when Matthew Bosse found out what you had done, you killed him."

Lionel leapt off the chair and wheeled around. He brought a fist down hard on the edge of the desk and stood over it a moment. Vicky could see the muscles twitching in his forearm, the blue vein standing out in his neck. She gripped the edge of her chair to keep from jumping up and running out. Silence filled the office. From down the hallway came the lazy thud of a door slamming.

Finally he turned to her. "Okay, so I sent you some threats."

"How did you get into my office?" Vicky asked.

The Indian smiled a long moment. Finally he said, "There's a real pretty little gal that cleans the offices in your building. Let's just say she likes me a lot. Anyway,

I was only tryin' to get you to back off. All it did was spur you on. But I had no intention of carrying out the threats. Whatever's been goin' on, I had nothing to do with it. Somebody shot Matthew, but it wasn't me. I don't know who'd do such a fool thing, just when we've about got this facility wrapped up, unless it was one of the enviromaniacs around the rez. Matthew was working for the facility just as hard as I was."

"You're saying Bosse agreed to bribe the consultants?"

"No. No. No." Lionel gave his head a hard shake. "Bosse wouldn't have gone for that. He thought the report was accurate, and he never found out otherwise."

"How can you be sure?"

"What are you, some kind of prosecutor?" Lionel leaned toward her, his eyes narrowed into black slits.

Vicky said, "I assumed he must've found the same information I found."

"Well, he didn't. He would've told me. Then he would've kicked my ass off the reservation. He wouldn't have wanted money, like you." Lionel straddled the chair again and smiled at her. "We're alike, you and me. We see a chance to make some real money, we grab it. There's a lot of opportunity here. Once the facility is built, I'll be the director, and that means I'll have a lot of, let's say, discretionary funds at my disposal. I imagine I'll need a smart lawyer working by my side. We'd make a hell of a team. Maybe we ought to get better acquainted." He reached his arm around the chair and took her hand. "You're a very sexy lady."

Vicky pulled her hand away. "Do you drive a black truck, Lionel?"

"What's this? You only sleep with guys who drive black trucks?"

"Is that what you drive?"

Lionel shook his head again, a little smile playing at his mouth. "I can buy one today, that's what you like."

"Who do you know who drives a black truck?"

Lionel drew back, still staring at her. After a long moment he said, "A lot of people, Vicky. Hell, Paul Bryant rented one at the airport a couple days ago. What's this got to do with you and me and our new partnership?"

Vicky picked up her purse and got to her feet. She'd taken enough depositions to have developed an ear for the truth. Truth had its own sound, its own authority. Here was a man filled with greed, willing to go a certain distance to turn a dream into reality. But did that distance include murder? She didn't think so. Murder was a line he probably wouldn't cross. But she had seen the look on his face when she asked about the black truck. Maybe he hadn't tried to kill her, but he knew who had.

That thought brought her back to the conspiracy theory. Who was he working with? If it wasn't Bosse, then who? Paul Bryant? A shiver ran through her. She didn't want to believe it was Bryant.

Vicky adjusted the wide black strap of her purse over one shoulder, hoping the Dictate button hadn't clicked off. "Do we have a deal for $250,000?"

"I want the documents you found."

"Of course."

"Plus . . ." Lionel laid one hand on her shoulder and moved it slowly, caressingly down her arm.

"This afternoon."

"That doesn't give me much time to get you a check." His fingers were running up and down her arm, like a pianist tapping the keys.

"Cash, Lionel."

He withdrew his hand. "Jesus, Vicky. That will take some time."

"Six P.M. At my office."

"What about your secretary?"

"I'll be alone."

"This will put an end to it? Your opposition to the facility? You'll even support it?"

Vicky swallowed hard. "Yes," she said, stepping past him, scarcely believing her bluff had worked. He must be under a lot of pressure, she thought, with Bosse's murder and the FBI agent asking a lot of questions, some of them undoubtedly about the facility. The last thing Lionel would want to surface was the kind of information she claimed to have.

Just as Vicky was about to open the door, she felt the hard pressure of his hand on her arm. "Your purse," he said.

Her heart gave a little lurch. Still gripping the metal knob, she turned slowly to face him. "What?"

"How do I know what's in your purse? How do I know you haven't been taping me? And I just spilled my guts."

Vicky stared at him. Slowly she began sliding the strap from her shoulder. She handed the purse to him. "I'm a lawyer," she said, struggling to keep her tone even. "I could be disbarred for the conversation we've just had. I could also be charged with a crime. Why would I be stupid enough to create the necessary evidence?"

He glanced at her, his hands gripping the purse.

"You're right about us being alike, Lionel. We want the money. It's there for somebody to take. Why not us?"

He was still watching her. Then he glanced down at the purse, hesitating. She felt as if her heart had stopped beating. The silence of death crept over the room. Abruptly he handed the purse back.

Vicky swung open the door and stepped out into the hallway. She started toward the lobby, aware of the sound of her own footsteps, her legs numb and shaky beneath her.

She was shaking all over as she turned the key in the ignition and willed the engine into life. The tape recorder was probably still running—she didn't dare to look. Lionel might be watching through a window. She waited until the Bronco was plunging down the highway, until the tribal office building had disappeared from the rearview mirror before she groped inside the purse, hit the stop button and then the rewind button. She had what she'd come for. She had the evidence to stop the nuclear facility.

◆ 28 ◆

Vicky parked the Bronco next to the curb in front of the FBI office in Riverton. She had kept an eye on the rearview mirror all the way from Ethete. No one had followed her, she was sure. For long stretches on Seventeen-Mile Road, the Bronco had been the only vehicle in sight. She had driven past the turn-off to St. Francis Mission, fighting back the urge to wheel to the right. There would be no more turning into St. Francis Mission.

She slammed out of the Bronco and ran up the side-walk. Inside the office next to the entry, the secretary was bent over an opened filing drawer. "Gianelli in?" Vicky asked from the doorway.

The secretary closed the drawer and started toward the desk. "I'll tell him you're here, Ms. Holden."

Vicky crossed the entry and ran up the stairs against the opposite wall. "Wait," the secretary yelled from the doorway.

In the center of one of the doors on the second floor she saw a plastic plaque with Gianelli's name. She rapped on the door. The muffled sounds of some opera floated toward her and mixed with the hard, quick sounds of her own breathing. Suddenly the door swung open. The agent stood beside it, one hand on the edge. "Vicky, what's happened?"

"I've got it." She stepped past him.

"What have you got?" Gianelli slammed the door and crossed the office. He sank into the squat, wide-backed chair behind the desk and gestured for her to take one of the two straight-backed chairs on the other side.

"I know what's been going on," Vicky began, the words coming in a rush. "Lionel Redbull bribed the consultants who prepared the environmental report for the nuclear storage facility. He admits he threatened me, and he may very well know who killed Matthew Bosse—"

"Wait a minute." The agent spread both hands in the air, palms toward her. "These are serious allegations."

"You bet they are." Vicky rummaged through her purse, extracted the recorder, and popped out the tape. She handed it across the desk. Gianelli picked it up and turned it slowly in his hand, black eyebrows knit together in a bushy line. "It's all there," she said.

The agent exhaled a long breath before lifting himself out of the chair and walking to the stereo cabinet. He flipped several switches. The music stopped, an abrupt falling off, as if the aria had ended in midnote. After a second, Vicky heard the sound of her own voice. Gianelli took his chair again, staring at her as Redbull's voice, then hers, wafted through the room.

The tape ended, and Gianelli was quiet, his eyes still on her. After a moment he said, "I can't believe you did that. Why in God's name didn't you bring your suspicions to this office? Do you realize the danger you've placed yourself in?" He sounded as if he were scolding one of his children.

Vicky leaned forward. "Lionel Redbull admitted what he's been doing. He never would have admitted it any other way, and you know it, Gianelli."

The agent raised his eyes to the ceiling a moment.

"Well, now you've started it, I guess we're going to have to finish it."

"Lionel will be in my office at six o'clock." She glanced at her watch—less than three hours to go. "I can tape him paying me the $250,000. You'll have all the evidence—"

"Hold on," Gianelli interrupted. "You're not going to be there."

"Of course I'll be there. How else can we prove he's using the grant money to pay bribes?"

The agent shook his head. "You heard what Redbull said. You're playing a dangerous game, Vicky. Somebody's stalking you, somebody's tried to kill you, and if it isn't Redbull it's whoever he's working with. We don't know how big this thing is, who might be involved. You've just set yourself up to be murdered. I'm not going to let you meet him and whatever thugs he happens to bring along. Forget it."

Vicky jumped to her feet and began pacing the small office. "I know the dangers," she said. "I'm willing to accept them."

The agent said, "Lionel can deny he meant anything on that tape, you know. He can turn the tables on you. He can claim you tried to blackmail him and he only went along to get the evidence on you."

Vicky stopped pacing and leaned over the desk, gripping the edges. "Not if you back me up. Don't you see, Gianelli? The facility must be stopped. This is the chance to stop it. When the joint council learns that critical information was deliberately left out of the report, the vote will be canceled. And everybody will start wondering what else was left out. They'll question all the data in the report; they'll start questioning the safety. It will be the end of the facility."

Gianelli set both hands on the desk and pushed himself to his feet. "You're a hard woman to convince, Vicky. You sure you understand what this involves?"

She nodded.

"Okay, I'll fix you up with a body mike. I'll be there, too."

"I have to be alone. If Lionel gets any hint you're around, he'll run for sure. Then he'll certainly deny everything on the tape."

"Is there someplace in your office where I can be out of sight? And I don't mean under the desk."

Vicky closed her eyes, trying to focus her mind on the office: the receptionist's office, her private office, the back hall, hardly big enough to turn around in, with a door to the restroom, another door to the back stairs.

"There's no place," Vicky said, opening her eyes. "He'd be sure to check the back hall and restroom."

"I don't like it, Vicky." Gianelli shook his head, and his entire upper body seemed to shake. "I can be outside somewhere, close by. And I can ask the Lander PD for assistance, but if anything goes wrong . . . I can't guarantee we can get up to your office in time."

Vicky sank into the chair. She didn't want to face Redbull alone—he frightened her. She had heard the crush of the desk under his fist. She understood a man's violence. She had been married to a violent man. She drew her breath in slowly. "Gianelli," she said, "I just don't see any other way."

The clouds clamped together, like a sheet of steel hung from the sky. A slow, rhythmic drizzle ran over the windshield. Father John stared past the wipers at the asphalt on Seventeen-Mile Road, shiny as a mirror. He stopped at the intersection, then joined the traffic heading into Riverton. At the corner of Federal Boulevard and Park Avenue, he wheeled left and continued for a few blocks, drawing up in front of the low-slung modern building that housed the Riverton Library.

The librarian raised both eyes over the rimless glasses perched at the end of her nose. A slim silver chain dangled from the earpieces and hung over her white sweater. "Father O'Malley, I believe you have some books overdue."

She was right. Two books, one on the Civil War, another on the war on the Plains, both waiting until he found the time. He never seemed to have the time. He fished in the small pocket of his blue jeans and brought out a dollar bill.

"Oh, I don't want your money," she said, pushing his hand away. "Keep it for those Indian kids. I'll just renew the books." She began tapping on the keyboard of the computer that occupied the counter.

"I'd like to see some old newspapers," he said.

She shook her head. "You history people. You don't like anything unless it's old. What's wrong with today's paper?"

"How about the *Central Wyoming News* from thirty years ago?" He clasped his hands and set them on the counter.

"Oh, dear me," the librarian said. "That will take some work. We don't have old newspapers on microfilm like some libraries. We're working on it, but it's a major job. And the cost . . ." She rolled her eyes.

"Do you have the newspapers?"

"Oh, yes, they're stored in the basement. They're bound in very large books. I'll have to ask someone to bring them upstairs. If you want to come back in a couple days, I'm sure I can make them available to you."

"What if I just looked at them in the basement?"

"Well, I don't know," the librarian said. "It's highly irregular."

"It won't take long."

She glanced around the reading room. They were the only ones there. "I'll show you."

He followed her down wooden stairs that felt solid beneath his footsteps. A strip of light shone through the open doorway above. Along one side was a wall of red bricks held together with thick cement, the foundation wall. He smelled the musty odors of mildewed paper and dried ink, the transmitters of history.

At the bottom of the stairs, the librarian flipped a switch, and a yellow light illuminated a space the size of a small gym. They walked across the cement floor, down aisles of metal shelving stuffed with books, papers, and cardboard folders.

"What are you looking for, Father?" The woman glanced over one shoulder, her voice reverberating in the cool space.

"A murder thirty years ago on the reservation." Polite conversation. He didn't want to go into details.

Another glance over the shoulder. "Good luck, Father. There are so many murders on the reservation."

They stopped in the shadows next to large bins along the far wall. Each bin held a stack of gigantic books bound in black cloth. On the spines, embossed in gold, were the words *Central Wyoming News* and dates. The earliest, 1880.

The librarian walked along the bins, touching the spines in a tender gesture. She stopped, her fingers resting on one volume. "This is what you'll want. You can work at the sorting table." She nodded toward a wooden benchlike table in the shadows next to the adjoining wall.

Thanking her, he lifted the volume from the bin and carried it to the table. The sound of footsteps filled the dead air as the librarian made her way back among the shelves and up the stairs.

He laid the top cover back gently. It crackled with stiffness, resisting the intrusion. He could smell the dust as he ran his hand along the top page, flattening the slight hump in the middle. January first. The murder would be front page news, he thought. He could skip quickly from front page to front page. Then the librarian's comment came to him: *so many murders on the reservation*. He would have to check all the pages, skipping only the sports and comics and classifieds. He sighed at the thick stack of newspapers beneath his hand as he began turning the pages. He glanced quickly down the columns.

Suddenly he stopped. What was he thinking? The cowboy had told him the exact date Tinzant Legeau was murdered. "I seen it all. Today's the day." Gabriel Many Horses had called the mission on the anniversary of the murder.

Father John lifted almost half of the newspapers and rolled the thick stack onto the side. He spread a smaller stack over the first hump, then thumbed through several more pages until he came to May sixth, the day of the murder. Locating the last page, he pushed that issue onto the hump and began scanning the front page of the next day's issue. No mention of a murder.

He found it on page four, a two-inch article tucked near the bottom under the headline RANCHER MUR- DERED. The basic facts: Tinzant Legeau, age 71, found murdered in the barn at his ranch in Wildhorse Flats. Head bashed in. Murder weapon appeared to be a shovel.

In the newspaper two days later, he located another small article with the headline COWBOY CHARGED IN RANCHER'S MURDER. Anton Hooshie—the article called him a drifter—was arrested and charged in the murder of Tinzant Legeau. Trial date was set for August four- teenth.

A flip through more pages, and Father John had the article about the murder trial. In the federal court in Casper, Anton Hooshie was found guilty and sentenced to life in prison. Testifying for the prosecution was the only eyewitness to the murder—Gabriel Many Horses.

Father John read through the article again, the cow- boy's words reverberating in his mind: *I seen what hap- pened.* An old murder, a lie that sent an innocent man to prison. A heavy weight to bear for thirty years. *I can't keep it inside no more.*

Father John took his time closing the volume, smooth- ing the pages section by section—the records of lives lived. He set the top cover in place. In his mind, the pat- tern was beginning to arrange itself into a logical se- quence. No one had benefited more from the death of Tinzant Legeau than his nephew and heir, Alexander.

And just as Alexander was about to reap his great- est rewards, the cowboy had reappeared. In a moment of spoken truth, Alexander Legeau's dream would have been destroyed. But Gabriel hadn't been sure where to find Anton Hooshie, the man he'd sent to prison. So he'd dropped a couple of postcards into the mail. He'd met Matthew at Betty's Place. And Matthew had confronted Alexander Legeau. Somehow Legeau had then arranged to meet the cowboy himself one night. He'd picked him up outside Betty's Place minutes after Many Horses had called the mission. The realization made Father John feel almost sick. It was always sickening to visualize the human face of a murderer.

Vicky was still in danger; she would be in danger as long as Legeau was free. Father John stuffed the volume of newspapers back into the bin and hurried through the aisles of metal shelving. He took the stairs two at a time and burst through the door. The librarian looked up, startled, as he ran across the library. "Find what you were looking for, Father?" she called as he slammed out the front door.

Gianelli's office was about a mile away. Father John was there in two minutes, tires squealing as he set the Toyota next to the curb. He jumped out, throwing the door shut behind him, and ran through the drizzle. He let himself in and started up the stairs just as the agent swung around the second story railing. He was in a dark slicker, the hood pulled around his face.

"Thank God you're here," Father John said.

The agent passed him on the stairs. "Whatever it is, John, save it for later. Call just came through. I have to get out to the reservation."

"This can't wait, Gianelli. I know who killed Bosse and Many Horses."

"For God's sake, John." Gianelli stopped about halfway down the stairs, gripped the bannister, and turned around. "We can talk later."

"Vicky's in danger now."

"Damn right she's in danger. How'd you know?"

"What?"

The agent drew in a long breath. "Vicky was supposed to meet Lionel Redbull at her office at six o'clock.

He thought she had some information about the Legeau ranch that would scuttle the facility. He was going to pay her for it, just like he paid off the consultants, and she would get the whole transaction on tape. We had it all worked out. Soon as it happened, I would've arrested him. Only . . ."

"What, Gianelli, what?" Father John could feel his heart thumping.

"Redbull was just found in his truck out in back of the tribal offices. Face shot off."

"My God, Gianelli!" Father John shouted. "Legeau killed him to stop him from talking to Vicky! And now he's going to kill her. How could you put her in that kind of danger? How could you let her do that?"

"Let her?" Now the agent was shouting. "You don't understand anything about that woman, do you? She was determined to do it! I just left a message on her answering machine that she should get the hell away from the office. And Eberhart's sending a couple cars over. They'll be there in minutes."

"What if Legeau gets there first?" Father John pushed past the agent and ran down the stairs. He could hear the other man's footsteps pounding after him.

"She'll be okay."

"God help you if she isn't!" Father John yelled as he slammed out the door.

◀ 30 ▶

Vicky stood at the window watching the intersection below. Cars and pickups rolled past, splattering in the rain. Other cars pulled up at the stop signs before dashing across Main: people on their way home from work. She slipped a hand past her blouse and felt again for the tiny microphone clipped to her bra between her breasts. Then she took in a long breath and exhaled slowly, trying to ignore the fear inside her. She glanced at her watch. It was already a few minutes after six, and none of the vehicles seemed to be stopping.

Maybe Lionel wasn't coming. He could've changed his mind and decided to go to the FBI himself, to accuse her of blackmailing him. But if he tried to turn the tables, he ran the risk of prompting an investigation on how he'd allocated the grant money. He couldn't win. He had no choice but to come for the documents.

The phone jangled in the outer office, startling her. Vicky kept her post by the window. She didn't want to miss Redbull's arrival. The answering machine would take the message. She'd turned down the volume so no other voices would interfere as the recorder taped whatever Redbull said.

The rain danced across the window, ran into little pools on the sill outside. Vicky debated about calling the tribal offices. Something might have delayed the project director, some unexpected meeting. That was it!

He'd been delayed, tried to call her, and she had allowed the machine to take the call. He probably thought she'd changed her mind.

Vicky pivoted around and hurried to the outer office. Just as she was about to push the Message button, she heard the slurry of footsteps in the corridor, soft and slow. Not what she had expected. She had expected Lionel to bound up the stairs and burst through the door, anxious to get the documents. It was his violence, she knew, that frightened her.

The footsteps crept closer. Vicky stood still, scarcely breathing, all her senses waiting for the next footstep to fall. So unlike Redbull. She pushed in the Message button, keeping her eyes on the door, expecting it to fling open. The message was barely audible. She leaned over the desk, close to the machine. For a moment, she didn't recognize the voice. Then she realized it was Gianelli's. A pang of fear shot through her; she had trouble catching her breath.

The agent repeated her name. "Vicky. Vicky. Vicky. If you're there, pick up. It's important." Her name again, then: "Get away from the office, do you hear me? Redbull's not coming. Somebody shot him. Get out of there fast."

Vicky jerked her head up, eyes still fixed on the door. The whir of the tape, the sound of her own breathing filled the office. A shadow moved across the frosted glass pane, the knob began to turn. In an instant, her mind calculated the distance to the door—to the bolt. Ten feet, twelve, a thousand. She couldn't make it.

She wheeled around and ran into her private office, slamming the door behind her. Then she was in the back hallway, as if she had materialized there. When had she passed her desk, passed the chairs? Her purse—where had she left it? Her keys were in the purse. "Oh, God," she said out loud. The purse was on her desk.

She dashed back to the desk. Someone was in the

outer office; she could sense the human presence. She grabbed the purse, gripping it in the soft underbelly. The contents burped out and spilled onto the floor. *God, the keys.* She dropped to her knees, running her hand across the carpet, searching for the little clump of metal. Her fingers closed on something; there was no feeling in her hand, but the keys were there, inert things, like her fingers. She jumped up, ran into the hallway, and hit the back door, pushing the bolt with all her strength. It slid sideways, a loud, grating sound, and she was outside, racing down the stairs to the parking lot.

She sprinted for the Bronco, stumbling once on the gravel, rain spitting at her face. The keys faltered in her hand, missed the lock. She forced herself to concentrate, to jam the key into the tiny slot. She yanked open the door and threw herself inside, jabbing the key now into the ignition. The engine growled, and she was wheeling the Bronco through the lot, down the side street, past the black truck parked at the curb, a dark blur in the rain.

She took a sharp right and headed west toward the police department. Eberhart's office was only a few blocks away. She was partway down the block when the black truck burst out of the alley, blocking her way. She slammed on the brakes, twisting the steering wheel into a U-turn. Tires screamed as the Bronco tore east, away from the police department.

She swung onto Main Street and drove north. As she made the right turn onto Highway 789, she glanced at the rearview mirror. The black truck was behind her.

Father John drove south through Riverton, stepping on the gas as the lights turned yellow, flying across intersections on the red. He swung west onto Seventeen-Mile Road. After a couple of miles, he headed south on Rendezvous Road, swerving around pickups, an occasional 4x4, any vehicle that got in the way. The air was heavy with clouds; the plains rolled past, as shiny as a mirror in the rain.

He let up on the gas pedal as he wheeled through Hudson, then stomped down for the final dash into Lander. He glanced at his watch: 6:25. The moment he turned into Main Street, he spotted the two police cars in front of the flat-roofed, two-story building squatting at the next corner. He parked behind one of the cars. The engine shuddered as he slammed out the door and started running up the stairway. A dim light glowed on the right. He swerved around the parapet and started down the corridor toward Vicky's office on the left.

A police officer in the light blue shirt and navy trousers of the Lander Police Department stood inside the doorway. Beyond him, Father John could see other policemen milling about. "Where's Vicky?" he yelled.

"Who are you?" The first police officer swung around as Detective Eberhart walked out of Vicky's private office.

"Father O'Malley," the detective called. "Any idea where Vicky might've gone?"

"She was supposed to meet Redbull here thirty minutes ago!"

Eberhart glanced at the uniformed officer. "We didn't get the call from Gianelli . . ."

"When did you get here?"

"Fifteen minutes ago." This from the uniform.

"My God. She was here alone." Father John could feel the perspiration on his forehead. His palms were clammy.

Eberhart said, "Gianelli left a message. She might've heard it and got out of here."

"What if she didn't?"

The detective rocked forward, both fists clenched at his sides. "We got cars on the street looking for a black truck. If it's out there, we'll find it."

"She could have gone home." Father John spun around and started down the corridor.

"She's not answering the phone if she did!" Eberhart yelled after him. "I got some cars on the way."

Father John wheeled the Toyota into the street, almost sideswiping a passing sedan. Traffic inched through Lander. He thumped the steering wheel with one fist, cursing under his breath, until he finally reached the turn into the residential neighborhood where Vicky lived. There was little traffic, and he pressed down on the accelerator.

Two other police cars stood at the curb in front of Vicky's house. He stopped behind the second car, the Toyota nudging the back bumper. He gave the door a sharp thwack and hurried up the sidewalk. The front door stood open about an inch. He pushed it into the living room and strode in after it. "Vicky," he called.

A uniformed policeman emerged from the hallway. "Who the hell—?"

"Father John O'Malley. A friend." The murmur of

voices floated down the hallway from where her bed-room would be. They had found her. For an instant, he stood frozen in space, as if his blood had drained away, leaving nothing alive inside him.

Then he threw himself across the room toward the policeman who dodged sideways and reached out one hand, as if to stop him. Pushing past it, he took the short hallway in a couple of steps, following the voices into the bedroom, aware of the other policeman stomping behind him.

Two officers near the foot of the bed turned almost in unison, like guards caught by surprise. Father John's eyes fell on the neatly made bed—a sea of reds and blues and golds that erupted into humps along the headboard and draped onto the carpet. In a glance he took in the entire room: the small chair with the blue cushions, the dresser covered with framed photographs, with glass bottles and little pink gadgets and gold tubes. An array of feminine paraphernalia that he only occasionally re-membered existed—when he came across an ad in a magazine or found himself in the wrong aisle at Wal-Mart.

He heard himself exhale. She wasn't here, yet she filled the room—the smell of her, the sense of her. And if he found her alive—she had to be alive—he would not lose her. It was a truth as real as the air he breathed.

"You're that priest from the reservation, right?" one of the officers asked. "No sign of Ms. Holden. We've been over the whole house. The detective's got every car in Lander on the alert for her—"

The phone on the table next to the bed emitted a loud jangle and, in two strides, the officer was beside it, lifting the receiver. "Burley here." He threw back his head and stared out the window. After a pause, he said, "House is clean, no sign of the occupant anywhere." Another pause, and he set the receiver in its cradle. He turned to the other officers. "Eberhart says they're headin' back to headquarters. Wants us back there, too. Except for you, Brandan." He looked past Father John toward the officer who had followed him down the hallway. "Wants you to keep circling the neighborhood. Watch the house, case she shows up or . . ." He stopped, gulped in air. "Case anybody else shows up."

Father John followed the officers outside. He sat in the Toyota, watching the two police cars roll down the street. He had to believe Vicky had gotten away—he couldn't bear to think anything else. He forced himself to concentrate on where she would go.

She would leave Lander and go to the reservation. Maybe to St. Francis. That train of thought came to a halt, as if it had hit a wall in his mind. Before this morning she might have gone to the guest house, but not after she'd run out of his study concluding God-only-knew-what about Sheila Cavanaugh. It had taken only a few minutes to let Sheila know he was not interested in lunch or anything else. But Vicky was gone. He doubted she'd ever return to St. Francis.

But she'd go to the reservation. Banner's men would be looking for her, he was sure, but they might not know about Aunt Rose or Grandfather Hedly and Grandmother Ninni. He started the engine and pulled into the street. Maybe he could catch Eberhart before he left Vicky's office. The detective could radio Banner.

Light traffic moved through the dusk: stragglers on the way home at the end of the day. Father John set the Toyota next to the curb. The police cars were gone. He hesitated before shutting off the engine, then decided to see if Eberhart had left a man upstairs.

He took the stairs two at a time and strode down the dim corridor, boots thudding against the floor. The door to Vicky's office was closed; the knob spun a quarter inch in his hand. He rapped hard on the frosted glass, waited, then rapped again. There was no sound inside, nothing but a sense of emptiness.

He turned and started back toward the stairs. In the glow of the light ahead, he saw the gun coming around the parapet, the squat silver barrel with a tiny hole. Then he saw the black glove that gripped the gun. He stopped, relief flooding through him—the killer had come back, which meant he hadn't found Vicky.

Slowly the figure emerged from behind the parapet. Father John could make out the long, dark raincoat, the cowboy hat pulled low, the gun raised. Alexander Legeau, he thought, ready to kill again to protect his dream. Then the figure moved sideways into the scrim of light, and Father John saw it was not Alexander Legeau.

◀ 32 ▶

"Lily."

"Don't pretend you're surprised, Father O'Malley." The woman gripped the gun in both hands and pointed it toward his face. From the street below came the thrum of a motor, the ratcheting of gears. Normal sounds. Everything must appear to be normal, he told himself, his eyes on the woman a few feet away. A madwoman. "I expected Alexander," he said.

"That's a lie." Lily tossed her head slightly. "Gabriel Many Horses told you what happened, didn't he?"

"I spoke with him," Father John said, moving slowly toward the woman. *Keep her talking*, he thought.

"I had no choice. Alexander could never bring himself to do what was necessary to save the ranch."

"So it was you who killed Alexander's uncle thirty years ago." He inched forward. If he could divert her attention, he might be able to knock the gun out of her hand.

"I knew you knew when you showed up on our doorstep. Just wanted to let Alexander know about the funeral of an old friend, you said. So disappointing, Father. I expected more from a Jesuit. What you really wanted was some sign that Gabriel had told you the truth. You and Vicky Holden are just like him, trying to destroy my husband's dream. What right do you have to destroy a man's dream?"

The woman stepped back. The gun rode against the folds of her raincoat. He could see the line of silver buttons down one side. "No one will destroy my husband's dream," she said. "I will not allow it. Alexander is weak. I have to protect him."

"Did you kill Tinzant to keep him from changing his will?" He was guessing, probing. *Keep her talking.*

"I didn't want to," Lily said. "I truly didn't. I searched for some other way. But those two white nephews had shown up, and he started talking about a new will. And after Alexander had worked on the ranch from the time he was twelve years old. Would that have been fair, Father? To cut him out because he was a breed? I tried to talk to Tinzant. I threw myself on the old man's mercy. But," the woman said as she shook her head, "he just laughed at me. We were in the barn, and when he turned away, I grabbed the shovel and . . . Well, you know the rest, don't you? Then Gabriel ran in like a fool and yanked the shovel away, but it was too late for the old man to change his will." A hollow sound came into her voice, as if she were speaking from a distance.

Somewhere on the street, an engine kicked over. "So you paid Gabriel to swear it was Anton Hooshie who killed Tinzant. Why Anton, Lily?"

"He was a drifter nobody cared about. For the right amount of money—Gabriel was a greedy son-of-a-bitch—he agreed to swear he saw Hooshie and Tinzant fighting. What a shame Gabriel decided to get religion after all this time, just when the best part of Alexander's dream was about to come true. Gabriel showed up at the ranch Monday afternoon. I hardly knew him. He looked terrible. He said he wanted to die with a clear conscience. I had to get him off the ranch before Alexander saw him, so I pretended to agree with him. I told him my conscience had been bothering me, too. It was time to tell the truth. I arranged to meet him later. I convinced him we would decide together on the best way to tell the truth. Of course the old man had to die. I had to take care of it, just like before."

"You picked him up at Betty's Place and drove him to the cabin. Then you shot him and cleaned out his pockets to make it look like a robbery." Father John was close enough to see the faint lines etched in her face.

"Stay where you are!" she shouted. "I know what you're thinking. I'm a very accurate shot, Father."

He stood still. "Why did Bosse have to die, Lily? Or Redbull?"

The woman gave a little snort. "Gabriel met with Bosse. He told him the whole story." She was quiet a moment, as if waiting for him to agree the murder made perfect sense. "Lionel was different. Such a fool. He thought the facility would just happen. He didn't understand you can't leave such things to chance. I had to direct him at every turn. Every turn." She shook her head slowly, a terrible burden. "He actually intended to hire the usual consultants. But, of course, we couldn't guarantee the results. And the moment Vicky Holden showed up saying she had some documents, he panicked. He couldn't see she was bluffing. He told her everything. And if he told her, well, he might tell the business council or that company president, what's his name, Paul Bryant, or the FBI agent. Don't you see, Father?" She drew in a long breath. "Lionel was about to destroy everything. When he called and told me Vicky had paid him a visit, well, I knew he had to die." She lifted the gun. "And now you have to die. I'm truly sorry."

"Give me the gun, Lily." Father John slowly stretched out his hand. "Gianelli knows the truth. Vicky taped her conversation with Lionel."

The woman stepped back, regarding him. "I'm disappointed, Father. Lionel told me he checked her purse. She didn't have a tape recorder."

"Lionel was lying."

"Please, Father. Don't try to bluff me. It stops here with you and Vicky Holden. No one else will ever know what happened."

A shiver ran down Father John's spine. He'd been wrong. This madwoman had taken Vicky somewhere and had come back for him, intending to kill them both. "Where's Vicky?" he asked, a hardness in the tone.

Lily's mouth broke into a thin smile. "I would have killed her awhile ago if she hadn't slipped out the back door. I caught up with her Bronco, but she's a very evasive driver. So now we're going to find her, you and I."

"I don't know where she is."

"You must think I just dropped from the blue sky, Father. I figured Vicky would tell you about her plan to meet Redbull, and you would come here to protect her. I was right, wasn't I? Now, I suspect, she's gone running to you. Shall we go to the mission?"

Lily waved the gun, motioning him toward the stairs. She stepped out of the way of his reach. Her footsteps mingled with his as they started down. "Keep moving," she said behind him.

A couple of pickups lumbered along the street, tires spraying water. Another car was approaching. He thought about whipping around, trying to hit away the gun, but he knew he wasn't faster than a bullet, and she was an expert with a gun. Even if he succeeded in shoving away her arm, she could pull the trigger. The bullet might hit someone in a passing vehicle.

They reached the Toyota, and she ordered him to stand at the driver's door while she walked around to the passenger side, the gun pointed at his face. Then she ordered him inside and let herself in beside him. He said a prayer that someone had noticed them, that someone would call the police.

◀ 33 ▶

The lights of oncoming cars glimmered on the wet hood as Father John drove across the reservation. He felt the weight of the metal weapon pressing through his jacket against his ribs. He was sure Vicky wouldn't be at St. Francis. He thanked God for the misunderstanding this morning, for creating such a stubborn woman.

He said, "It's not too late for you, Lily." He used the tone of a counselor talking someone through a crisis. There was so little time. They would be at the mission in twenty minutes; the woman was likely to fly into a rage when she saw Vicky wasn't there.

"Don't try to con me." The gun pressed harder.

"You've only been trying to help your husband, Lily. You didn't really intend to commit murder; you just didn't see any other way. I'm sure Alexander would understand. He loves you. He would want you in a place where you could get the care and treatment you need. But if you kill Vicky and me, the FBI will have no choice but to see that you're charged with first-degree murder. Think of Alexander, how hard it will be on him. We can go to Gianelli's office right now and clear up everything."

The gun pushed so hard he felt a stab of pain. "Would you like to die now, Father? I can always find Vicky on my own."

He guided the Toyota along the dark stretches of Rendezvous Road. He knew the woman was capable of pulling the trigger, stomping on the brake, and pushing him out onto the asphalt. Time, he thought, time was what he needed.

He bore east on Seventeen-Mile Road and swung into Circle Drive. Light glowing from the overhead lamps gave the mission the eery feeling of another world. There were no vehicles in sight, and he breathed easier. Vicky wasn't here. The mission looked deserted; the administration building was dark, and only a dim light shone in the windows of the residence. His assistant was probably having dinner in the kitchen. It was the quiet time between the work day and the evening meetings. He slowed in front of the administration building.

"Over there." Lily jabbed against him.

He stared past the windshield at the rainy grounds. "Where?"

"The old school."

"It's locked, Lily. We don't use it anymore."

"You have keys. Park at the side. Vicky'll see your pickup."

"We can wait in my office." Someone might come along, he was thinking. He might still get the chance to grab the gun. He did not want to go into the old school with its long hallways, stairs with missing boards, and broken bannisters. He wasn't even sure the lights still worked. The last time he'd been inside at night he'd run off a couple of teenagers trying to roast hot dogs in a little campfire on the second floor.

Lily jabbed the gun into him again. "We don't want anyone interrupting us in your office, do we?"

He pushed down on the accelerator and guided the Toyota around the gravel drive. He stopped next to the old building, switched off the ignition, and removed the key. All his keys—the keys to the mission—hung on the round silver loop in the palm of his hand.

Their footsteps squished against the wet stone as she followed him up the steps and across the narrow porch to the front door. He located the key in the shadows and jammed it into the lock. The gun pushed against the small of his back.

Inside, he ran one hand along the stucco wall until he found the hard plastic switch and flipped it up. A dim, cloudy light, like white mist, flickered out of the glass fixtures marching along the ceiling. Shadows fell over the far reaches of the hallway and the wide stairway that curved to the second floor. The old building had a faint odor of gas and damp stone.

Lily said, "Upstairs."

Father John started to turn toward her, but the gun was against his back, some hard thing permanently attached.

"You're a very difficult man," she said, pushing the gun into him. "I want to see my old classroom, can't you understand? So many dreams there when I was young. And I made them come true, all of them— Alexander, the ranch, our position here. Seems a fitting place to make the last dream come true, wouldn't you agree? Vicky will find us."

"Her Bronco's not here," Father John said, starting up the stairs, running one hand along the railing. The bannister moved beneath his palm. The wooden steps creaked into the silence.

Shards of light filtered up the stairs behind them. At the top, she nudged him toward the first doorway down the hall. He stepped into the classroom and groped for the light switch. "We don't need it," she said. Another nudge forward. A thin light from the street lamps worked its way through the windows on the opposite wall and fell over the rows of small, wooden desks with silver-rimmed ink wells, the teacher's desk against the right wall, the floorboards that rose and fell in little waves. Just as the Arapaho elders remembered the classroom, that was how they insisted upon keeping it.

He realized some of the light must be coming from the porch fixture. The downstairs switch had also turned on the outside light. It gave him a sense of hope: No one used the old school, the lights were never on. Geoff would see them and know something was wrong. Anyone driving into the mission would know.

But if Vicky drove in, she would also see the lights. She would spot the Toyota, and she might come to find him. He forced himself to remember how she'd run out the door this morning, to convince himself she would not come back.

The floor shivered as the woman kicked the door shut behind them. "Sit down," she ordered.

Time, a little more time, he was thinking. He said, "What was it like going to school here?" as he slid down the wall onto his haunches.

She backed around the rows of desks toward the window, the pistol glinting in her hand. "I was a child," she said after a moment. "It's very hard to be a child. I dreamed always of growing up, so I could be in control." Keeping the gun on him, she stole a quick glance out the window. "Someone's walking this way."

"Gianelli."

Another glance, and then she turned back toward him. The light caught the whiteness of her teeth as she smiled. "Wrong, Father. It's your girlfriend."

He could hear the *thump, thump* sound of his own heart. If it was Vicky, time had run out. "You're not a child anymore, Lily," he said, struggling for a tone that concealed the desperation he was feeling. "You're in control now. It's not too late to save yourself. I can help you. I'll talk to Gianelli, make sure he understands you weren't responsible—"

"Stop it!" She started across the room as the thud of a slamming door reverberated through the floorboards.

She cracked open the classroom door, allowing a sliver of light to run inside and melt into the light from the window.

"John, where are you?" It was Vicky. He could hear her footsteps across the lower hall. "Are you all right?"

"Call to her." The words hissed through the room.

Father John pushed himself slowly up the wall, his jacket catching on the old stucco. He said nothing.

"I said call to her!" It was a yell, high and piercing, like the cry of a coyote in the night. Then came the sound of footsteps running up the stairs.

"Vicky, go back!" he shouted. "Get out of here!"

Lily crouched down, one hand on the knob ready to yank the door open, the other gripping the pistol pointed at him. "You fool." She spit out the words. "Die, damn you."

A sharp crack sounded, like a burst of thunder. Heat exploded next to his face as Vicky crashed through the door, crashed into Lily, who spun sideways diving for the pistol that clattered across the floor. Father John threw himself between Lily and the gun. He grabbed her from behind, wrapped his arms around her, engulfing her, holding her tightly as she twisted and jerked against him—so small a woman, so much strength. A long howl sounded into the room, like that of a wounded animal, as Vicky dodged past and scooped up the gun.

"Lily, Lily," Father John said soothingly into the woman's ear. "It's over now. You're okay. Everything will be okay."

The howling had fallen into a low moan as the woman relaxed against him. He felt himself gradually loosen his hold, aware of Vicky standing against the wall, gripping the gun at her side. Suddenly Lily twisted out of his arms. He grabbed for her, but she jumped sideways, her body pulling away from him. She was out the door, racing toward the stairs. "Lily, wait!" he shouted, running after her.

She started down the stairs, reeling into the bannister, grabbing for the railing. Father John reached for her again, but the bannister was already collapsing, a snapping and splintering of wood that gathered momentum as the railing and supports began falling into the hall below, the woman falling with them, arms outstretched, a long wail echoing through the old halls. Then came a hard thud and silence.

Father John ran down the stairs. Even before he sank onto one knee beside the woman, before he lifted the limp and broken wrist and tried to locate the pulse, he saw the splayed and twisted way she had landed, the blood at the side of her mouth, the broken neck.

Vicky stood beside him; he felt her hand on his shoulder. "She's dead." It was almost a whisper.

Father John dropped his head onto his knee and prayed silently for the woman who was now in the hands of God, beyond human help, human justice. Then he said a prayer of thanksgiving that it was over, that Vicky and he were still alive.

From outside came the sound of sirens and tires crunching gravel. "The police," Vicky said. "I called them."

Father John waited on the porch under the eaves at the edge of the cold drizzle. He needed the fresh air. From inside came the clatter of footsteps on the wood floors, the sound of Chief Banner barking orders to the uniformed officers. Alexander Legeau had arrived with the police, and the old man's sobs were almost more than Father John could take. He'd tried to find some words of comfort—words were so inadequate—but the man had wanted only to be with the broken body of his wife. The medics were probably loading Lily onto the stretcher now. Gianelli was still inside with Vicky, taking her statement. His statement would be next.

Circle Drive was filled with vehicles: the white ambulance, Gianelli's Blazer, four BIA police cars. Red and blue lights circled the cottonwoods, the wet grasses, the old school. Through the car windows came the static sound of radios crackling, voices jabbering. Beyond the police cars were other vehicles. People milled around—a crowd drawn by the sirens. He thought he saw Paul Bryant at the edge of the crowd, talking with Father Geoff.

Suddenly the police officers filed across the porch, followed by the medics who carried the stretcher down the stone steps to the ambulance. Alexander moved alongside, quiet now, as if he were walking in his sleep.

Gianelli stepped out on the porch and came toward Father John. "Looks like one of your theories finally hit the bull's-eye, John. But that doesn't mean . . ."

Father John nodded. He knew the rest of the sentence: He should stick to his own work. Let the FBI and police do theirs. He wondered if Vicky had come outside, if he had missed her in the crush of police officers. He glanced at the crowd around the cars. She must still be in the old school.

"Vicky called the minute she got to the guest house," the agent said.

"She was at the guest house?" The thought sent a chill through Father John. He had clung to the belief she would not come to the mission. Had he dreamed she was here, he would never have brought Lily. He would have done something else; he should have done something else. Lily might have spotted the Bronco. Vicky would have died here tonight, and he was the one who had put her in danger.

"Her call was patched to Banner at Fort Washakie just as we were questioning Alexander Legeau about Redbull's murder. Didn't take much to figure out Legeau wasn't the one skulking around her office, not with him sitting in front of us. But Legeau caught on right away. It was Lily who always drove their black truck.

You could see on the man's face the way things started falling into place. I felt sorry for him. Anyway, Vicky was afraid the killer would show up at St. Francis. She was more worried about you than herself. Banner and I hightailed it over here. Didn't arrive soon enough, though. Heard the shot soon as I turned into the mission. That crazy lady might've killed . . ."

Just then Vicky appeared in the doorway, hugging her coat around her, glancing over the crowd, as if she were looking for someone. Father John stepped past the agent, who grabbed his arm. "I need your version of what happened," Gianelli said.

For a moment, Father John caught Vicky's eye. Then she looked away, hurried across the porch and down the steps. He jerked his arm free and started after her, unsure of what he wanted to say, knowing only he did not want her to leave.

"Now, John, while everything's fresh." Gianelli fell in alongside.

"Give me a minute." Father John started toward the steps, but the agent set a hand on his shoulder. The grasp was firm.

"We've got to talk now."

"Look, Gianelli, I'll tell you everything I know, but there's something I've got to do first."

A look of understanding came into the agent's eyes. "Okay," he said, removing his hand.

Father John hurried down the steps and stopped, his eyes searching the crowd milling about, parting around the ambulance that had started to back around Circle Drive. Vicky was nowhere in sight.

He darted past the crowd and the police cars and ran down the drive toward the guest house, in and out of the circle of overhead lights, barely conscious of the sound of footsteps behind him.

"Hold on, John!" Father Geoff yelled. "She's gone."

Father John stopped and whirled around, facing the other priest.

"She left," Father Geoff said, gulping in air.

"What?"

"She left with Paul Bryant. He stopped by the residence to see you. I'd just shown him into your study when we heard the gunshot. Then those police cars came racing into the mission. I didn't know what in God's name was going on."

"Vicky left?" Father John said, as if to convince himself.

"Bryant ran out and collared one of the police officers. He found out you and Vicky were inside the old school with a murderer. He tried to get in, but the police made him stay outside. He waited, and the minute she came out, he was beside her, walking her over to his truck. They just drove off."

Father John turned away and stared past the splotches of light and shadows, past the long expanse of darkness that stretched across the reservation to the rim of the mountains outlined against the silver sky. He felt the other man's grip tightening on his shoulder.

"Believe me, John, it's better this way."

❮ 34 ❯

The midmorning sun slanted across the papers and folders on Father John's desk. He thumbed through the summer schedules for the adult literacy classes, the religious education programs. Most of the volunteers who had taught spring semester had agreed to stay on, but he still needed a few teachers. He'd have to make some phone calls, pay a few visits. Setting the schedules aside, he got to his feet and walked over to the window. Walks-on was rolling in a clump of grass across Circle Drive. The sky was an endless expanse of blue. It had suddenly started to feel like summer.

He'd been missing Boston lately, the long ripening of spring, and he was looking forward to going back. He would make his retreat there, take the time to step away and think, to pray over the direction of his life. The Provincial had agreed with his decision, and, to his surprise, had even offered to pay the expenses.

Father John had wanted to leave immediately, but he'd delayed his departure a week. It had been a week of funerals. The services for Lionel Redbull and Lily Legeau had been small and private. A few family members, some friends, all in shock and grief. Matthew Bosse's services had taken three days, and featured all the rituals and ceremonies for the funeral of a good man. A good man, Father John thought, who had tried to do what he thought was best. Almost everyone on the reservation had attended the services, even Vicky, although she'd stayed at the edge of the crowd, and he hadn't had the chance to talk to her.

He'd thought about calling her. He wanted to thank her for crashing through the door the way she did, when she should have turned and run out of the old school to save her own life. Instead, she'd saved his. But he hadn't called. He knew Paul Bryant would be there. And at some point her Bronco had disappeared from in front of the guest house, and he had understood that Bryant had probably brought her to the mission to retrieve it.

He'd tried to put it out of his mind. There was so much to think about. All week he had watched for the mail, hoping for a response from some of the benefactors he'd written to. Hoping for a miracle. And yesterday the mail had brought in enough donations to pay Ralph for repairing the church roof and to catch up on some old bills. Enough to keep Father Geoff's plans at bay—the thought made him smile. His own brand of financial planning wasn't so bad after all.

Even the collection on Sunday had been larger than usual. The elders had taken him aside and told him the extra money should go to plaster over the bullet hole in the classroom before the evil intention of Lily Legeau invaded the whole mission. Such symbols of evil could not be ignored. He had to repair the wall immediately.

The reverence the Arapahos had for the old buildings, for St. Francis Mission, filled him with a kind of awe. He reminded himself he was just the caretaker here, one in a long line of caretakers, and whatever his own feelings might be, he had a job to do. He also reminded himself that he was fortunate. It was a job he loved.

Outside, the golden retriever pushed to his feet—a momentary struggle—and bounded across the grass, as if he expected a red Frisbee to come sailing overhead at any moment and was determined to be ready to pluck it out of the air. Elena would take care of his dog while he was gone, even if Father Geoff buried himself in his numbers and forgot. At least his assistant had agreed to take over for the Eagles. The kids were in for precision and drill while he was gone, which might not be much fun, but they'd get the details down.

While he was gone. The thought brought a sharp stab of pain. He knew he would miss this place more than he could say. He hadn't even left yet, and he was already beginning to miss it.

A black truck turned into Circle Drive and caught his attention. He watched it pull up in front of the administration building. Paul Bryant leapt out, giving the door a hard slam. Another slam of the front door sent a shiver through the old building, and then Bryant was standing in the doorway to the office, dressed in tan slacks and blue sport coat, looking as relaxed and confident as usual. "Ah, Father O'Malley. I'm glad I caught you."

"What can I do for you?" Father John had to make an effort to keep his tone civil, to mask his dislike for this man who had appeared out of nowhere and had changed the direction of his own life. He wasn't sure how his life might have gone, but a part of him resented the fact that this stranger seemed to have had a say in the matter.

Bryant strode across the room and stopped in front of the desk. "I'm sure you know the joint council has canceled the vote on the nuclear waste facility."

Father John didn't respond. They both knew the canceled vote didn't mean that a nuclear waste facility might not be proposed for some other site on the reservation.

"Regardless of what you may think, Father O'Malley, I was as appalled as you must have been at what happened here. My company lost a great deal of time as well as money in the effort to prove out the Legeau ranch. Our efforts would have been better spent elsewhere. Time is of the essence. We have to build an interim facility soon."

"On the reservation?" Father John asked. He didn't doubt the other man's capacity for pursuing his plans.

Bryant shook his head and smiled. "It doesn't belong here. I understand that now. It wouldn't fit with the culture of the people. But Wyoming is a large and empty place." He threw out both hands. "Somewhere in this state, I'm confident, we can construct a storage facility that will be as safe as science can make it."

The man cleared his throat as he slipped one hand inside his sport coat and removed a white envelope. "We seem to have gotten off on the wrong foot for some reason, Father. I had stopped by the residence the other evening hoping we might have a quiet talk. I also intended to give you this." He held out the envelope.

Reluctantly Father John took it and opened the flap. The check inside was written for the largest amount St. Francis had ever received at one time, large enough to run the mission for six months.

Bryant said, "Since I arrived here, I've heard nothing but good about St. Francis Mission. And during the time I've spent with Vicky this week, she's talked almost nonstop about you and your work here. Helping people to help themselves is the kind of charity my company likes to support. I want you to know you can expect checks such as this from time to time."

Father John handed the envelope back to the other man. "I don't want your money," he said.

Surprise flickered in Bryant's eyes before giving way to a glint of understanding. He was quiet a moment, as if he were rehearsing in his mind the exact words. Finally he said, "I'm aware of the fact that we both find Vicky Holden a rare and beautiful woman, Father O'Malley. You, however, are in no position to do anything about it. I am not in any such position, and I want very much to get to know her better. I hope to convince her to move to Chicago. She can take a job in our legal department—one I'll create, of course. For the moment, she says she prefers to stay here, but I hope that in time she'll come to see I'm not such a bad fellow." He shrugged, then continued. "I expect to spend a good deal of time in Wyoming while we pursue other sites. I can assure you I have no intention of allowing someone so rare and beautiful to slip away."

Bryant tossed the envelope onto the desk, turned quickly, and walked to the door. He stopped and looked back. "Keep the check, Father O'Malley. I expect you'll discover that you need it."

Father John stepped to the window and watched the pickup as it began its slow glide around Circle Drive. In a moment it was lost in the shadows of the cotton-woods. It was as it should be, he thought. Bryant had fallen in love with her—a man with something to offer her—and she had every right to love such a man, to carve out a space of happiness for herself.

His own life would continue in the direction it was meant to go. He was scheduled to fly out of Riverton to-morrow morning after the early Mass. He would spend the next two weeks on retreat—he was looking forward to the quiet time of prayer and reflection.

When he came back, there would be so much to do at St. Francis. New classes and programs he'd been thinking about starting for a long time. A class on cen-tering prayer. Perhaps another class on Christian spiri-tuality. Maybe a day care program, or even senior care. And new activities for the kids. The girls needed a soft-ball team to play on, and he wanted to start a social club for the teenagers. There would be a thousand things to do. A thousand things to fill up his mind and heart.

When he came back, he thought. When he came back.